HYPERACTIVE

CREATED AND WRITTEN BY SCOTT CHRISTIAN SAVA
WITH ART BY JOSEPH BERGIN III

& JONAS PUBLISHING

IDW

PRESENT:

WORTHWHILE
B O O K S

www.WorthwhileChildrensBooks.com

ISBN: 978-1-60010-313-1

11 10 09 08   1 2 3 4 5

Layout by Neil Uyetake • Edited by Justin Eisinger

Worthwhile Books, a division of Idea and Design Works, LLC. Editorial offices: 5080 Santa Fe Street, San Diego, CA 92109.
Any similarities to persons living or dead are purely coincidental. Printed in Korea.
Worthwhile Books does not read or accept unsolicited submissions of ideas, stories or artwork.

Jonas Publishing, Publisher: Howard Jonas
IDW, Chairman: Morris Berger • IDW, President: Ted Adams • IDW, Senior Graphic Artist: Robbie Robbins
Worthwhile Books, Vice President and Creative Director: Rob Kurtz • Worthwhile Books, Senior Editor: Megan Bryant

"To Joey Caram... Always take time
to slow down and enjoy each moment."

Scott Christian Sava, 2008

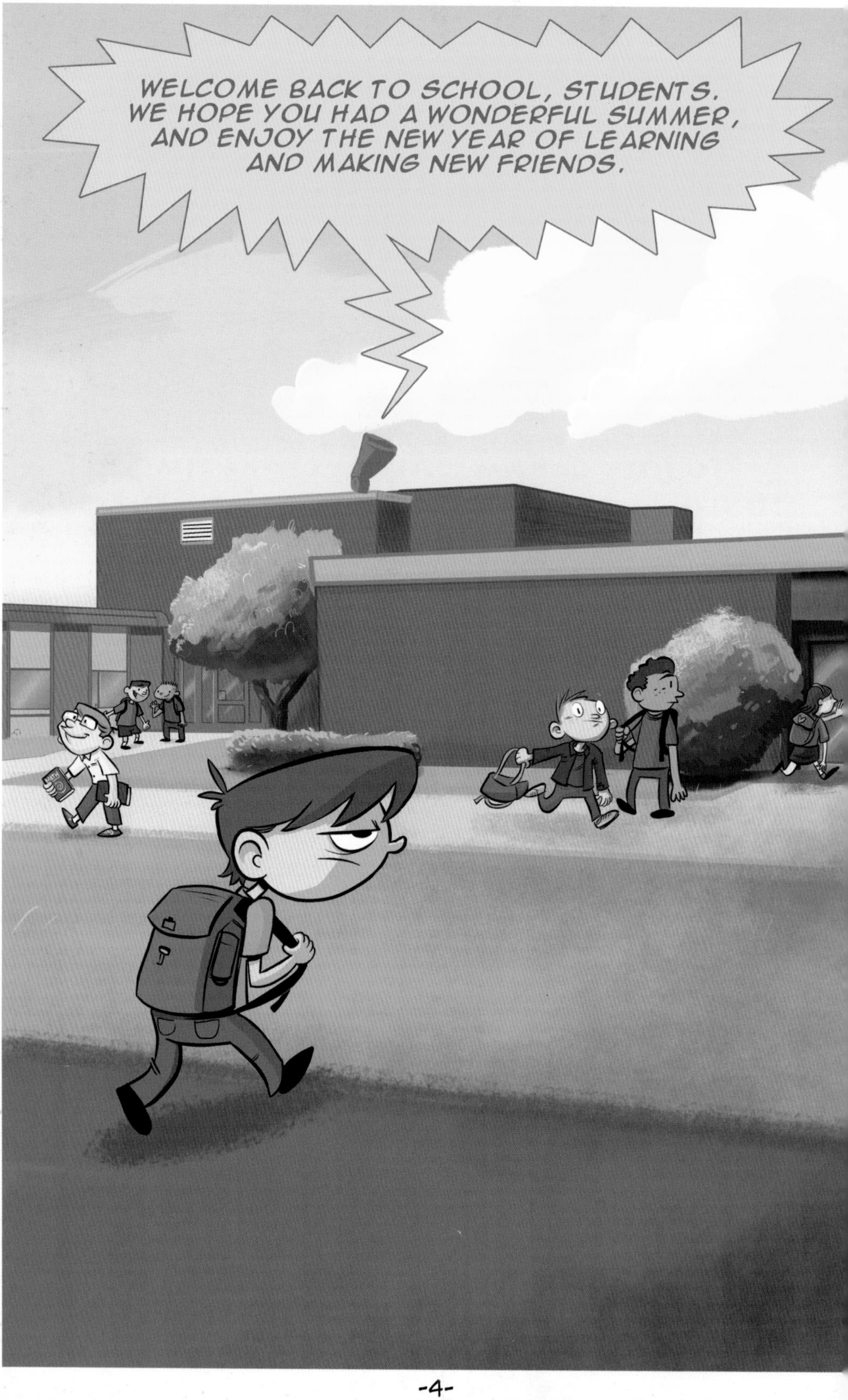
WELCOME BACK TO SCHOOL, STUDENTS. WE HOPE YOU HAD A WONDERFUL SUMMER, AND ENJOY THE NEW YEAR OF LEARNING AND MAKING NEW FRIENDS.

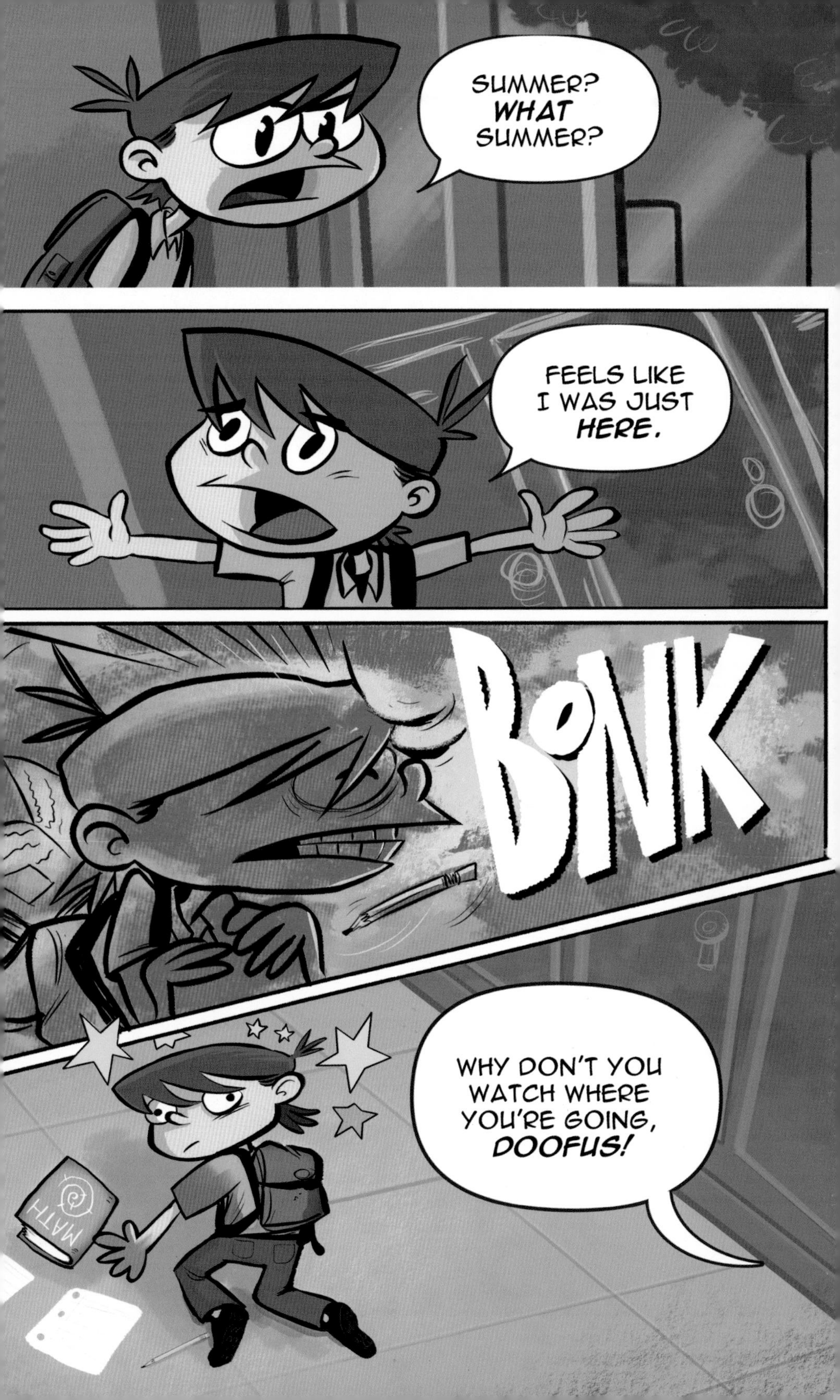
SUMMER? WHAT SUMMER?
FEELS LIKE I WAS JUST HERE.
BONK
MATH
WHY DON'T YOU WATCH WHERE YOU'RE GOING, DOOFUS!

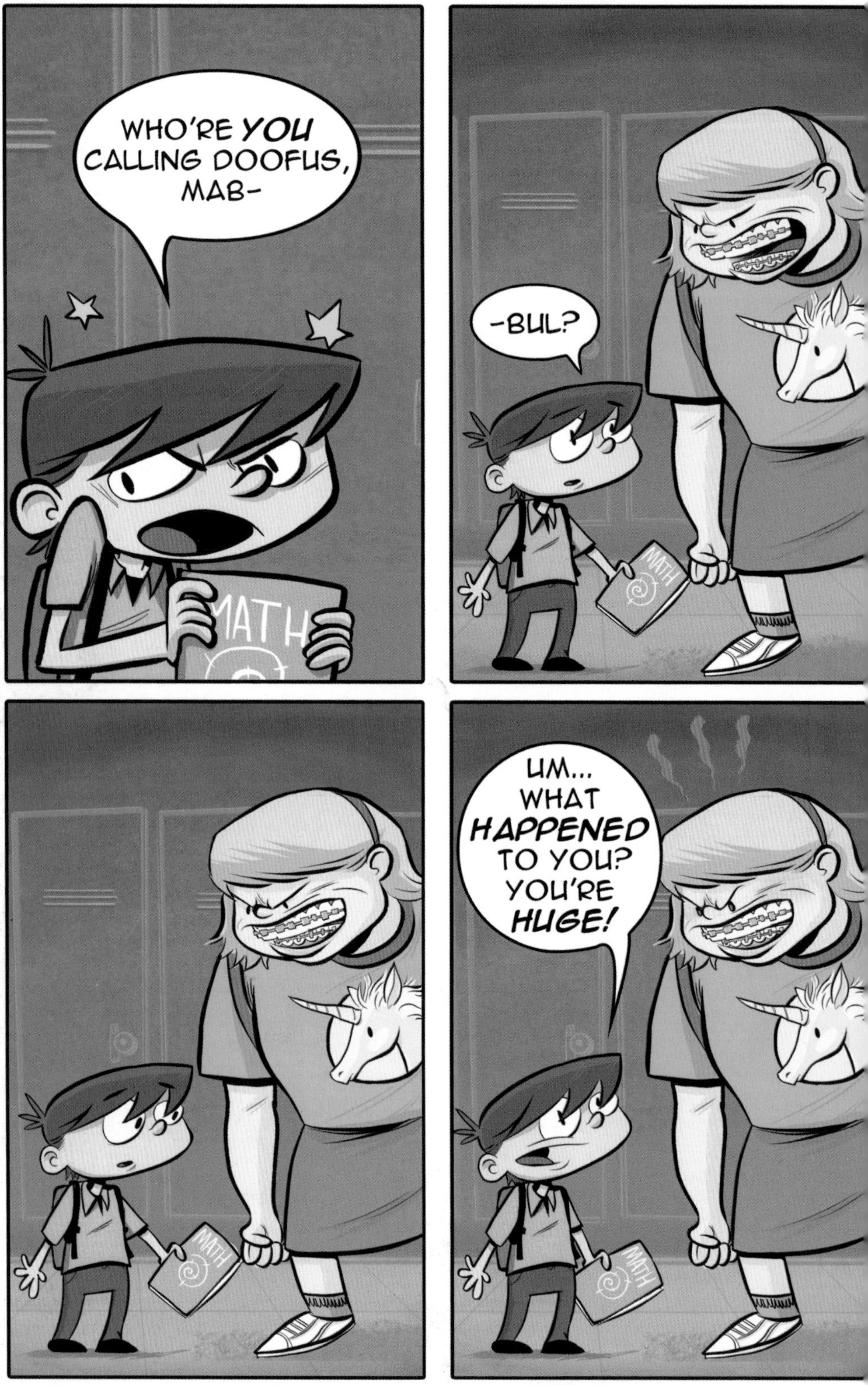
WHO'RE *YOU* CALLING DOOFUS, MAB-
-BUL?
UM... WHAT *HAPPENED* TO YOU? YOU'RE *HUGE!*

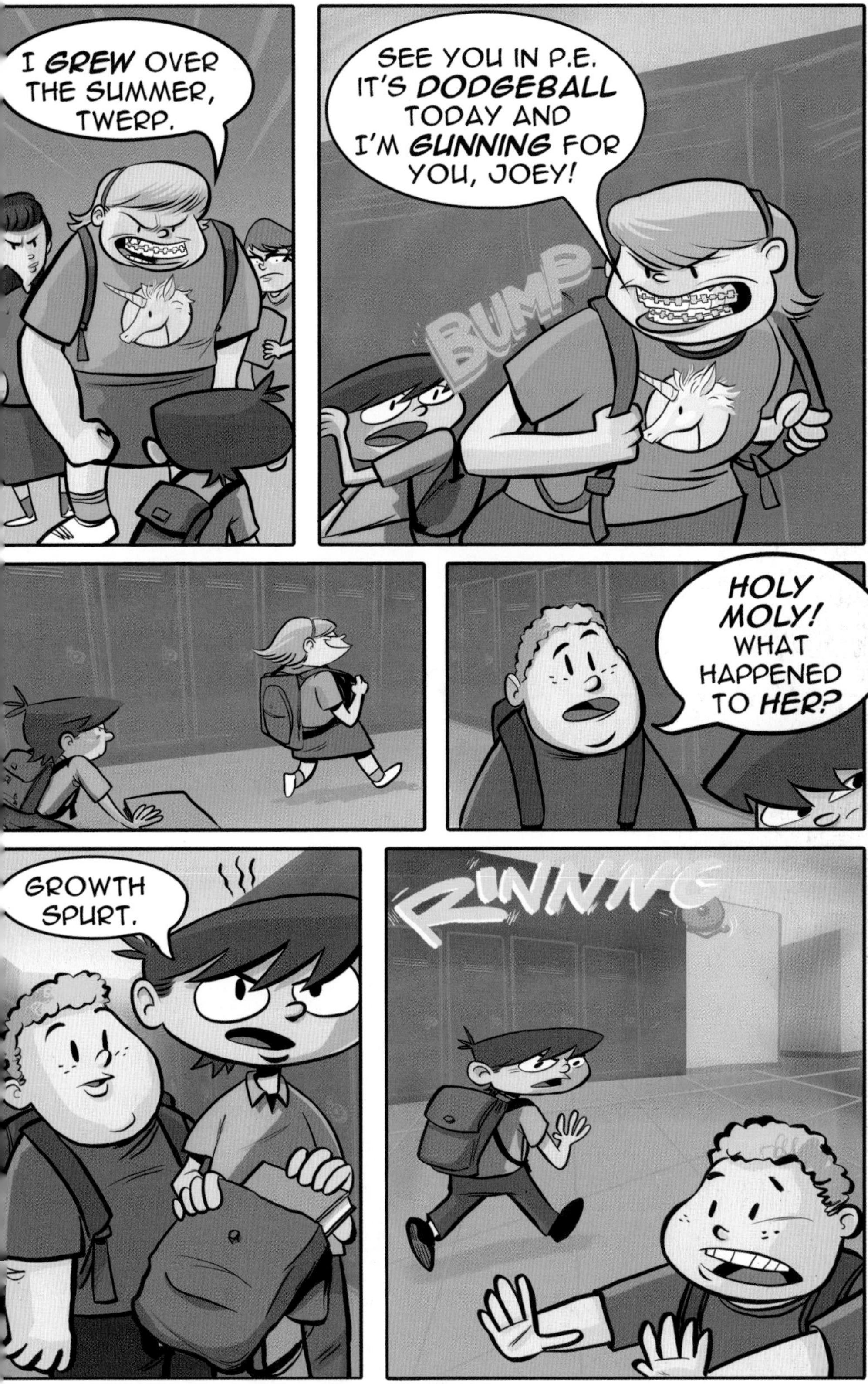
I GREW OVER THE SUMMER, TWERP.
SEE YOU IN P.E. IT'S DODGEBALL TODAY AND I'M GUNNING FOR YOU, JOEY!
BUMP
HOLY MOLY! WHAT HAPPENED TO HER?
GROWTH SPURT.
RINNNG

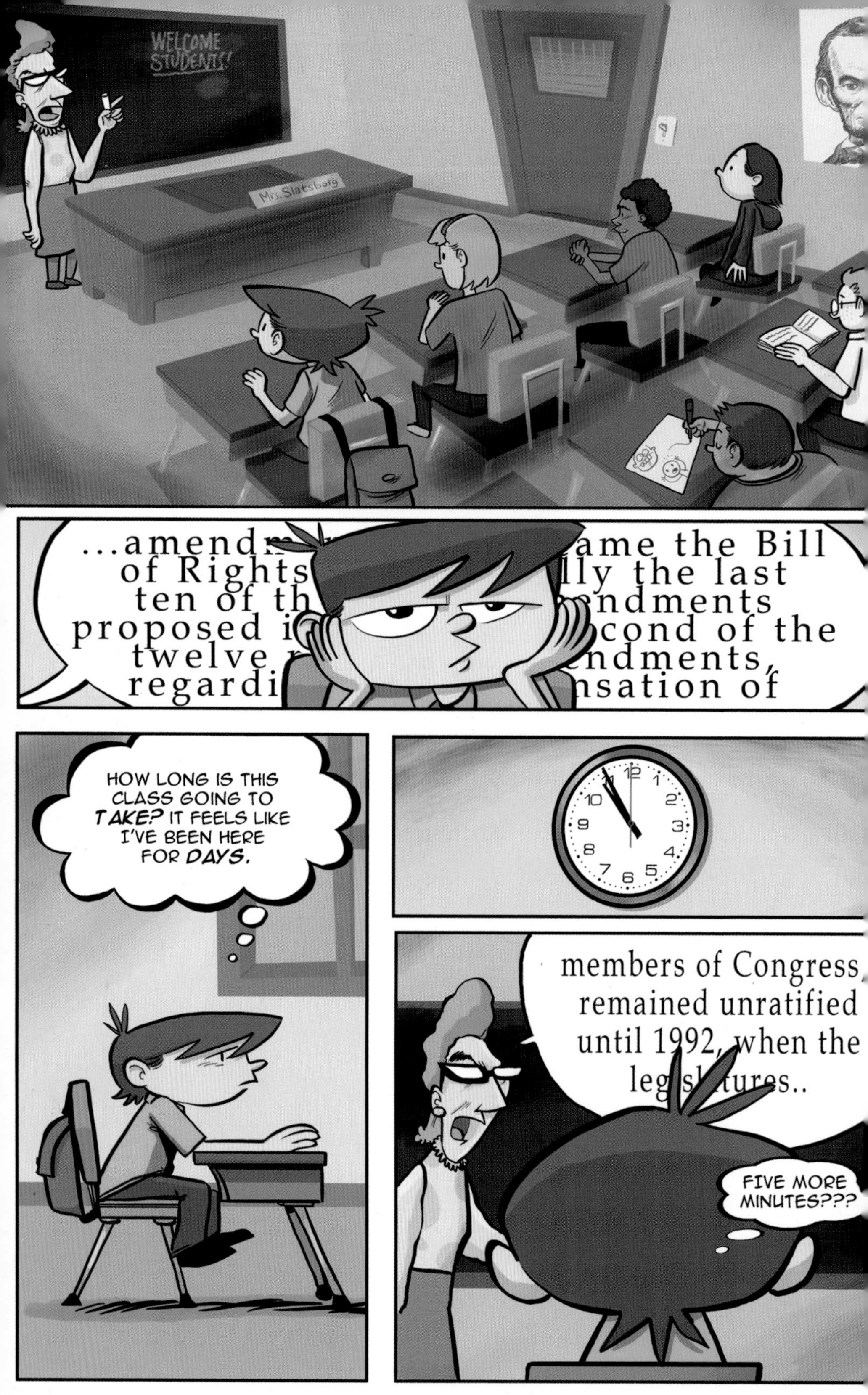
WELCOME STUDENTS!
Mrs. Slatsborg
...amendm ame the Bill of Rights lly the last ten of th endments proposed i cond of the twelve endments, regardi nsation of
HOW LONG IS THIS CLASS GOING TO TAKE? IT FEELS LIKE I'VE BEEN HERE FOR DAYS.
members of Congress remained unratified until 1992, when the leg tures..
FIVE MORE MINUTES???

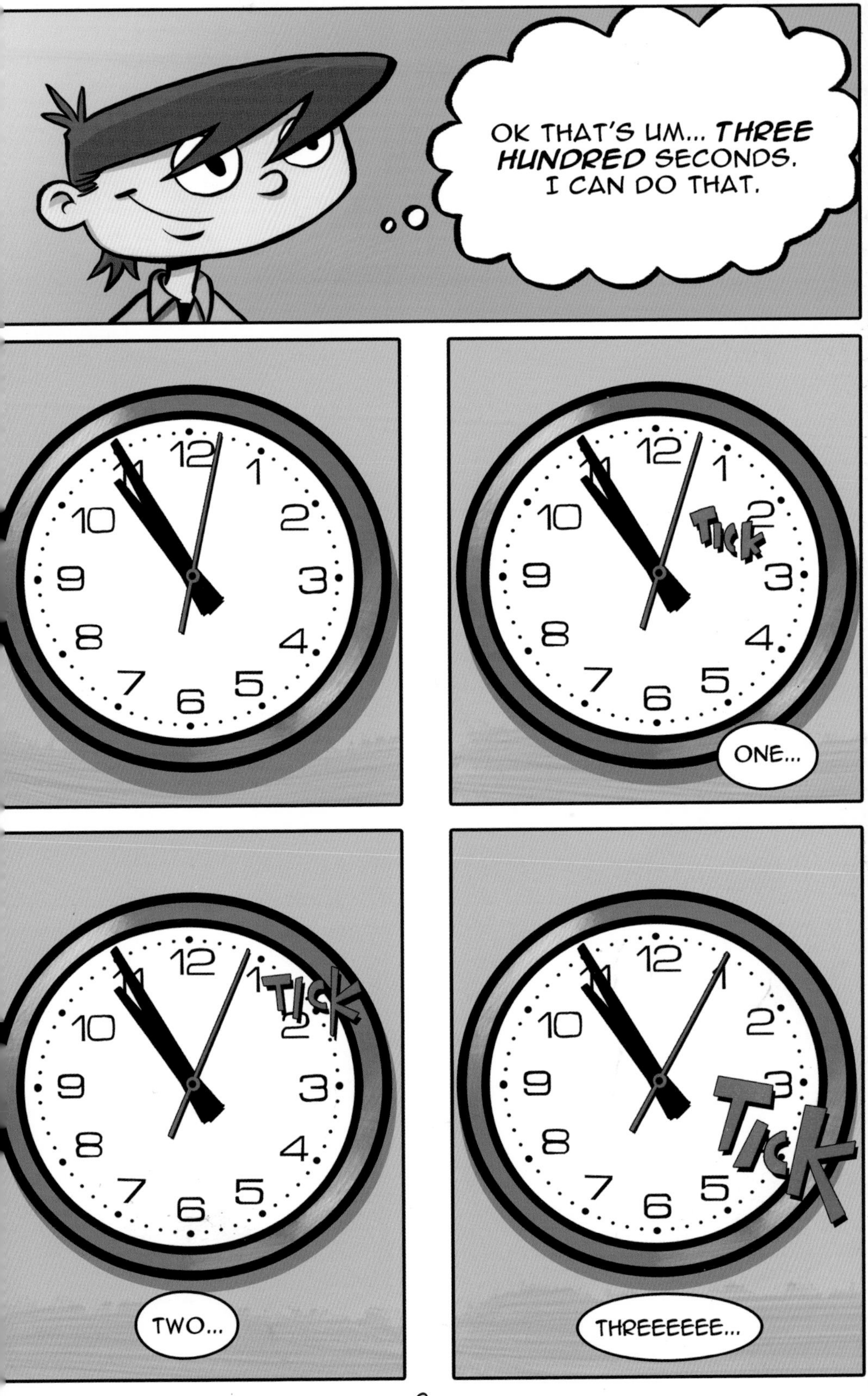

OK THAT'S UM... ***THREE HUNDRED*** SECONDS. I CAN DO THAT.
TICK
ONE...
TICK
TWO...
TICK
THREEEEEE...

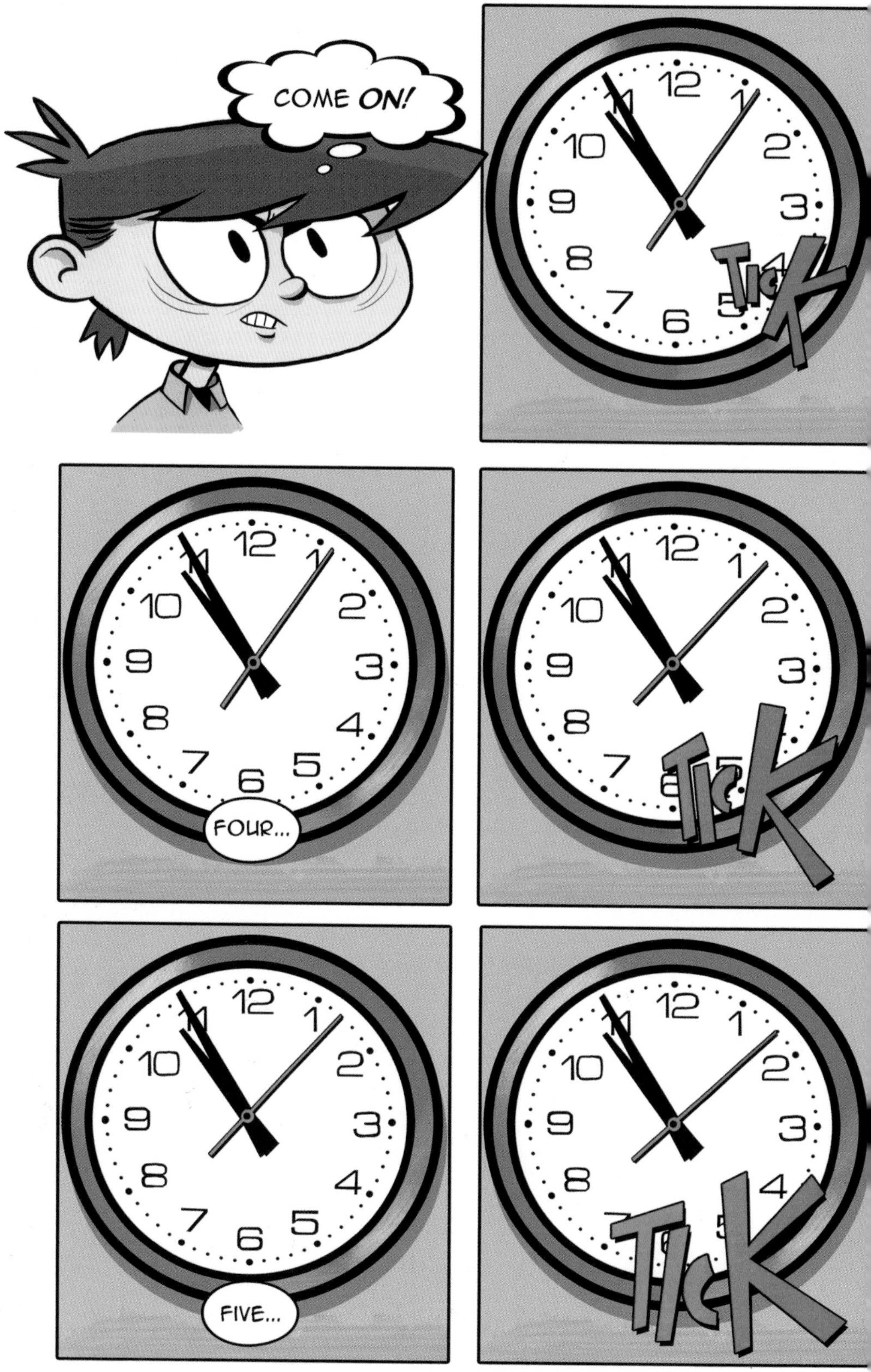

COME ON!
TICK
FOUR...
TICK
FIVE...
TICK

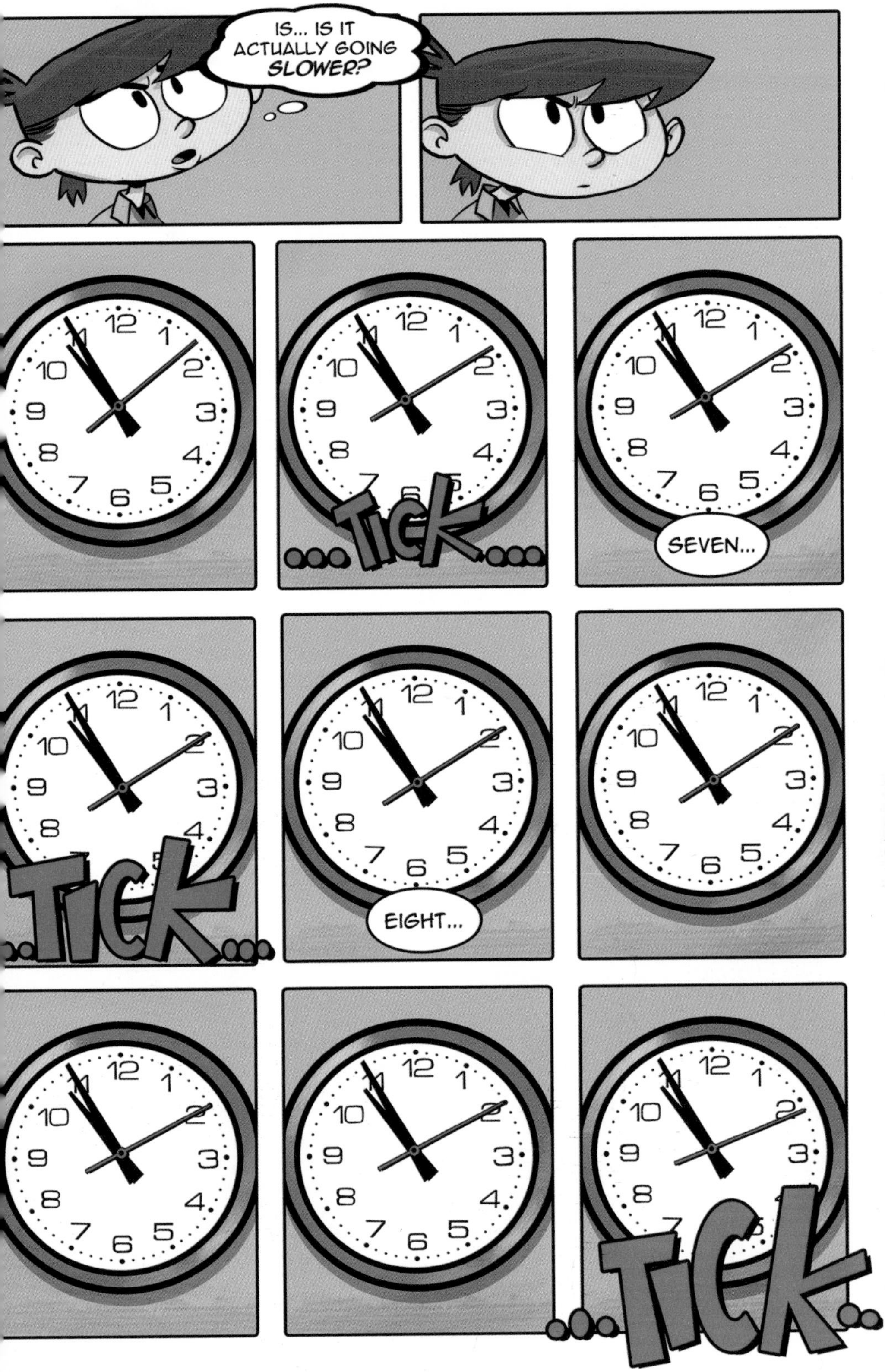

IS... IS IT ACTUALLY GOING SLOWER?
TICK
SEVEN...
TICK
EIGHT...
TICK

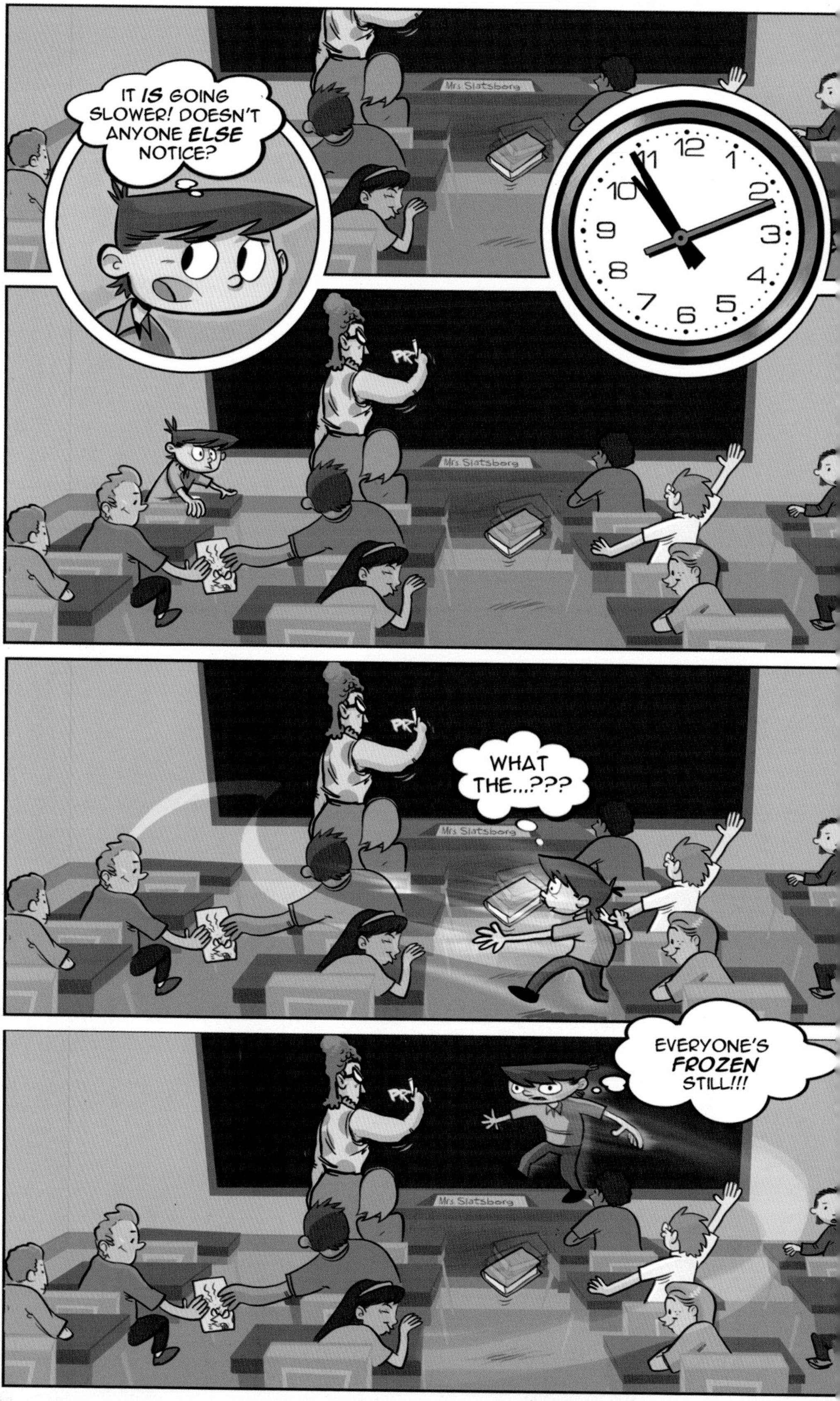
IT IS GOING SLOWER! DOESN'T ANYONE ELSE NOTICE?
Mrs. Slatsborg
PR
WHAT THE...???
EVERYONE'S FROZEN STILL!!!

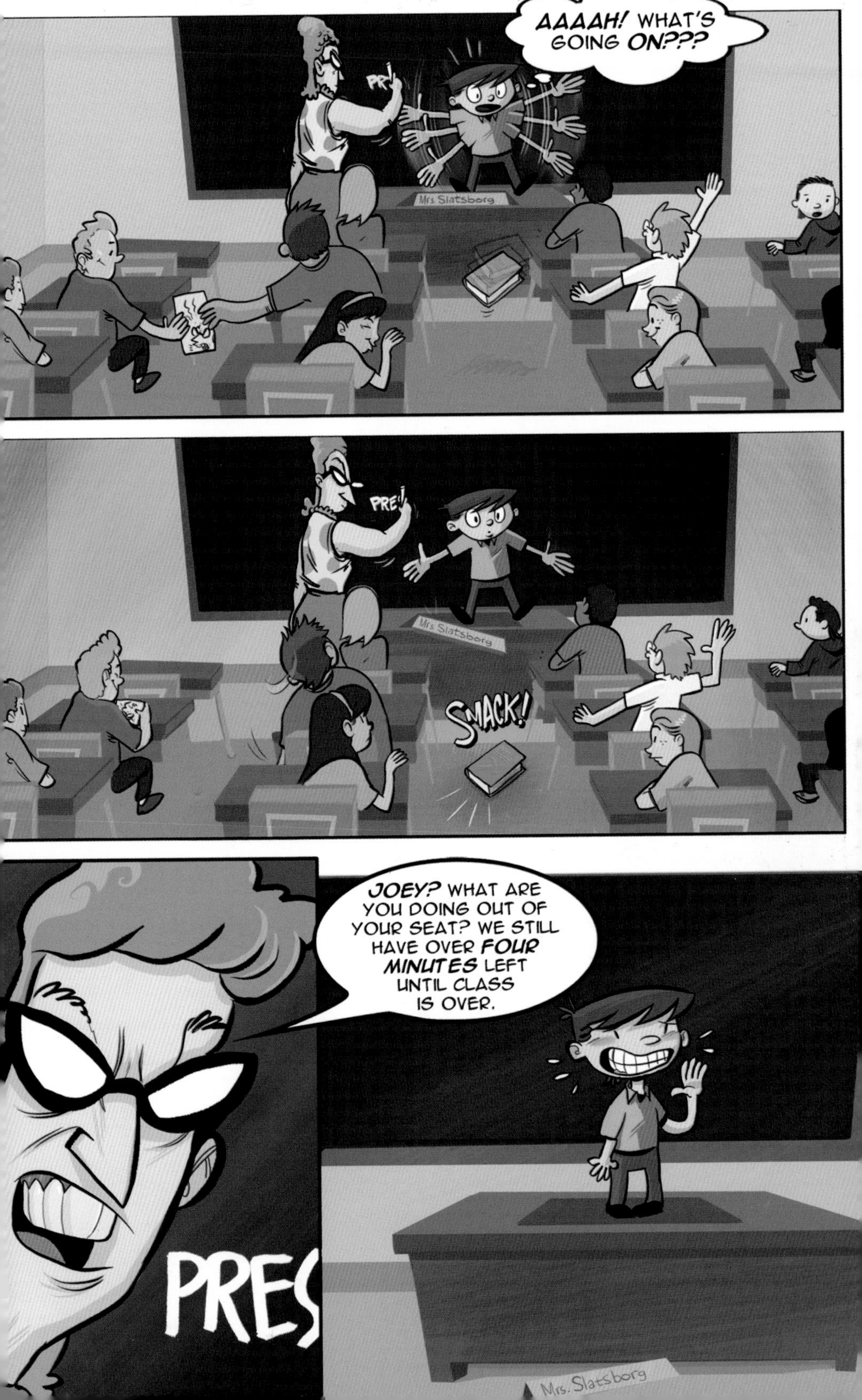
AAAAH! WHAT'S GOING ON???
PRE
Mrs Slatsborg
PRE
Mrs Slatsborg
SMACK!
JOEY? WHAT ARE YOU DOING OUT OF YOUR SEAT? WE STILL HAVE OVER FOUR MINUTES LEFT UNTIL CLASS IS OVER.
PRES
Mrs. Slatsborg

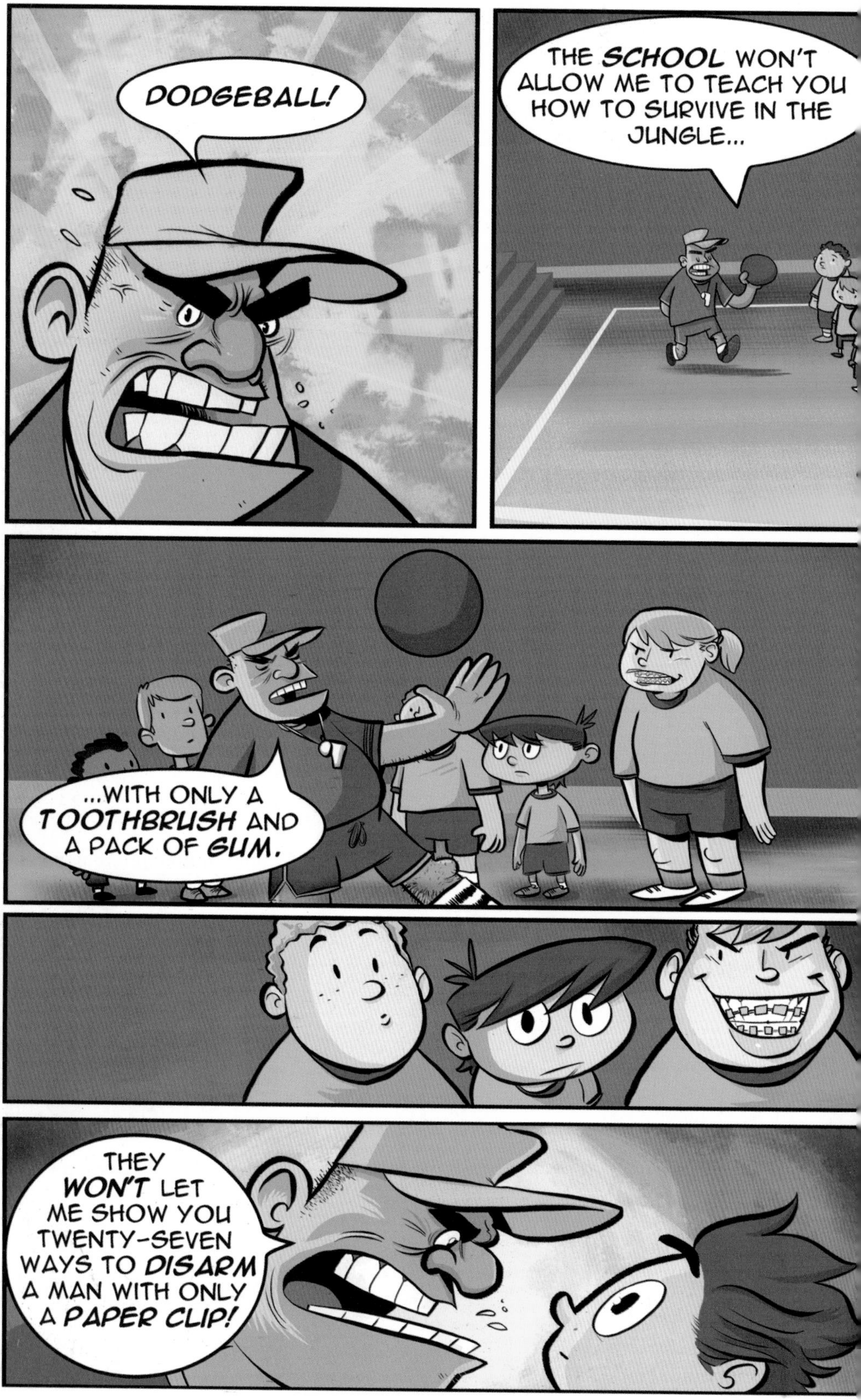
DODGEBALL!
THE SCHOOL WON'T ALLOW ME TO TEACH YOU HOW TO SURVIVE IN THE JUNGLE...
...WITH ONLY A TOOTHBRUSH AND A PACK OF GUM.
THEY WON'T LET ME SHOW YOU TWENTY-SEVEN WAYS TO DISARM A MAN WITH ONLY A PAPER CLIP!

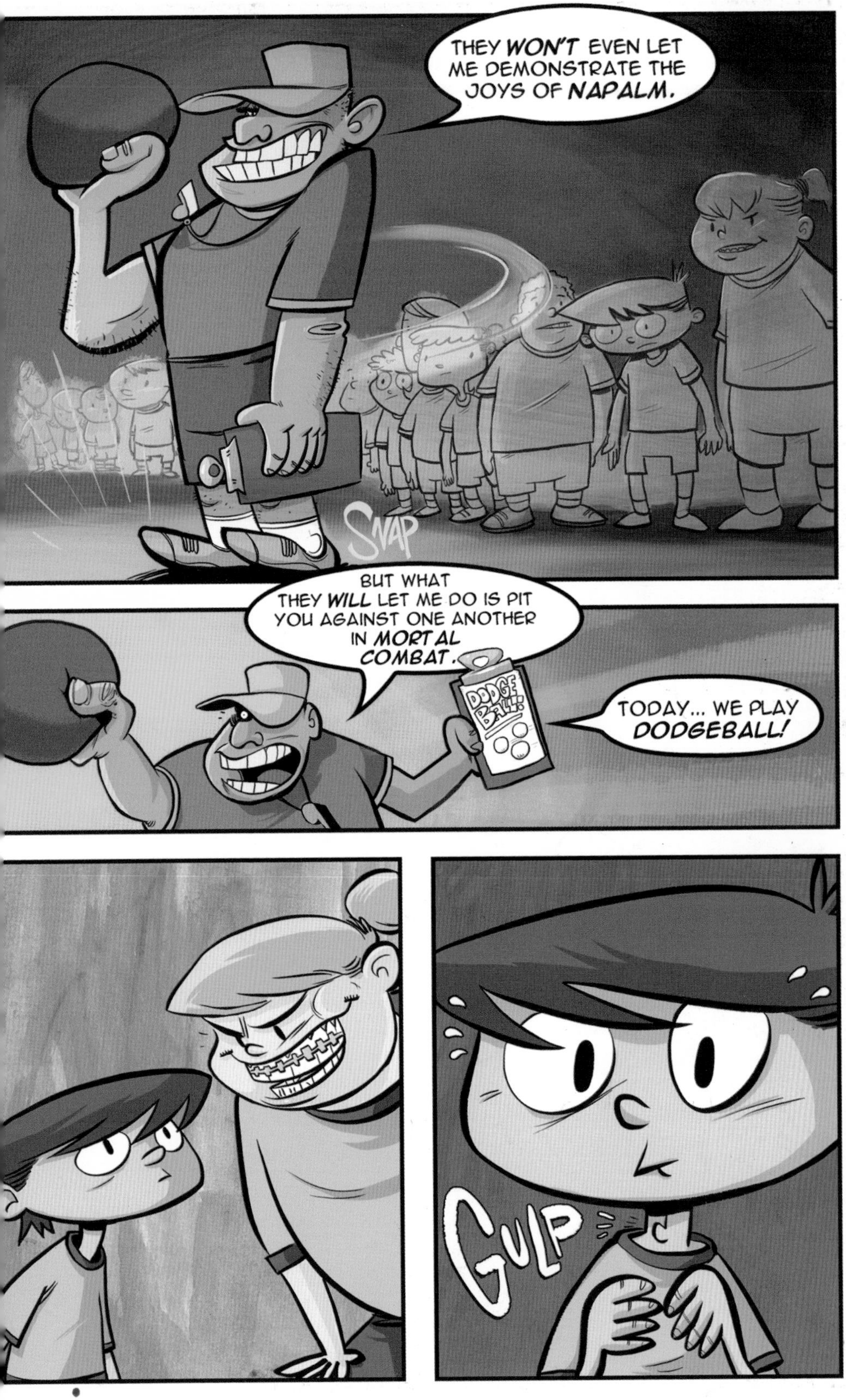
THEY WON'T EVEN LET ME DEMONSTRATE THE JOYS OF NAPALM.
SNAP
BUT WHAT THEY WILL LET ME DO IS PIT YOU AGAINST ONE ANOTHER IN MORTAL COMBAT.
DODGE BALL!
TODAY... WE PLAY DODGEBALL!
GULP

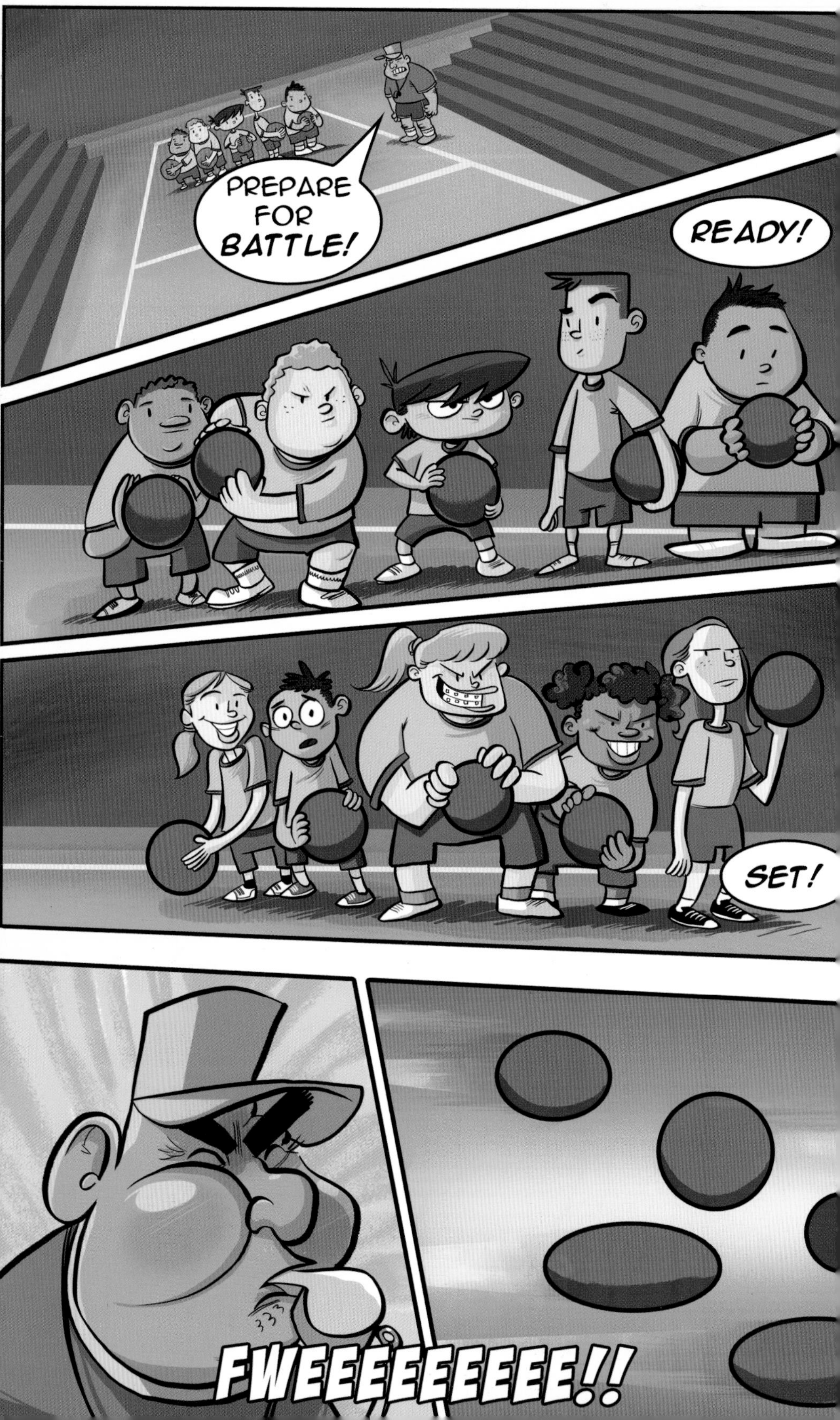
PREPARE FOR BATTLE!
READY!
SET!
FWEEEEEEEEEE!!

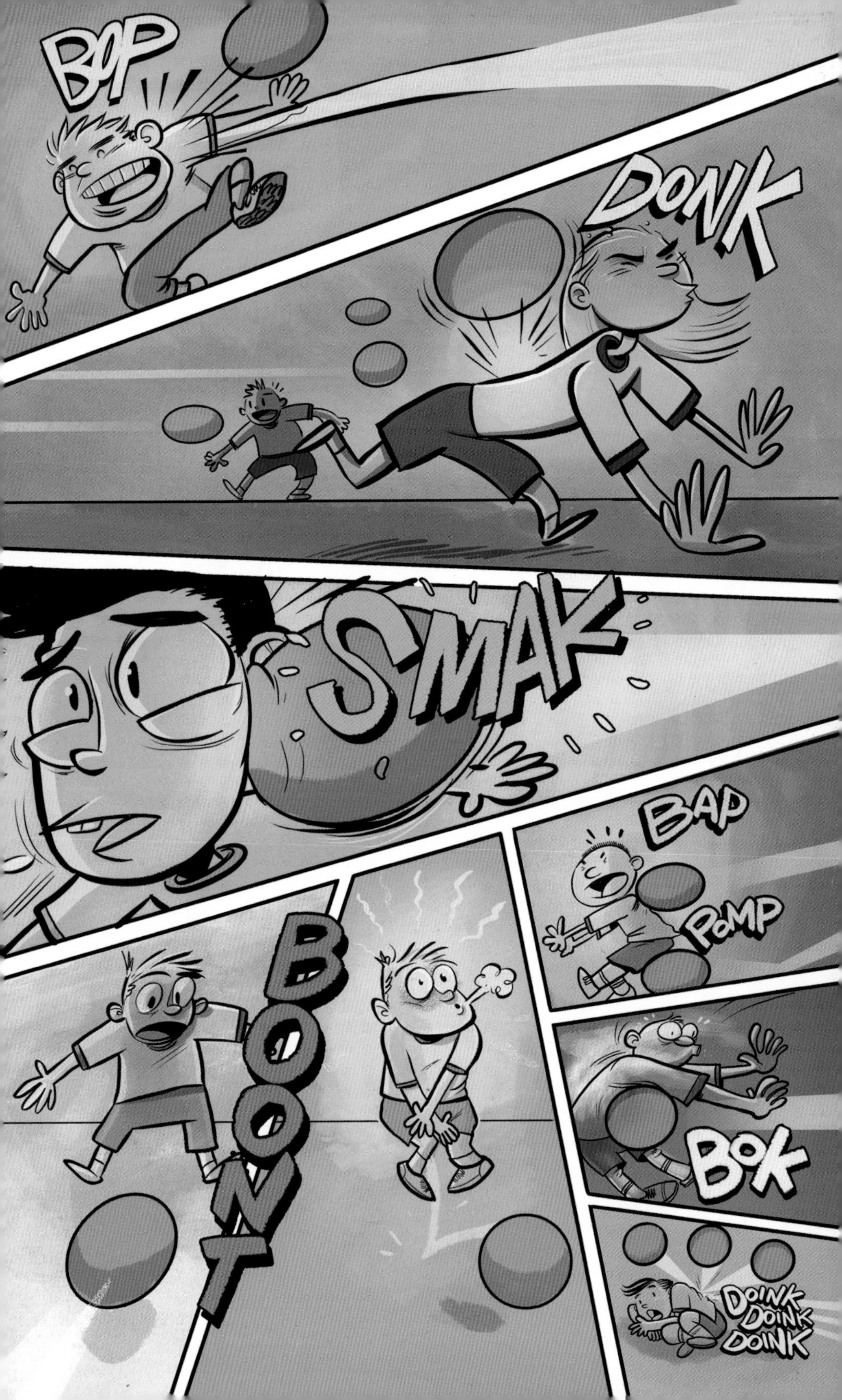
BOP
DONK
SMAK
BAP
POMP
BOOINT
BOK
DOINK
DOINK
DOINK

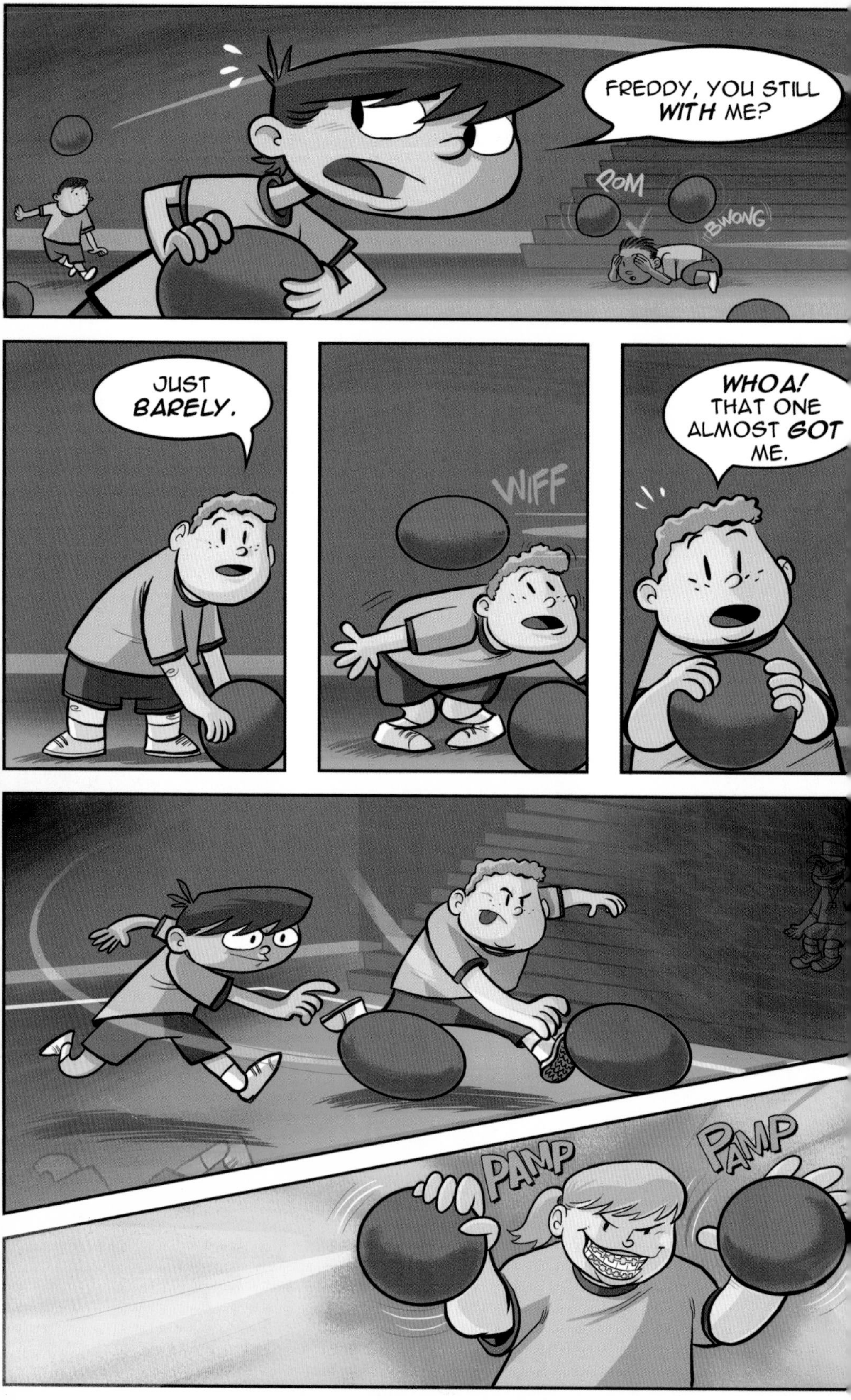
FREDDY, YOU STILL WITH ME?
POM
BWONG
JUST BARELY.
WIFF
WHOA! THAT ONE ALMOST GOT ME.
PAMP
PAMP

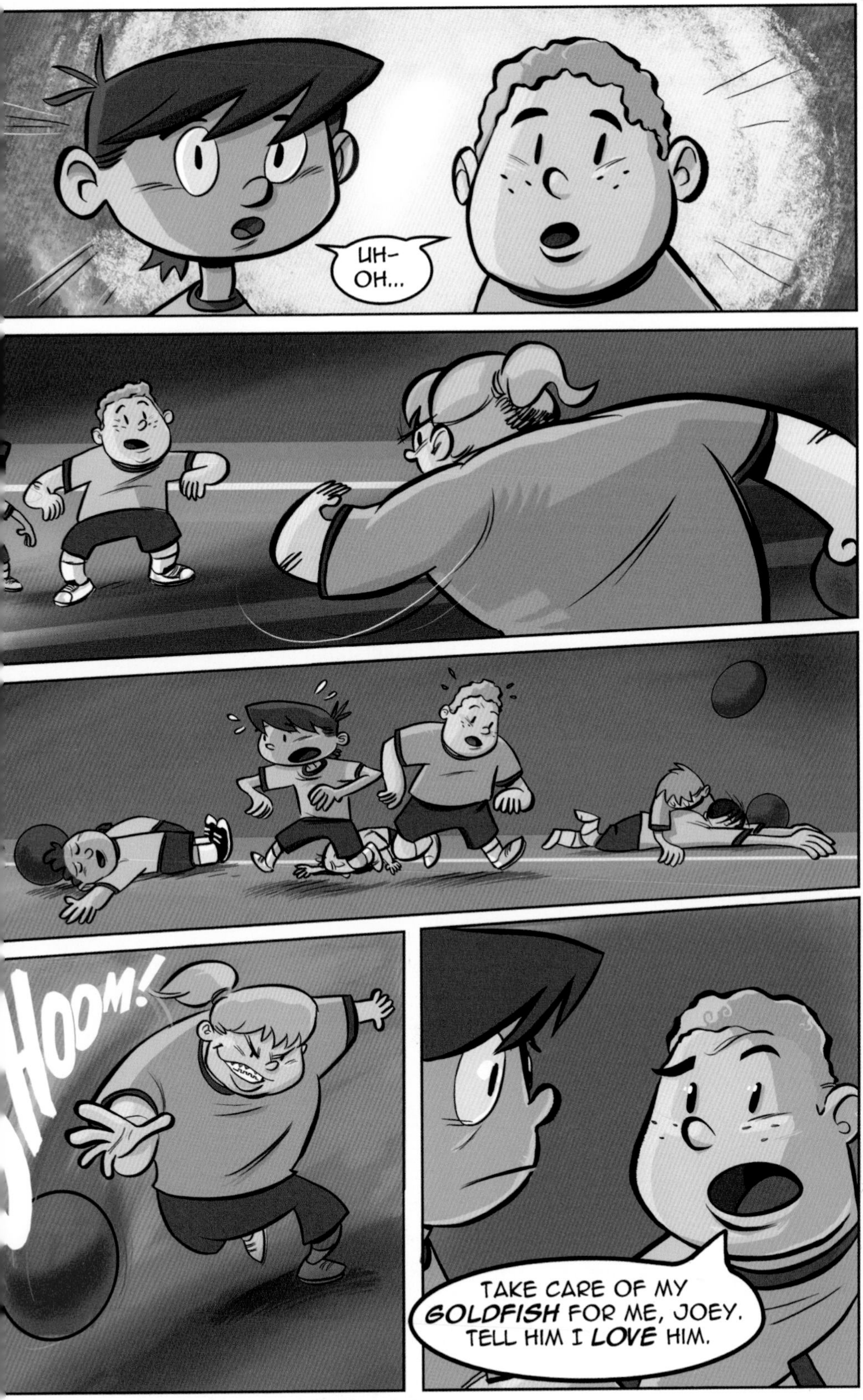
UH-
OH...
SHOOM!
TAKE CARE OF MY GOLDFISH FOR ME, JOEY. TELL HIM I LOVE HIM.

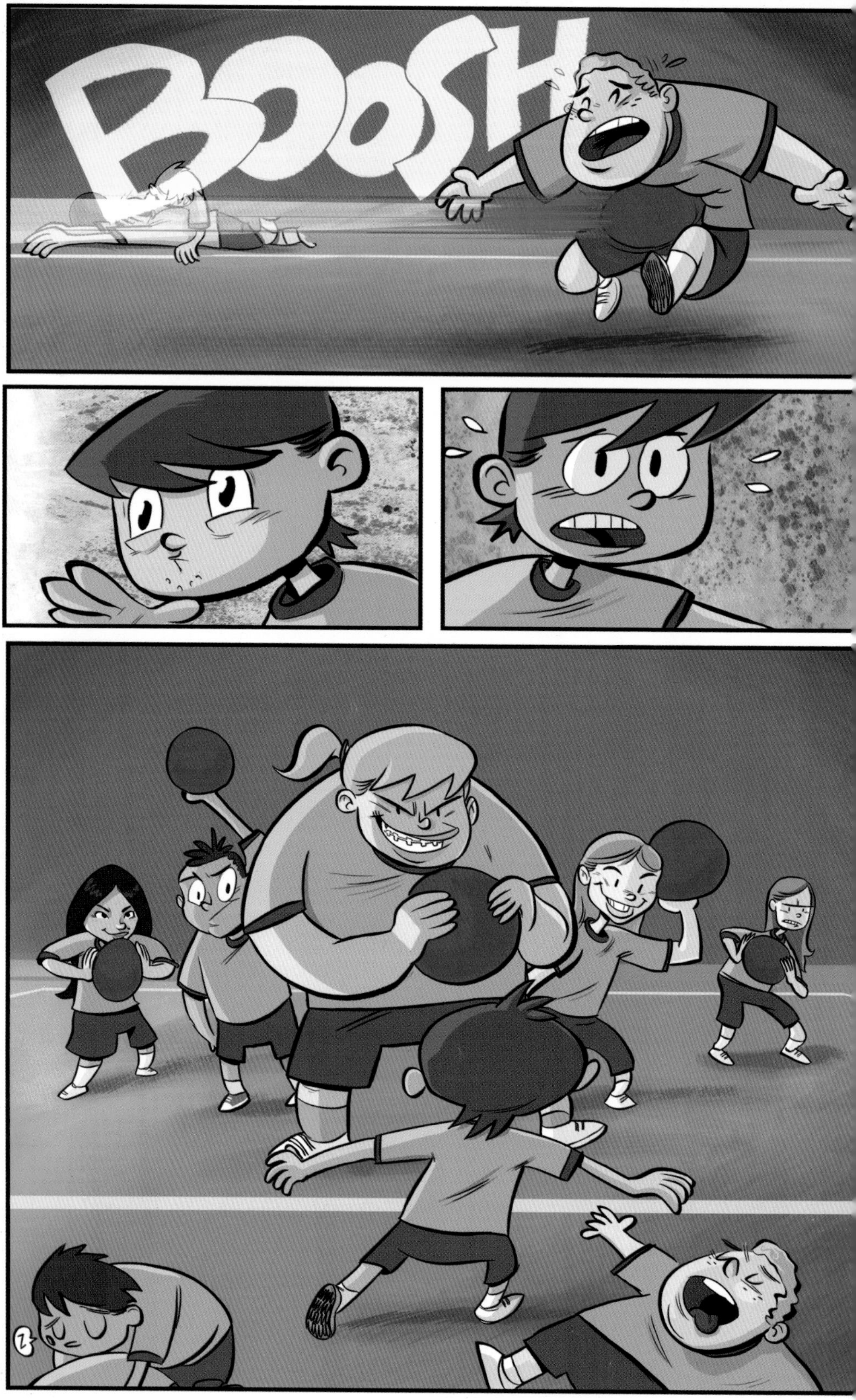
BOOSH
Z

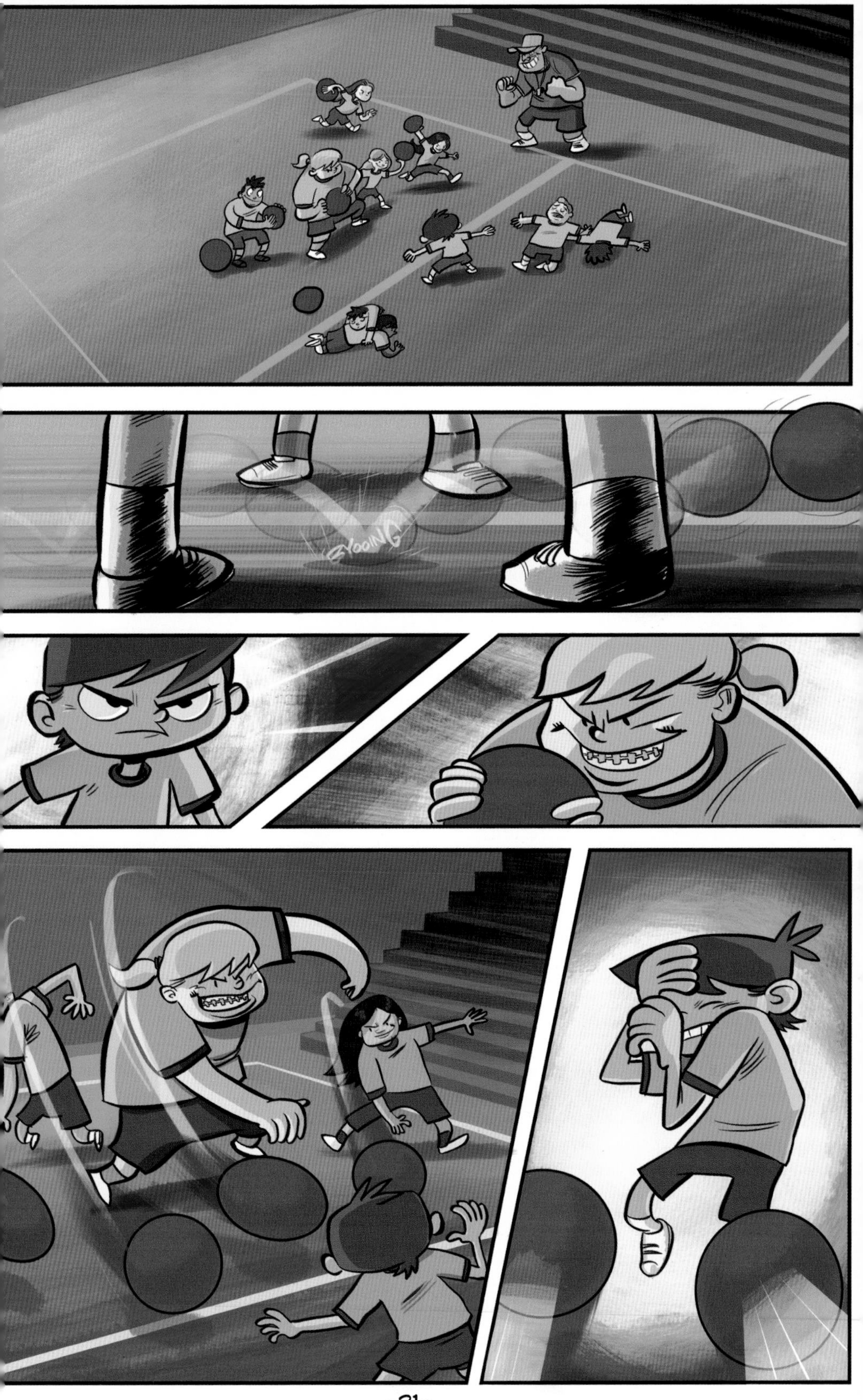
BYOOING

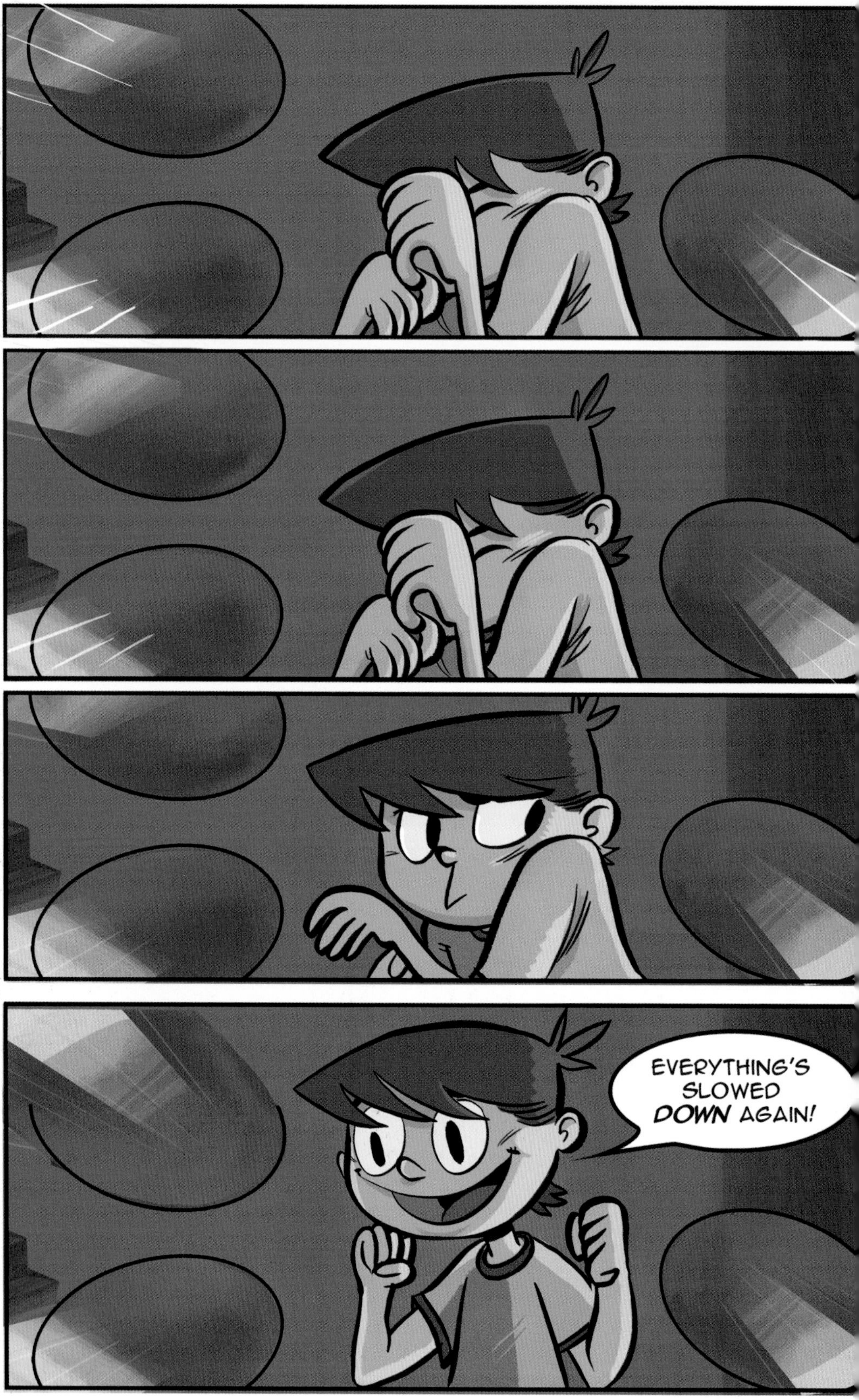
EVERYTHING'S SLOWED *DOWN* AGAIN!

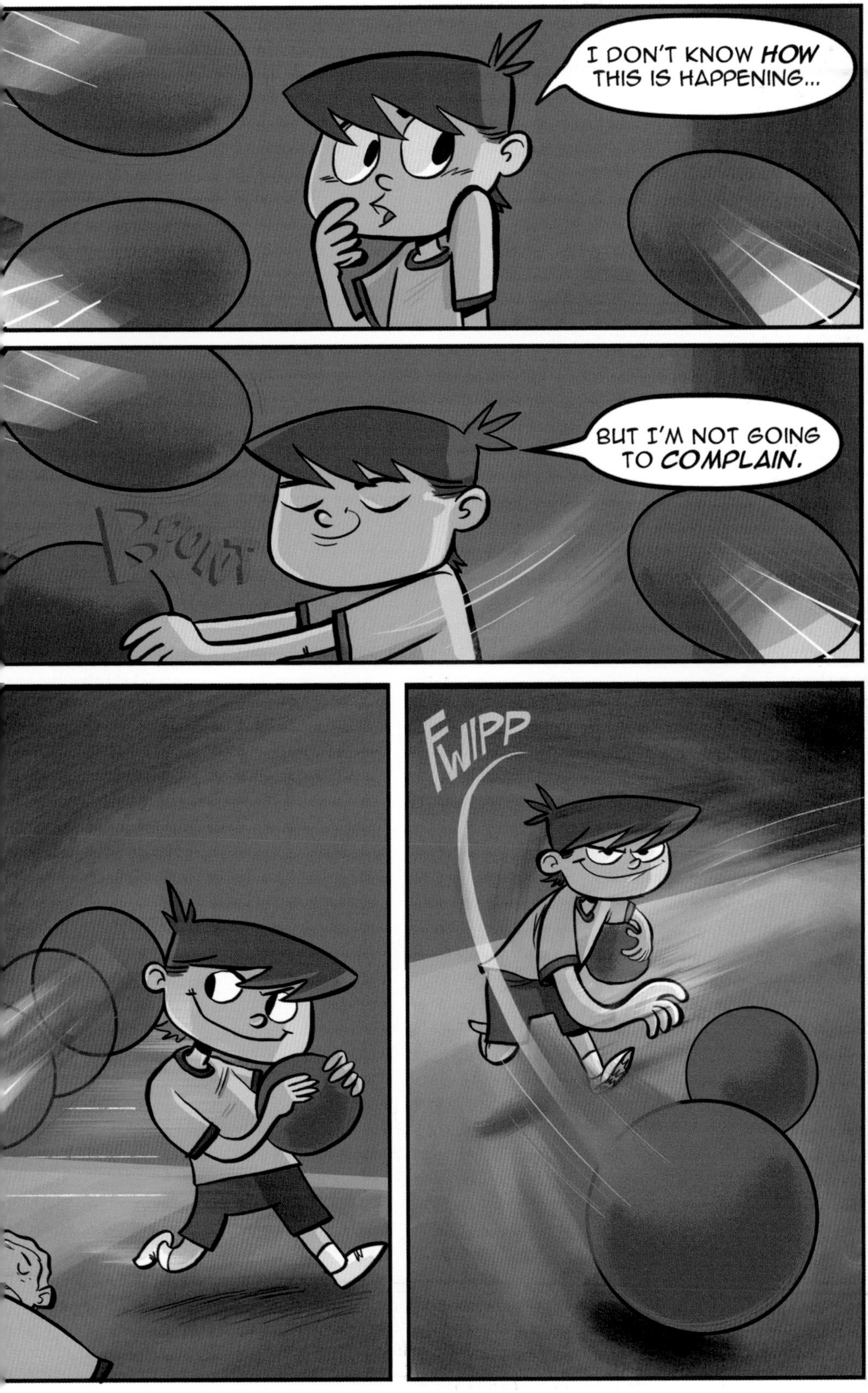
I DON'T KNOW *HOW* THIS IS HAPPENING...
BUT I'M NOT GOING TO *COMPLAIN.*
FWIPP

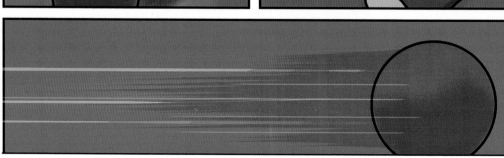

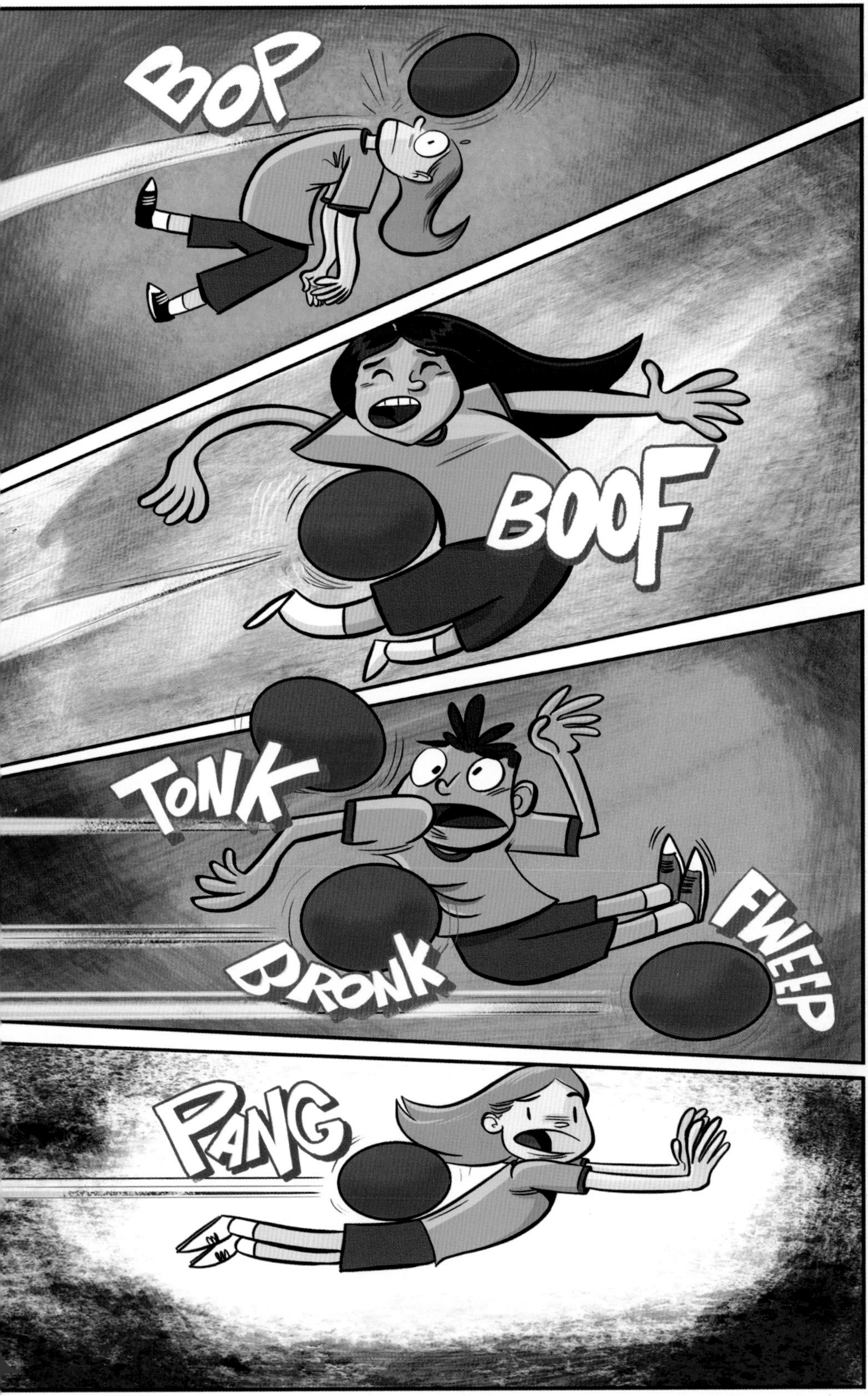
BOP
BOOF
TONK
BRONK
FWEEP
PANG

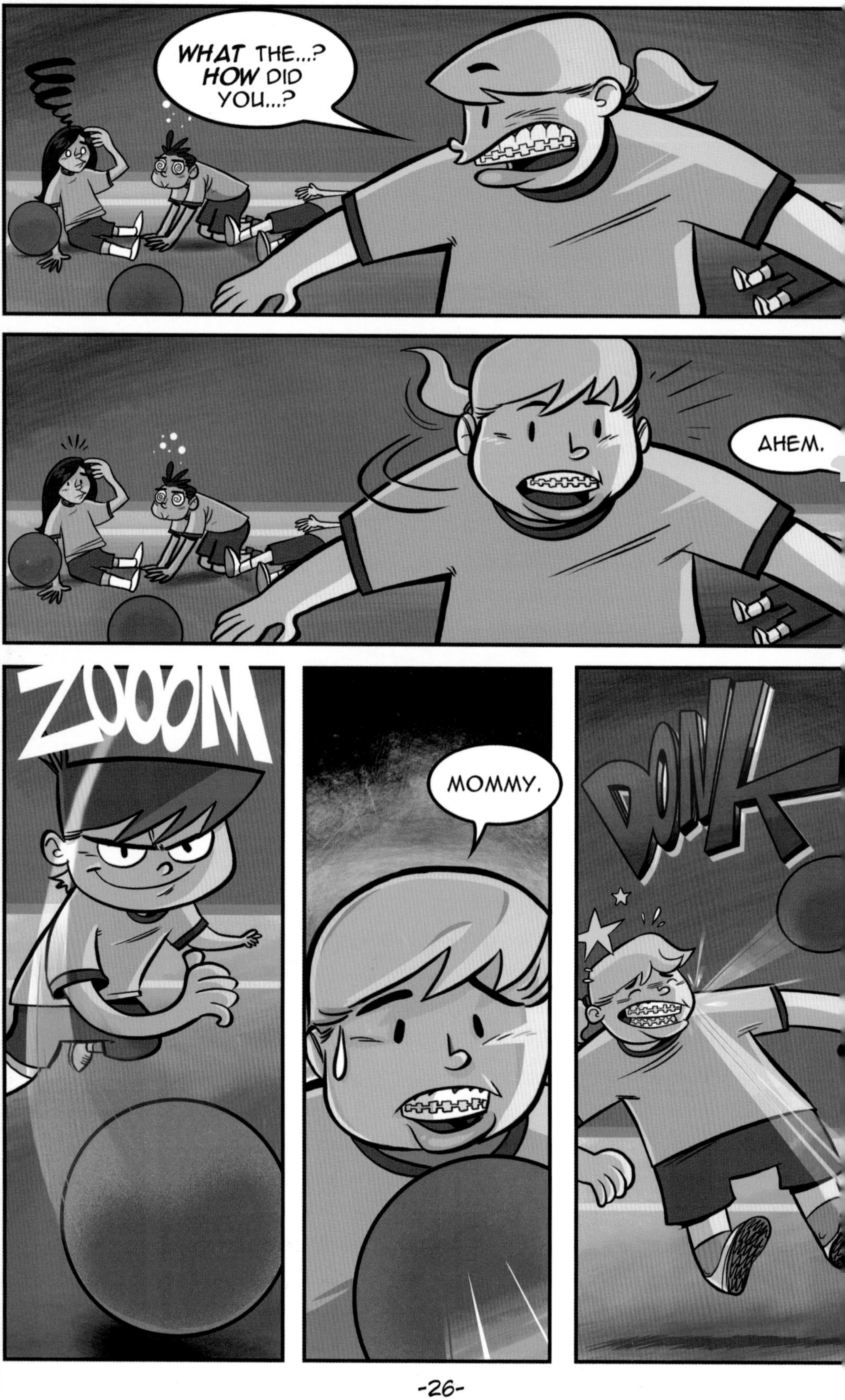

WHAT THE...? HOW DID YOU...?
AHEM.
ZOOOM
MOMMY.
DONK

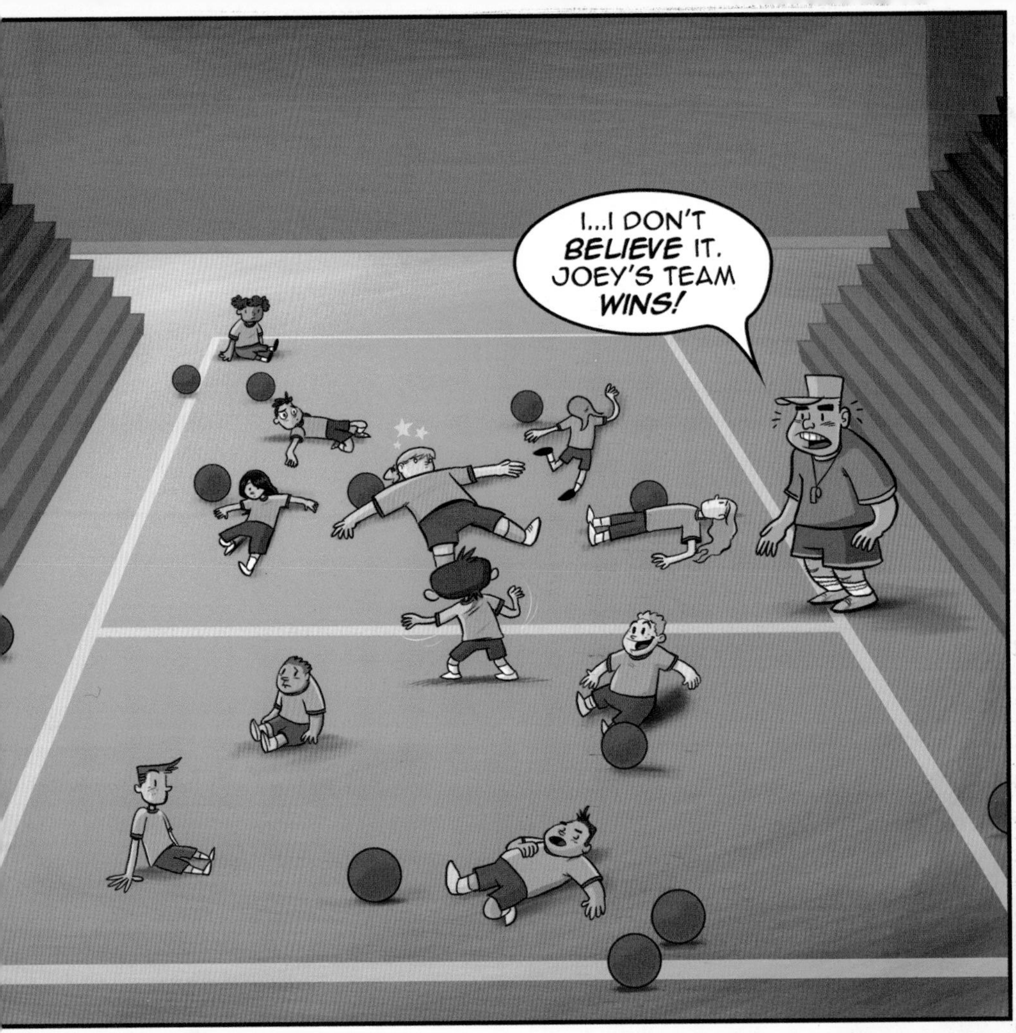
I...I DON'T BELIEVE IT. JOEY'S TEAM WINS!

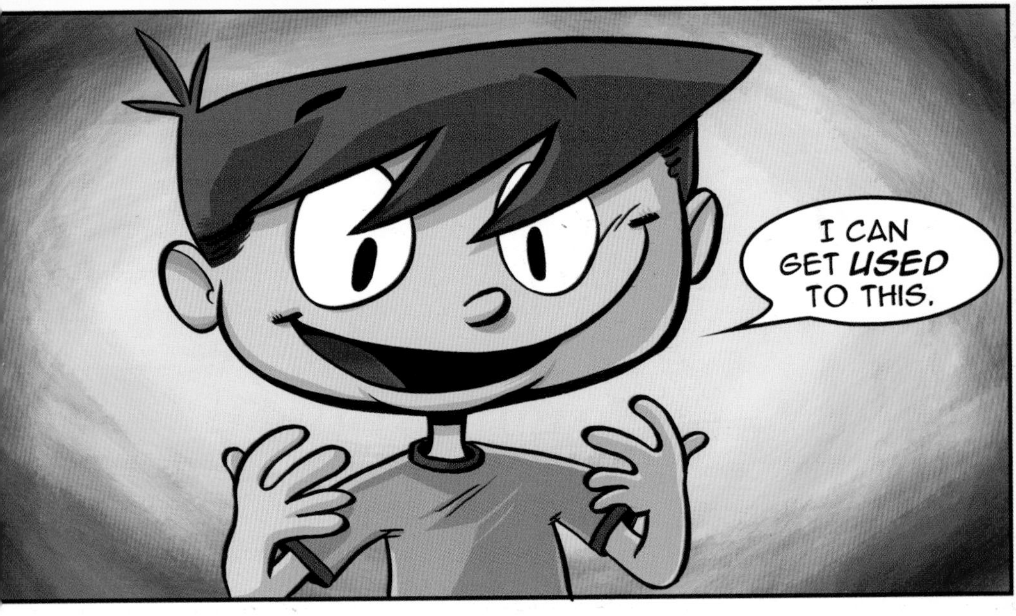
I CAN GET USED TO THIS.

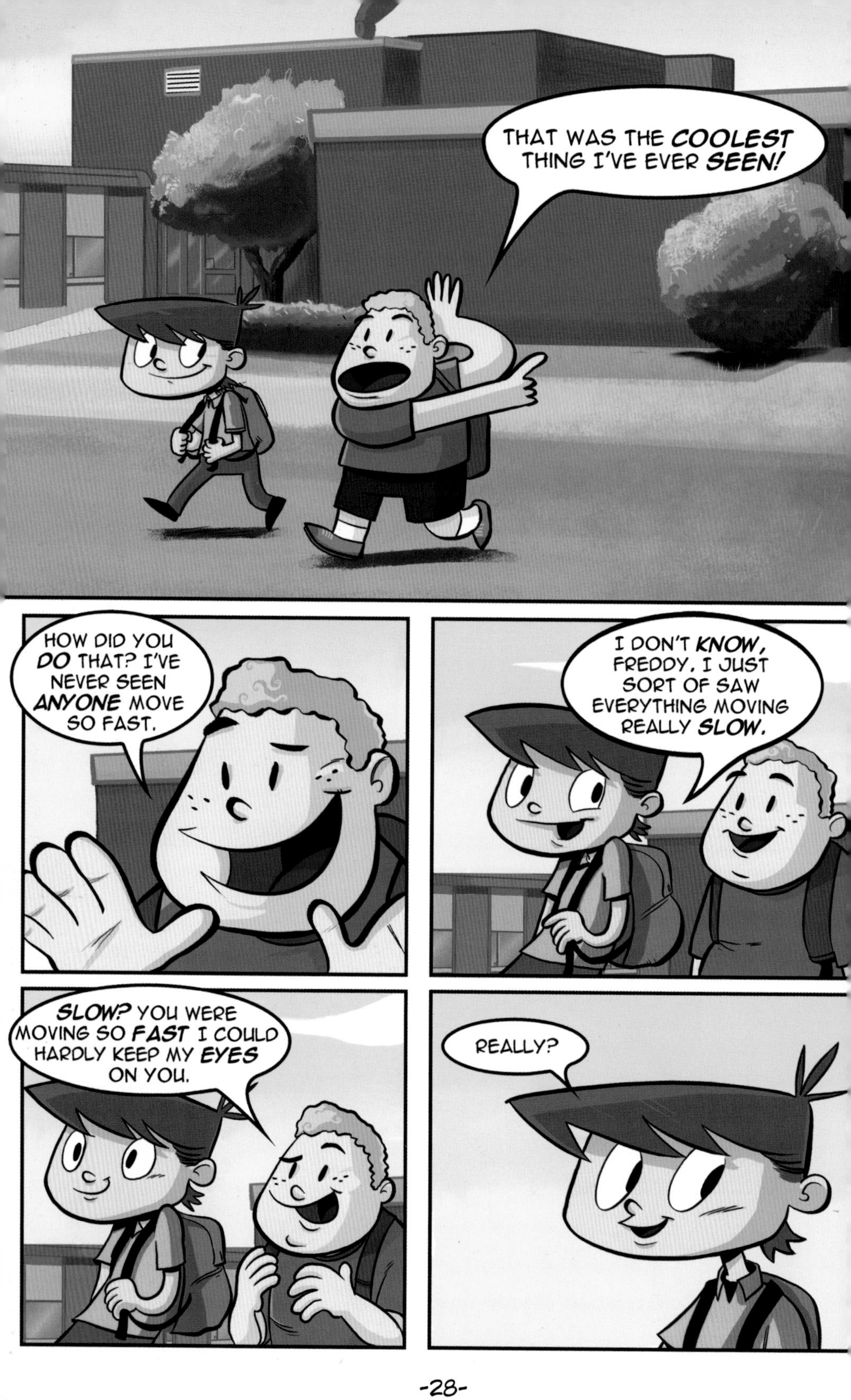
THAT WAS THE COOLEST THING I'VE EVER SEEN!
HOW DID YOU DO THAT? I'VE NEVER SEEN ANYONE MOVE SO FAST.
I DON'T KNOW, FREDDY. I JUST SORT OF SAW EVERYTHING MOVING REALLY SLOW.
SLOW? YOU WERE MOVING SO FAST I COULD HARDLY KEEP MY EYES ON YOU.
REALLY?

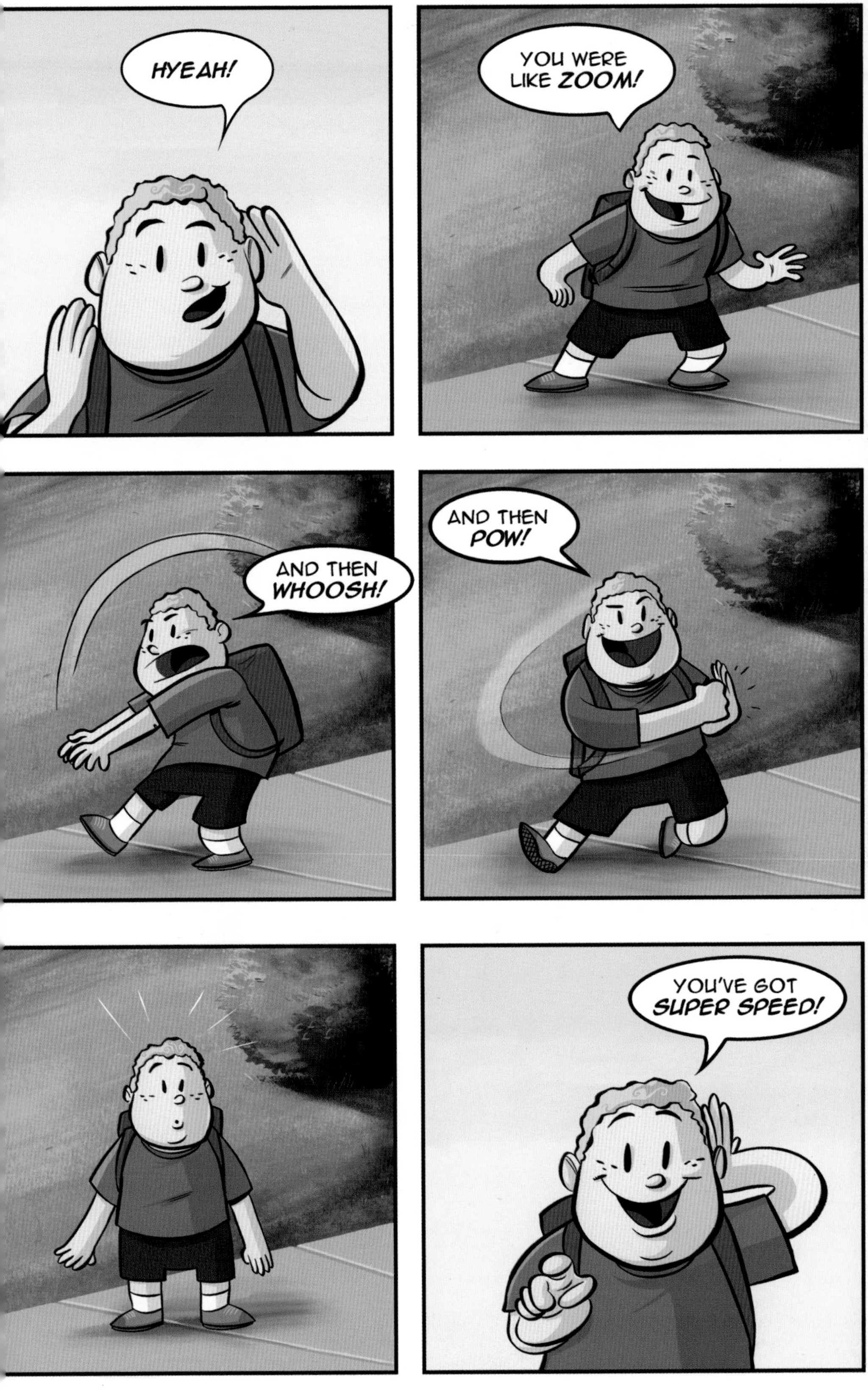
HYEAH!
YOU WERE LIKE ZOOM!
AND THEN WHOOSH!
AND THEN POW!
YOU'VE GOT SUPER SPEED!

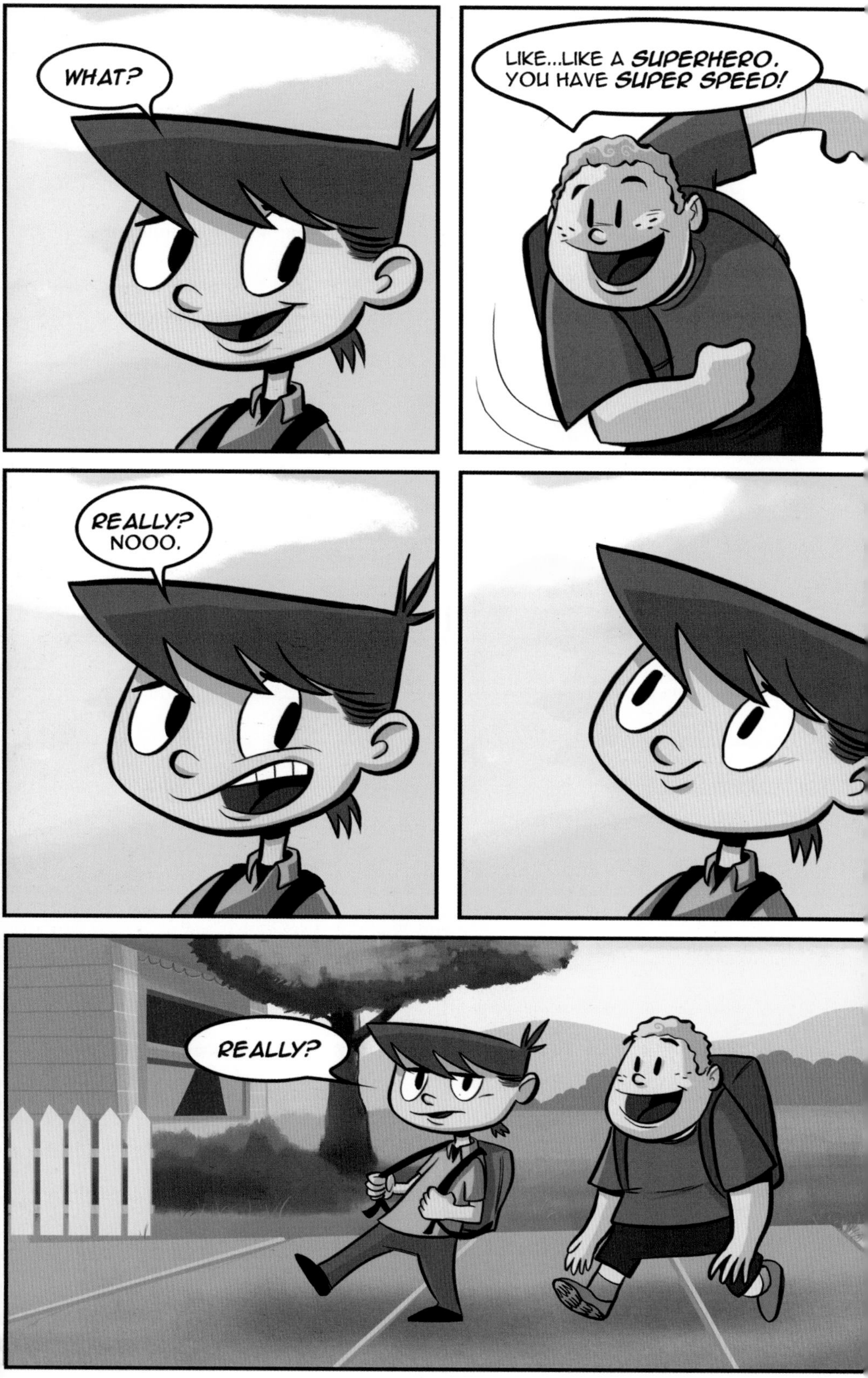
WHAT?
LIKE...LIKE A SUPERHERO. YOU HAVE SUPER SPEED!
REALLY? NOOO.
REALLY?

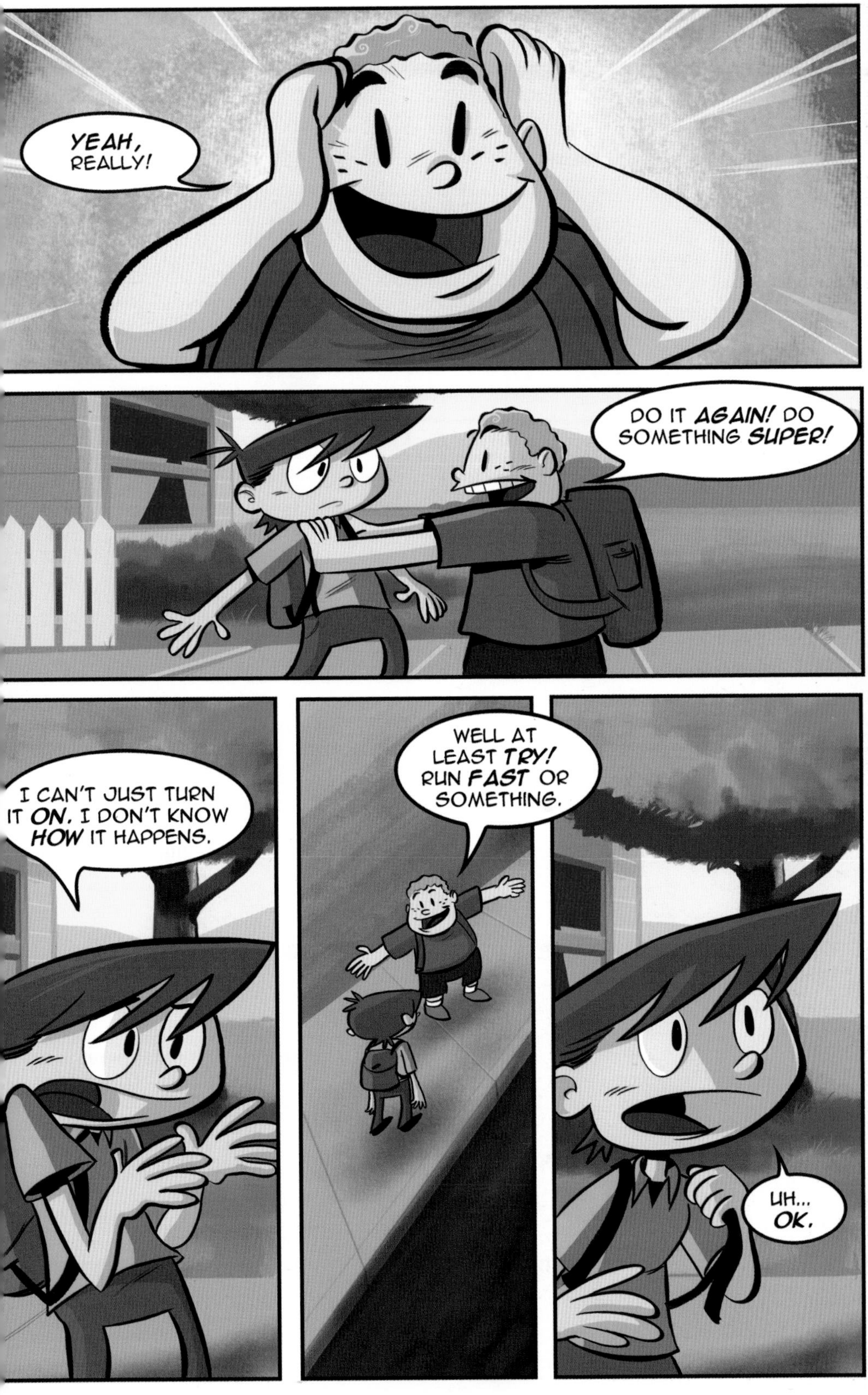
YEAH, REALLY!
DO IT AGAIN! DO SOMETHING SUPER!
I CAN'T JUST TURN IT ON. I DON'T KNOW HOW IT HAPPENS.
WELL AT LEAST TRY! RUN FAST OR SOMETHING.
UH... OK.

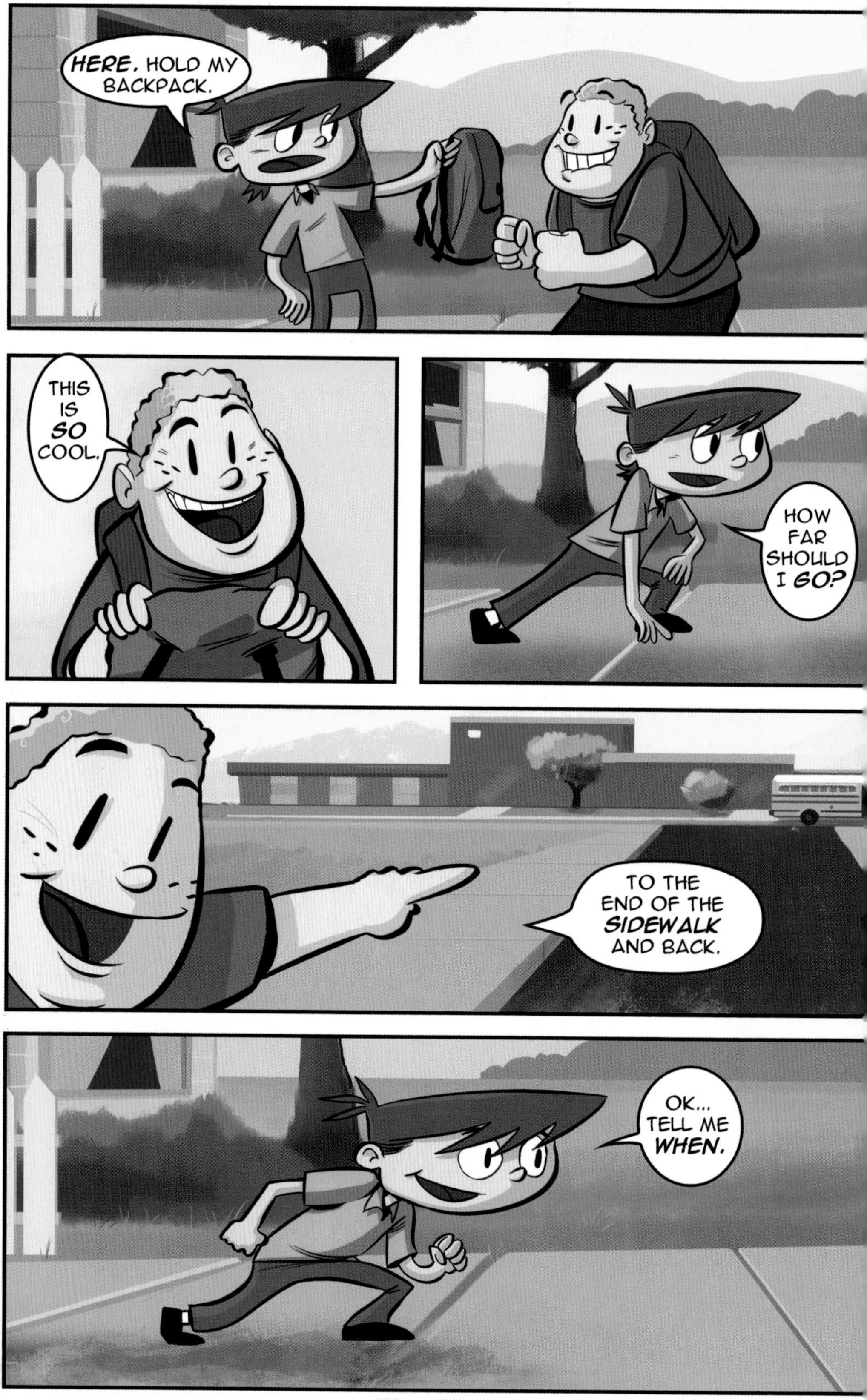
HERE. HOLD MY BACKPACK.
THIS IS SO COOL.
HOW FAR SHOULD I GO?
TO THE END OF THE SIDEWALK AND BACK.
OK... TELL ME WHEN.

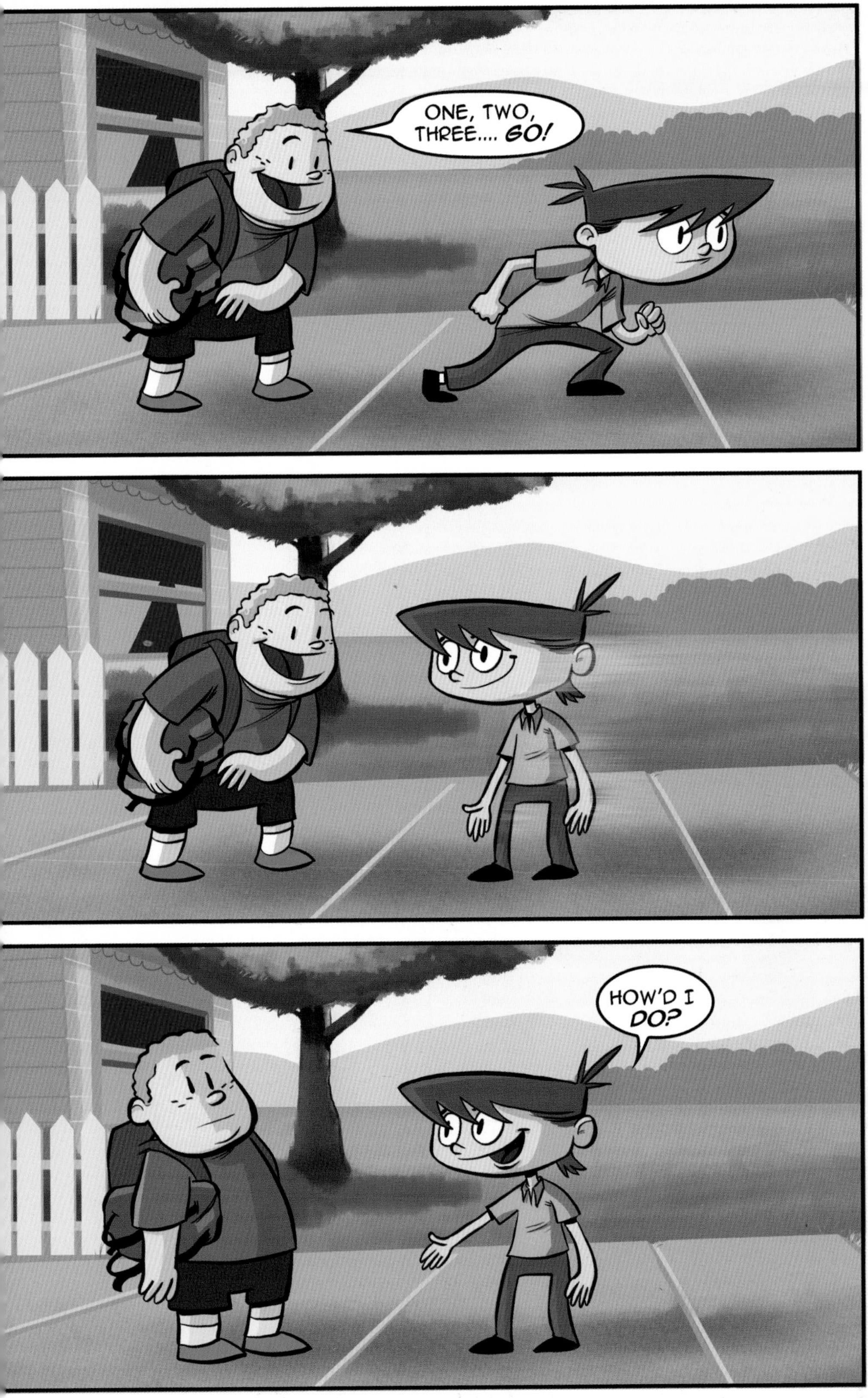

ONE, TWO, THREE.... GO!
HOW'D I DO?

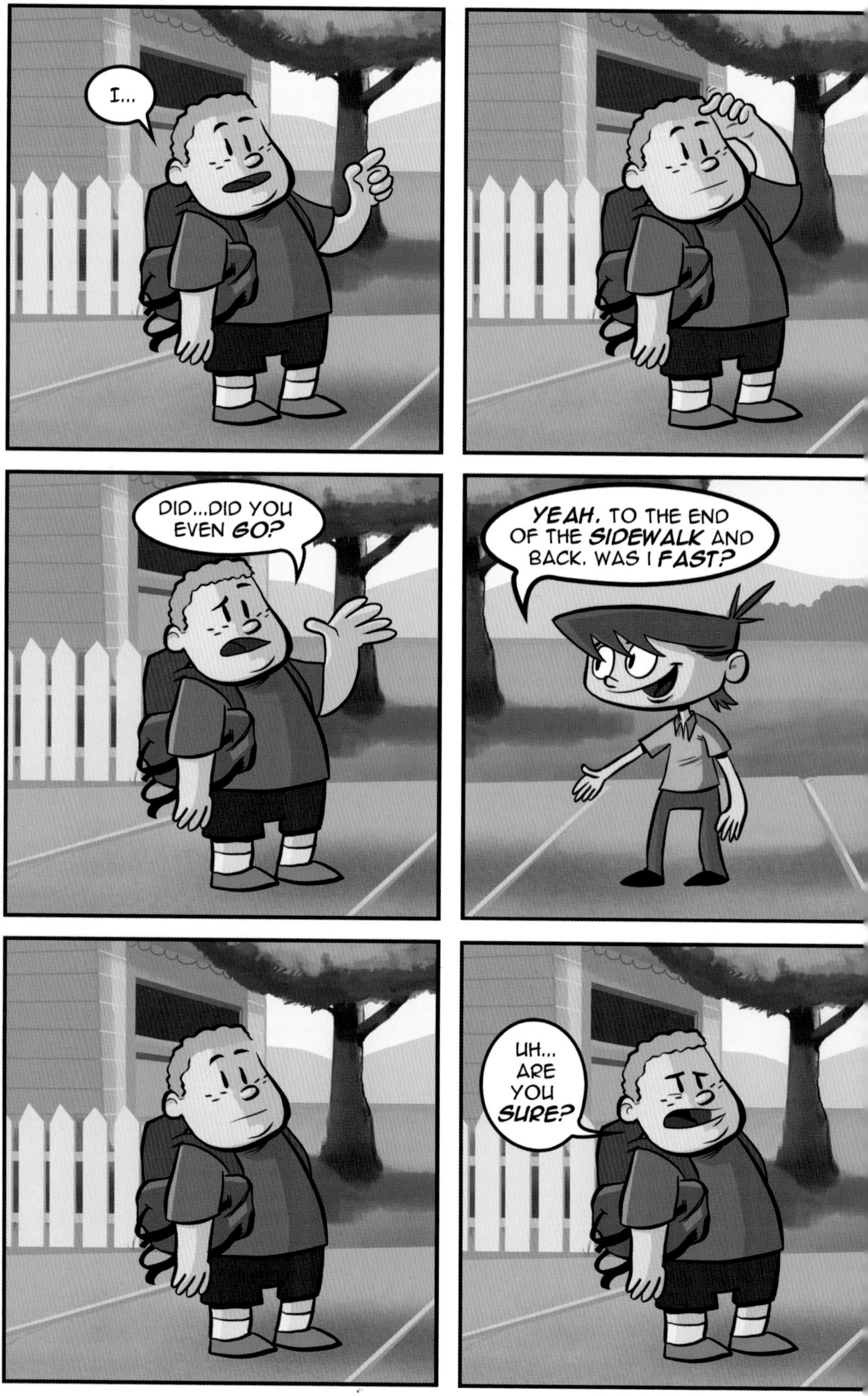
I...
DID...DID YOU EVEN GO?
YEAH. TO THE END OF THE SIDEWALK AND BACK. WAS I FAST?
UH... ARE YOU SURE?

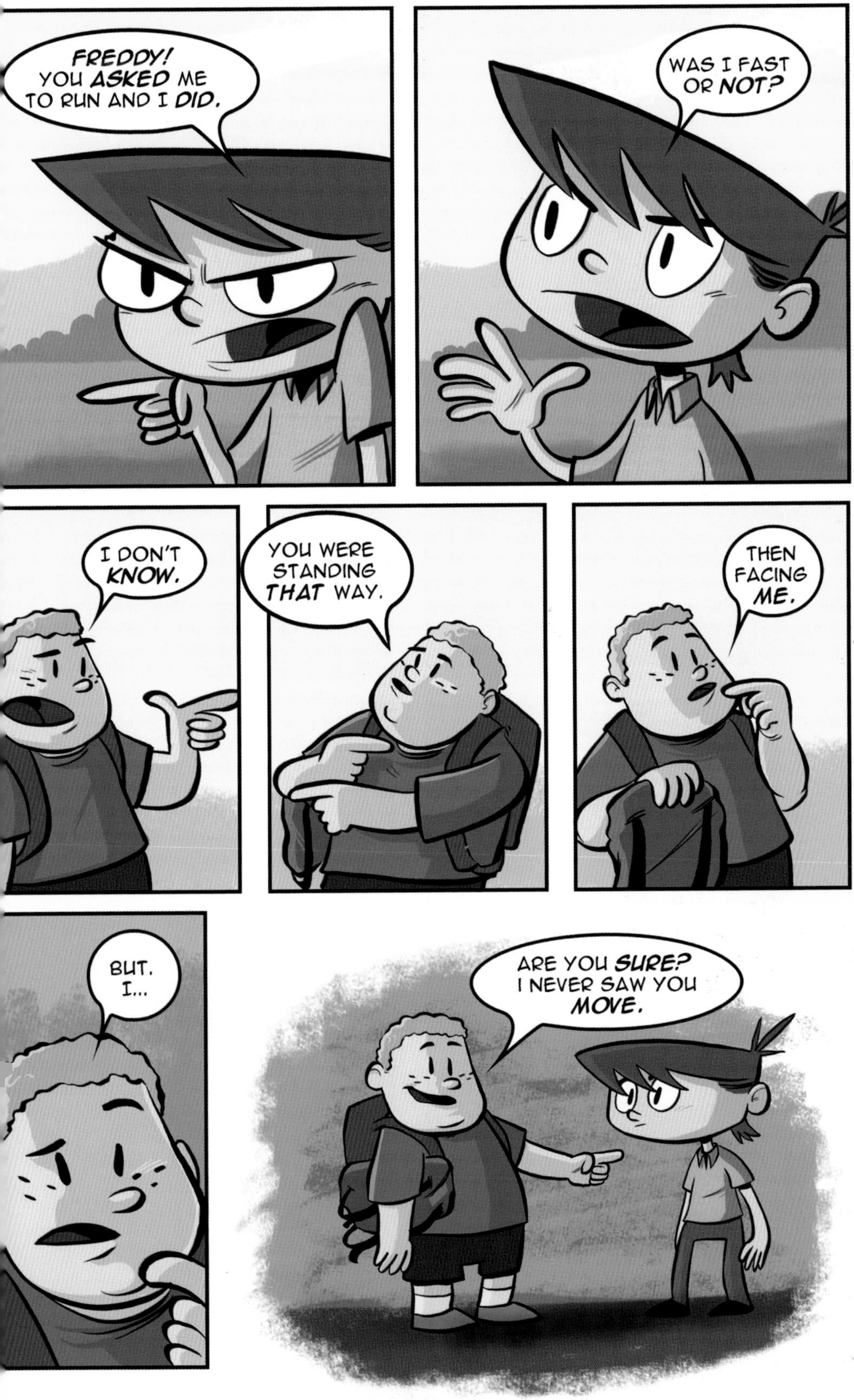
FREDDY! YOU ASKED ME TO RUN AND I DID.
WAS I FAST OR NOT?
I DON'T KNOW.
YOU WERE STANDING THAT WAY.
THEN FACING ME.
BUT. I...
ARE YOU SURE? I NEVER SAW YOU MOVE.

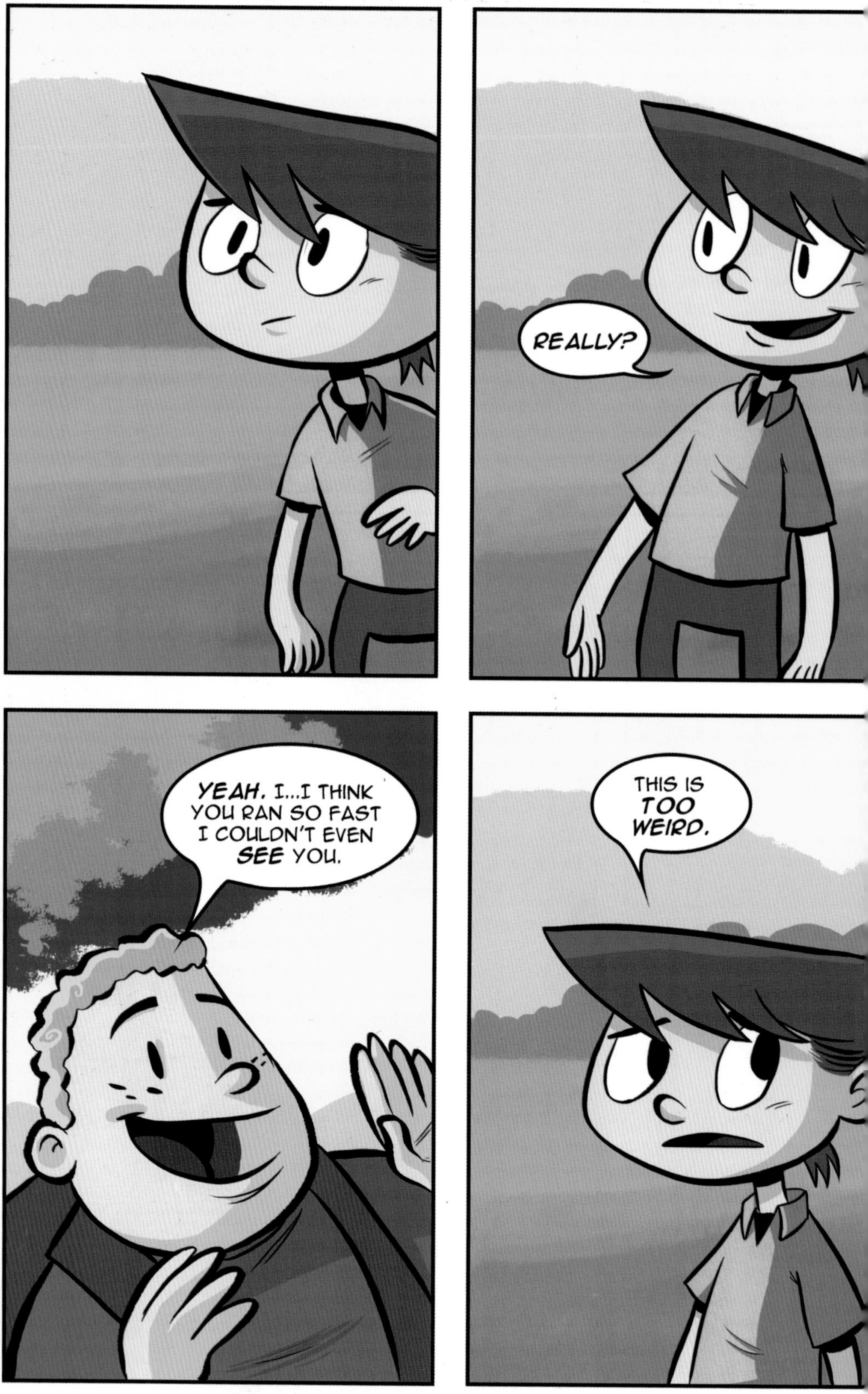
REALLY?
YEAH. I...I THINK YOU RAN SO FAST I COULDN'T EVEN SEE YOU.
THIS IS TOO WEIRD.

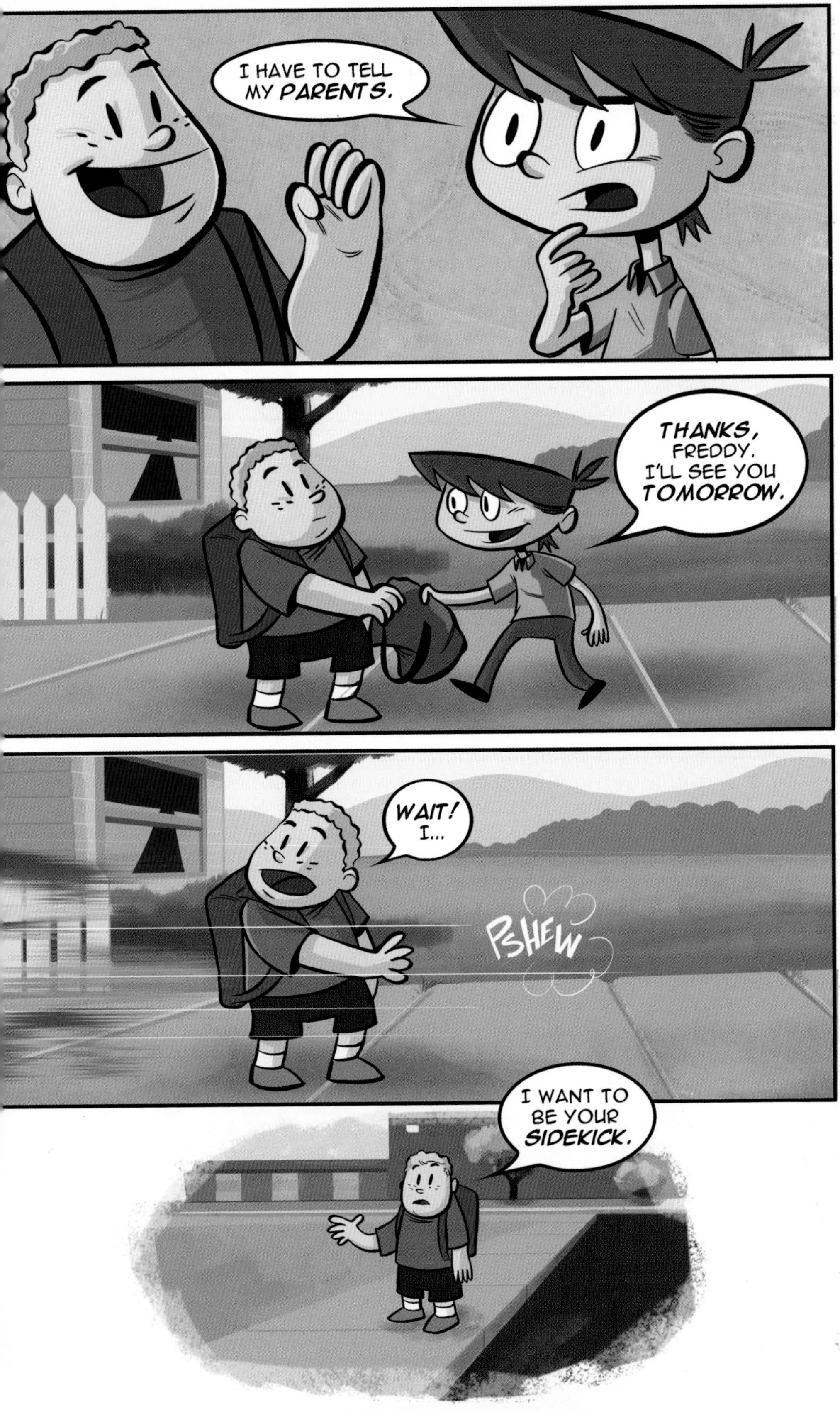
I HAVE TO TELL MY PARENTS.
THANKS, FREDDY. I'LL SEE YOU TOMORROW.
WAIT! I...
PSHEW
I WANT TO BE YOUR SIDEKICK.

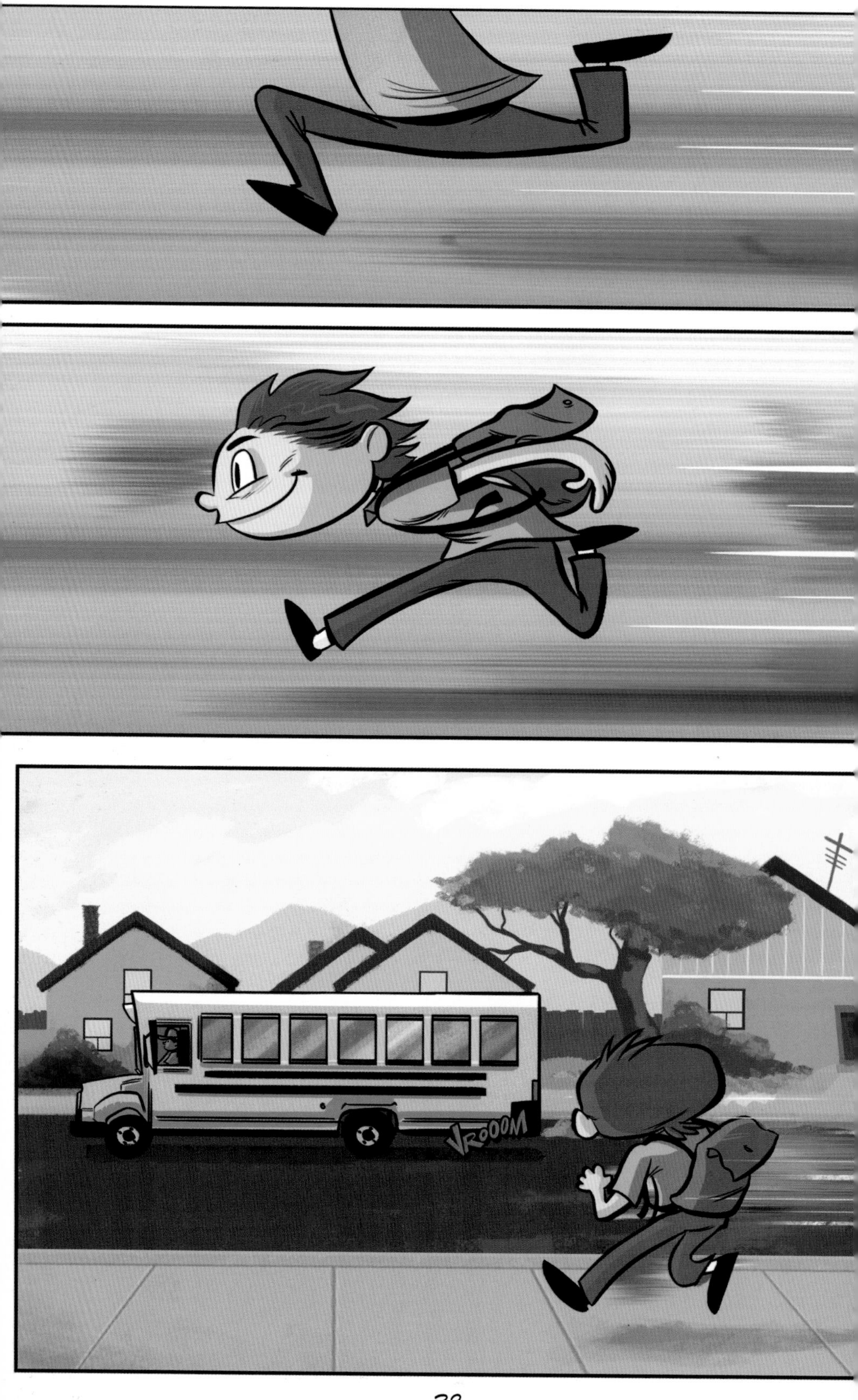
VROOOM

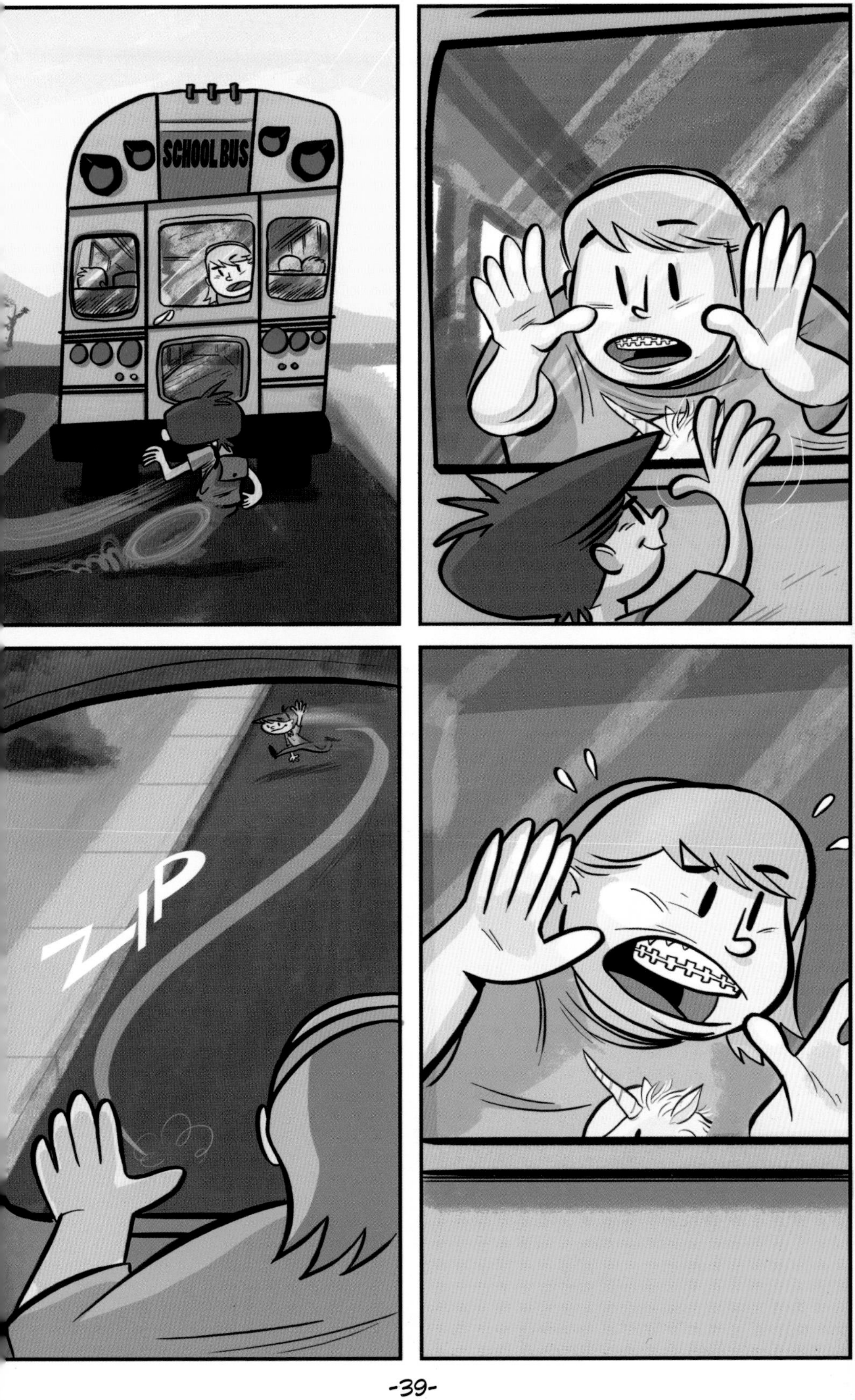
SCHOOL BUS
ZIP

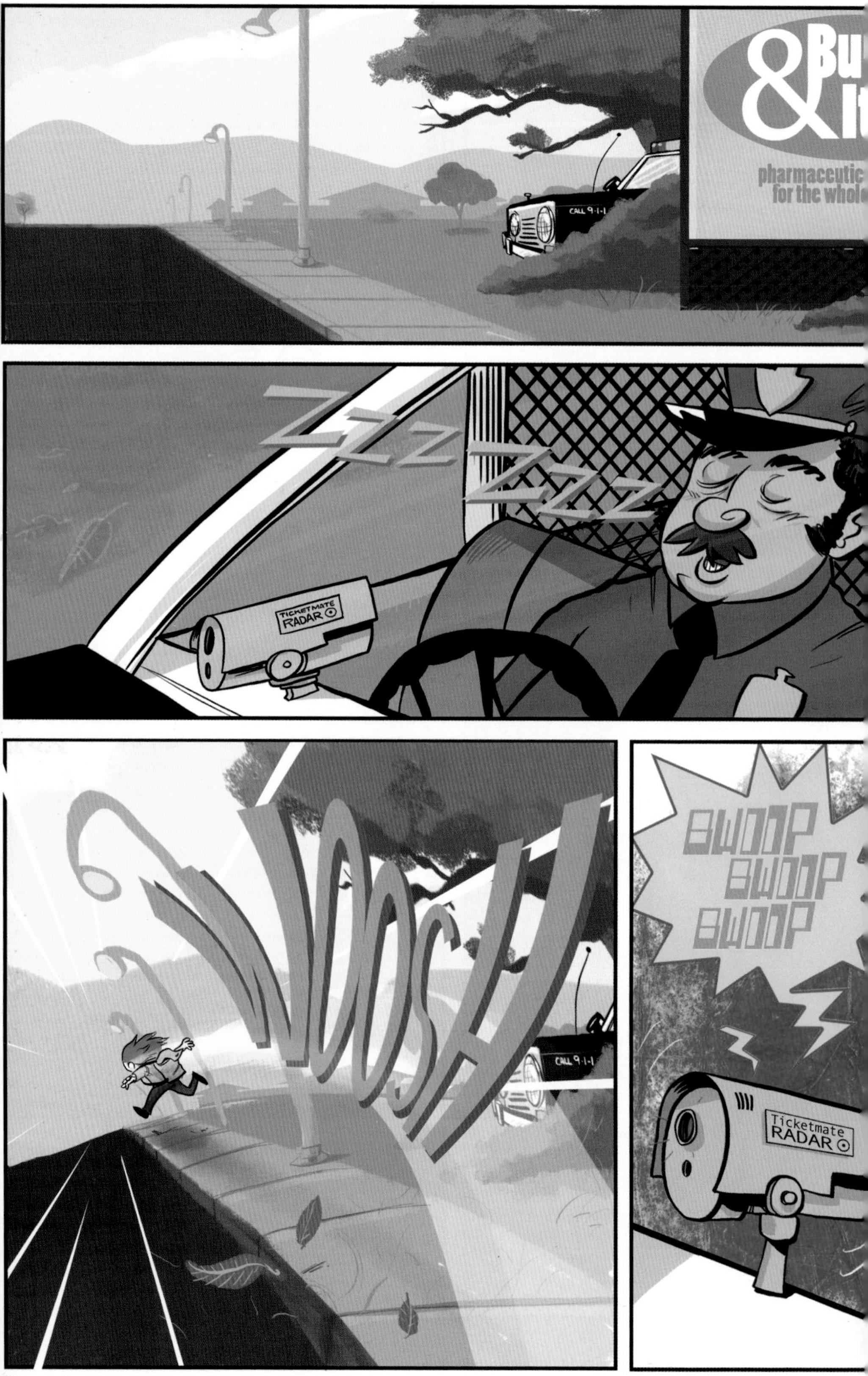
CALL 9-1-1
ZZZ ZZZ
TICKETMATE RADAR
WOOSH
CALL 9-1-1
BWOOP
BWOOP
BWOOP
Ticketmate RADAR

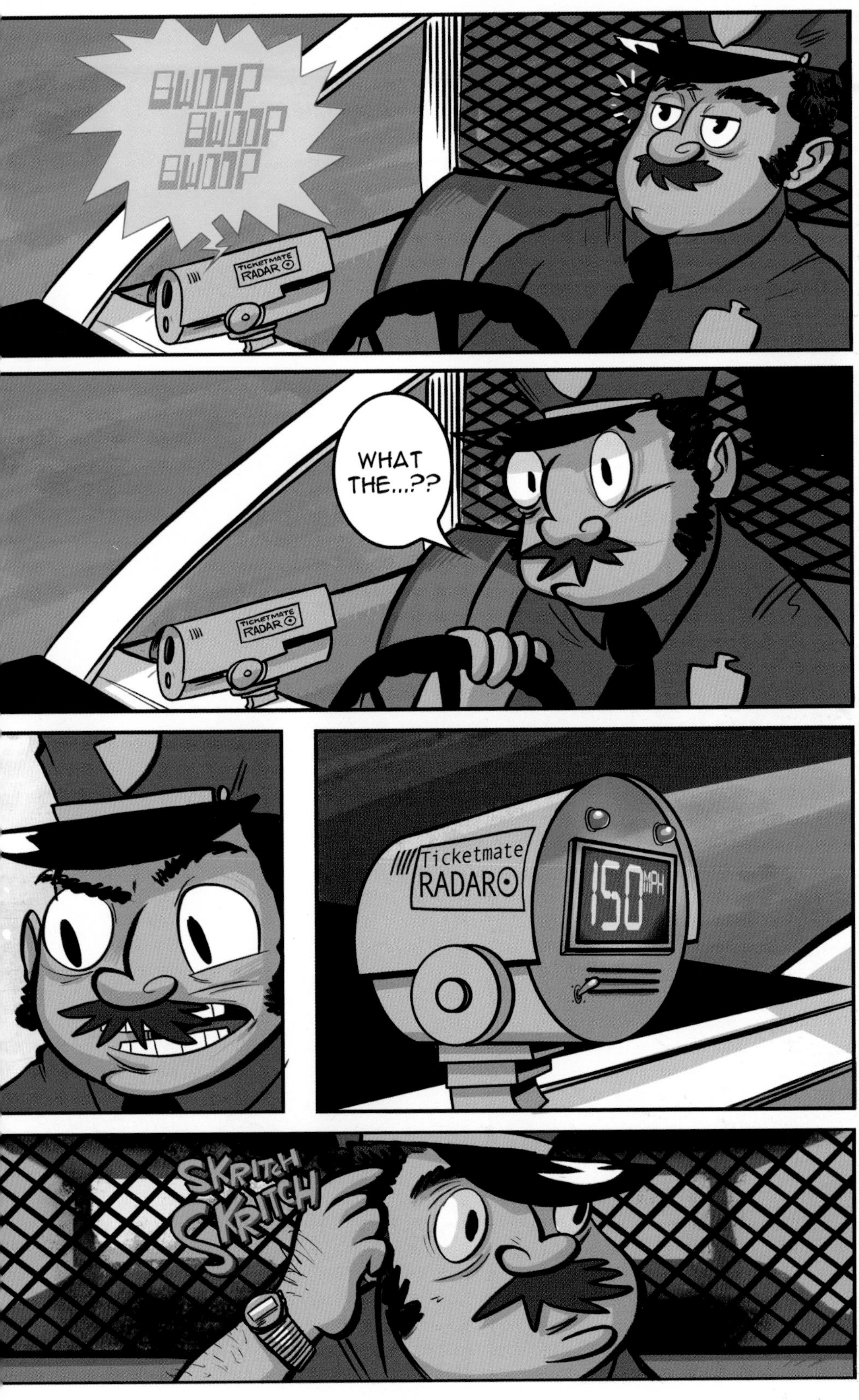
BWOOP BWOOP BWOOP
TICKETMATE RADAR
WHAT THE...??
TICKETMATE RADAR
Ticketmate RADAR
150 MPH
SKRITCH SKRITCH

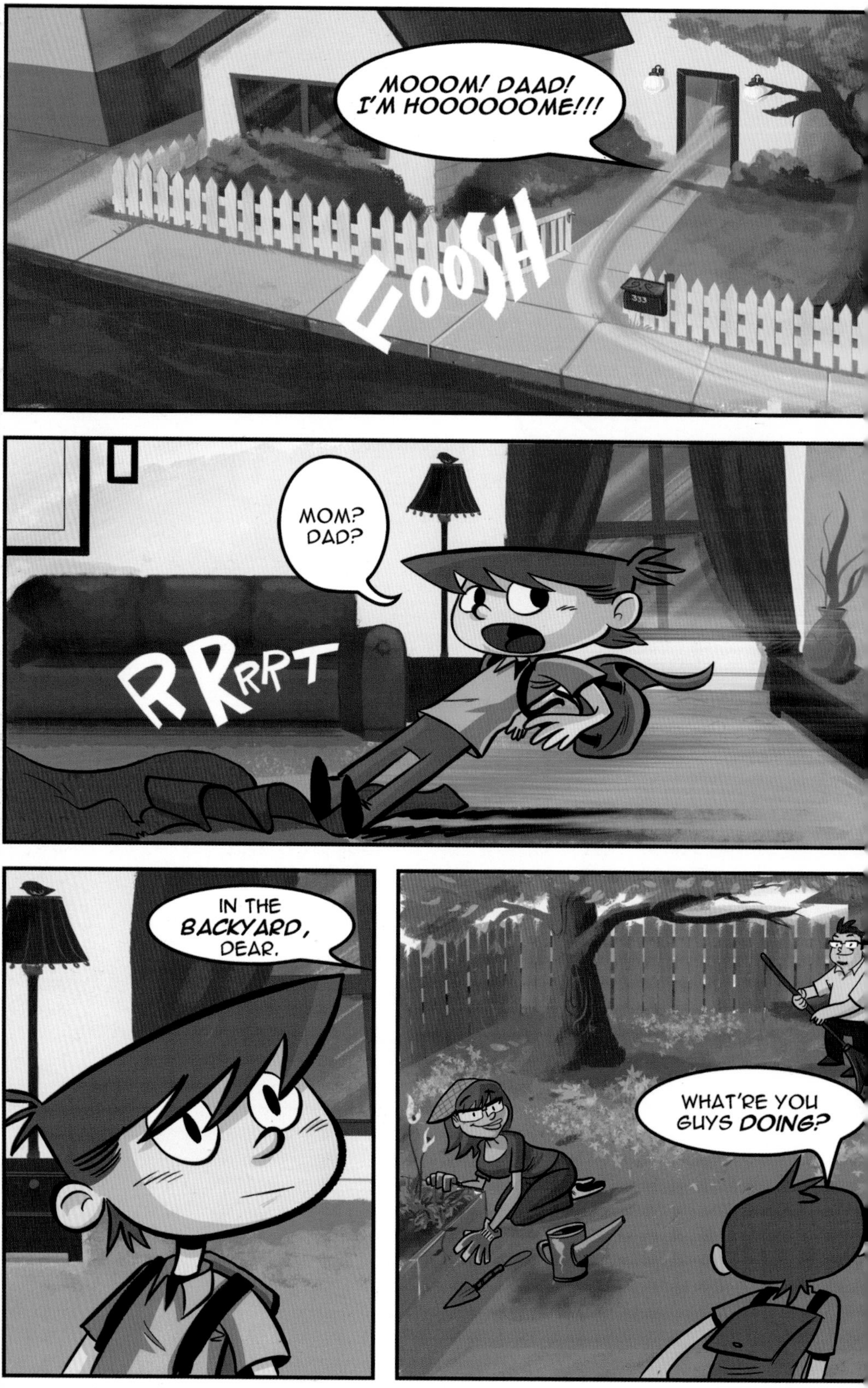
MOOOM! DAAD!
I'M HOOOOOOME!!!
FOOSH
MOM?
DAD?
RRRRT
IN THE
BACKYARD,
DEAR.
WHAT'RE YOU
GUYS DOING?

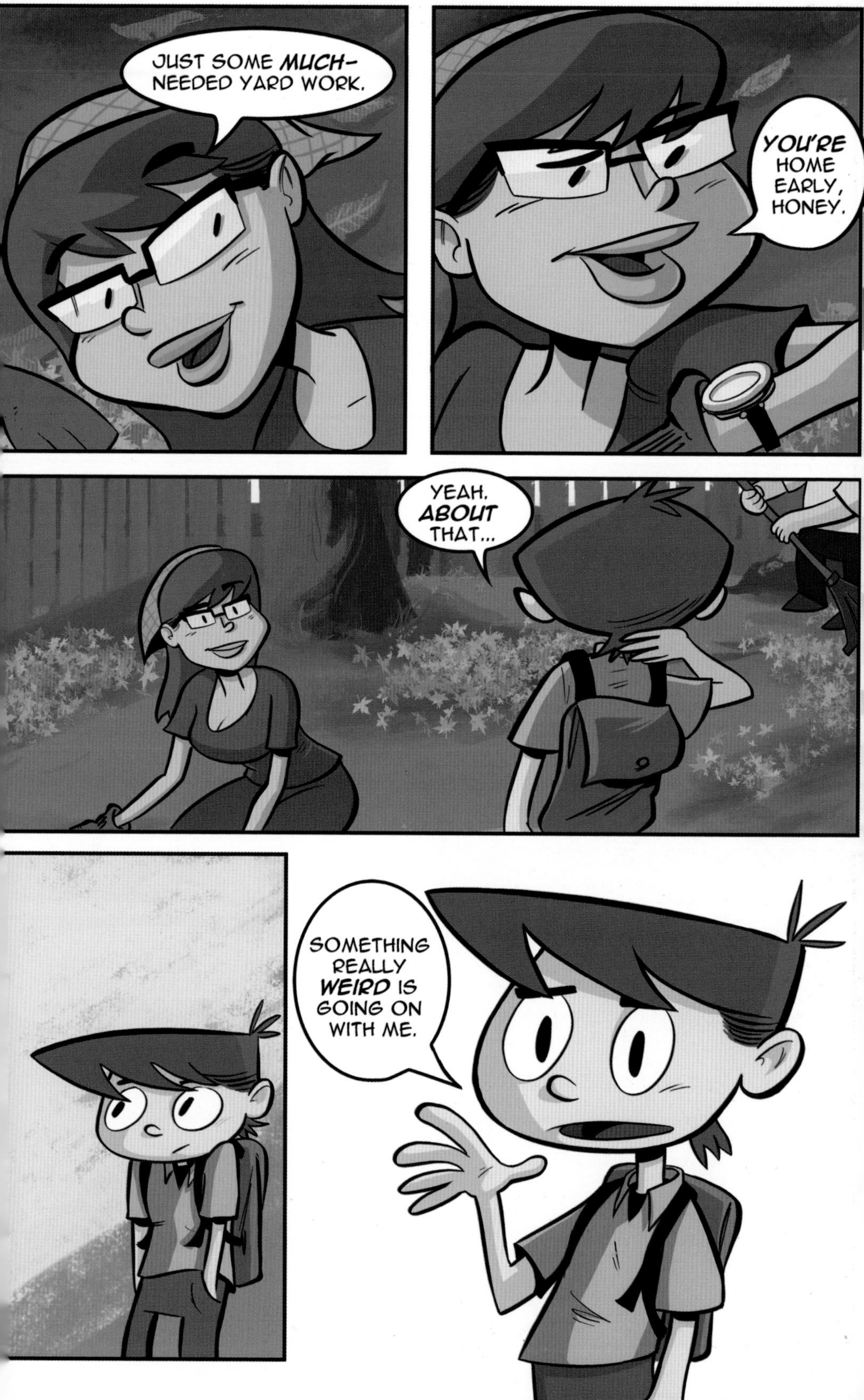
JUST SOME MUCH-NEEDED YARD WORK.
YOU'RE HOME EARLY, HONEY.
YEAH. ABOUT THAT...
SOMETHING REALLY WEIRD IS GOING ON WITH ME.

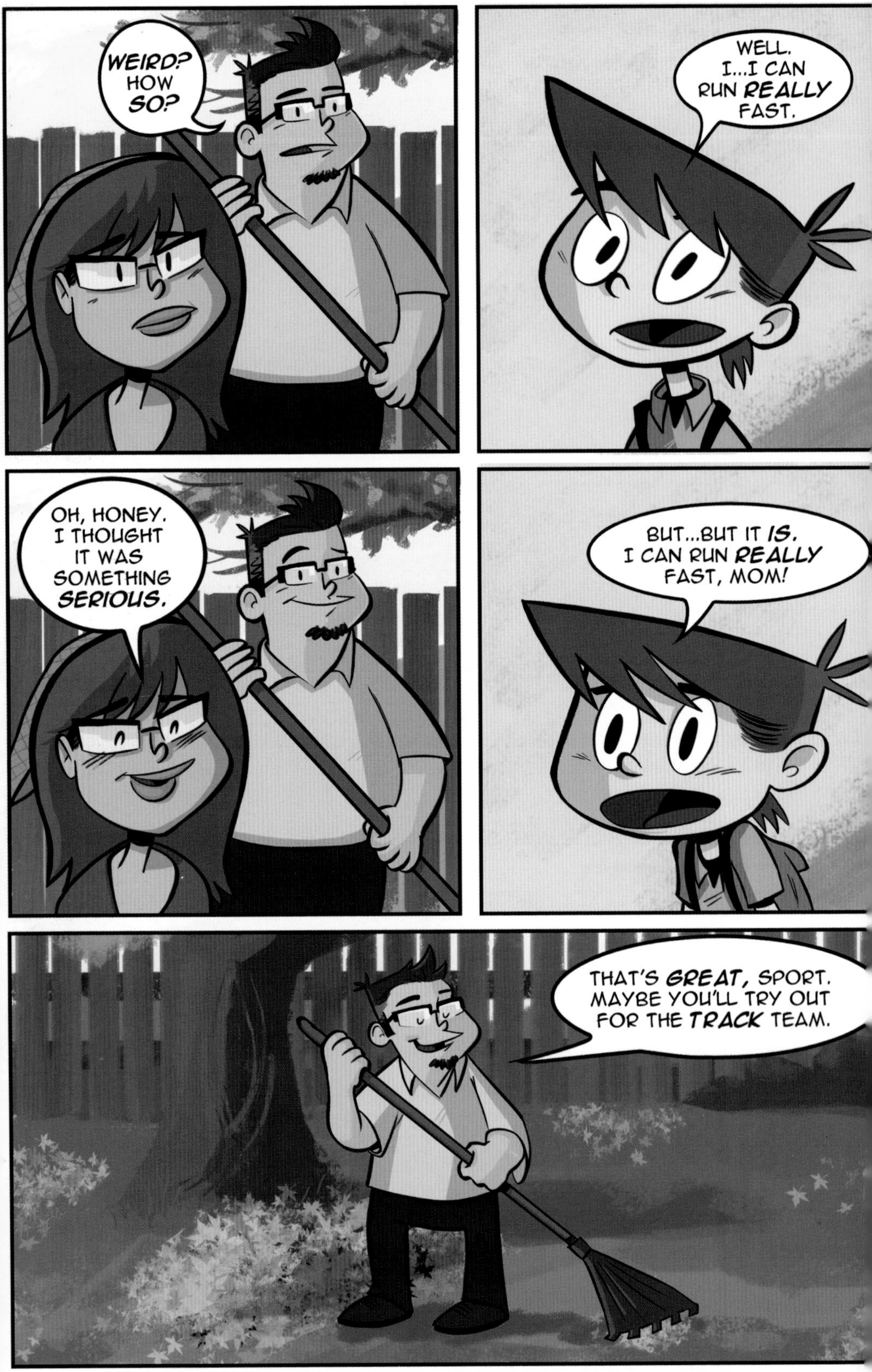
WEIRD? HOW SO?
WELL. I...I CAN RUN REALLY FAST.
OH, HONEY. I THOUGHT IT WAS SOMETHING SERIOUS.
BUT...BUT IT IS. I CAN RUN REALLY FAST, MOM!
THAT'S GREAT, SPORT. MAYBE YOU'LL TRY OUT FOR THE TRACK TEAM.

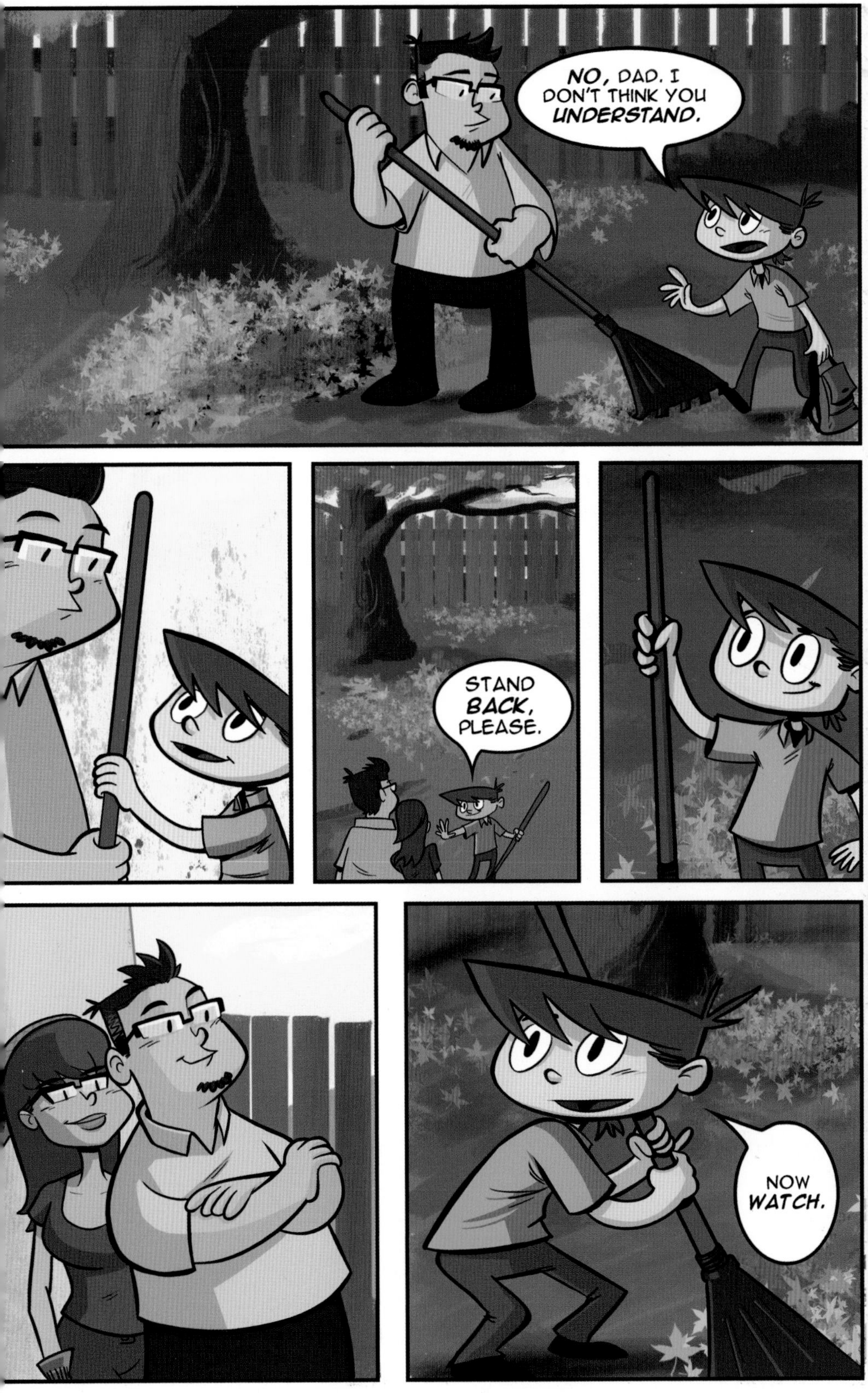
NO, DAD. I DON'T THINK YOU UNDERSTAND.
STAND BACK, PLEASE.
NOW WATCH.

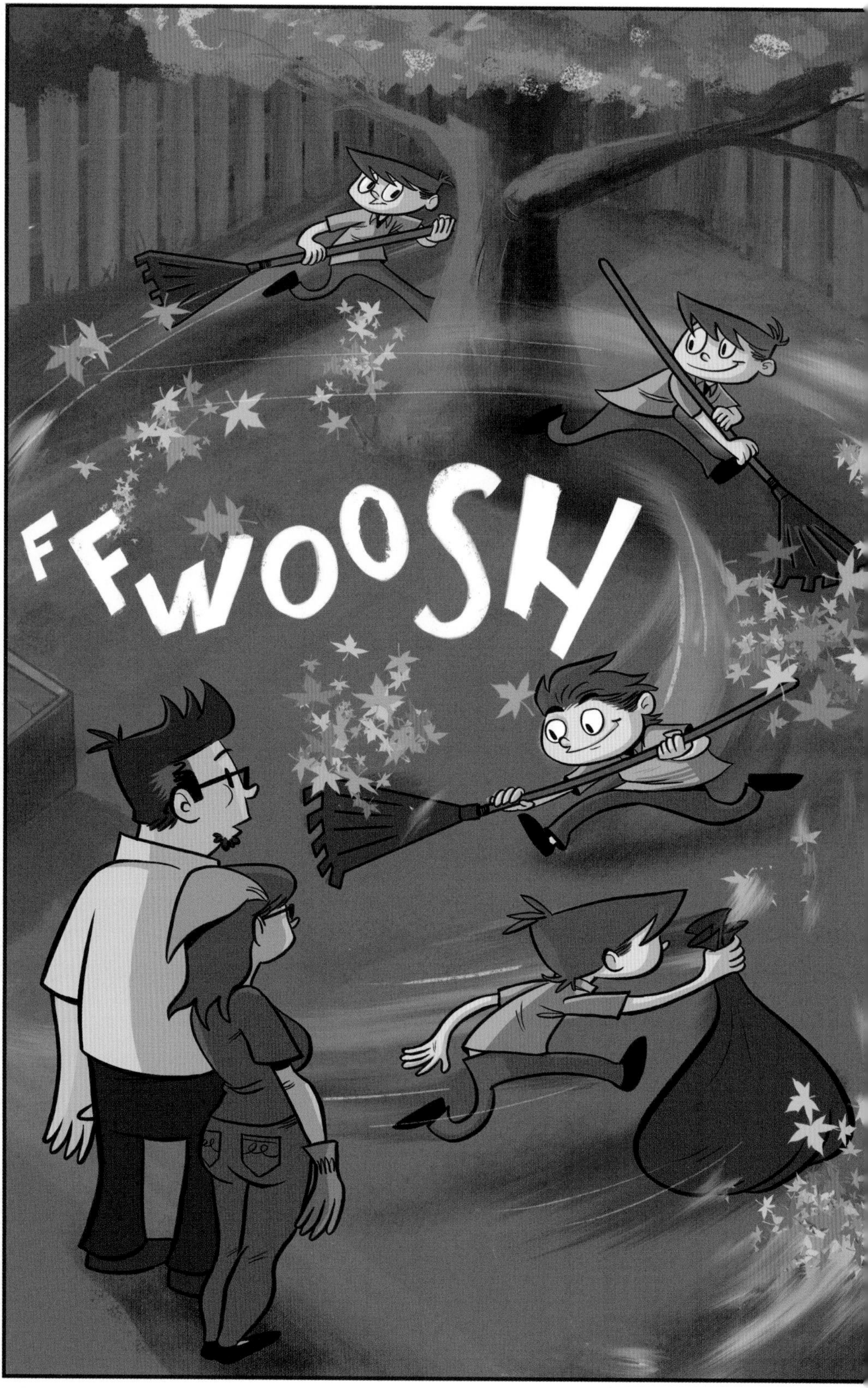
FFWOOSH

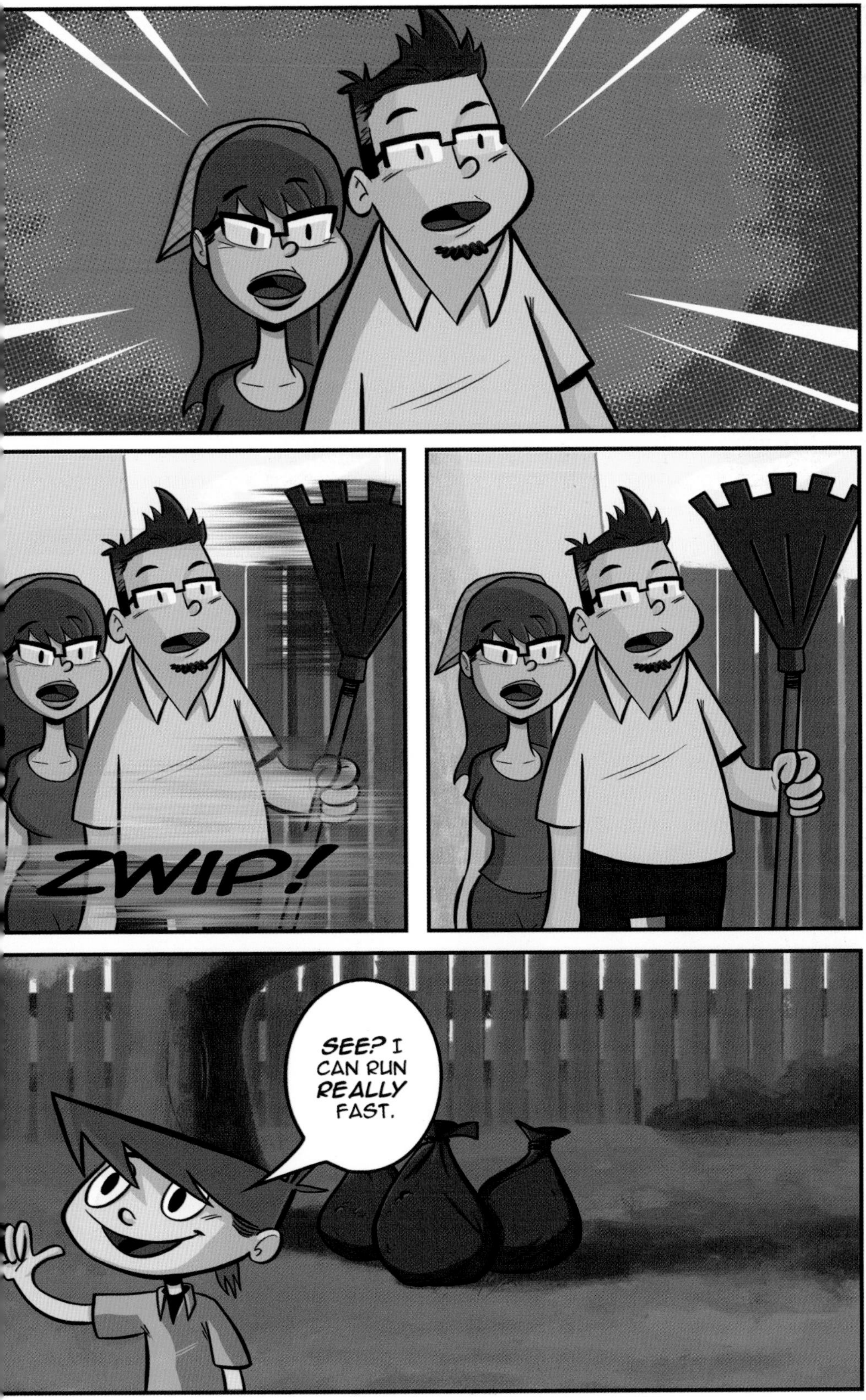
ZWIP!
SEE? I CAN RUN REALLY FAST.

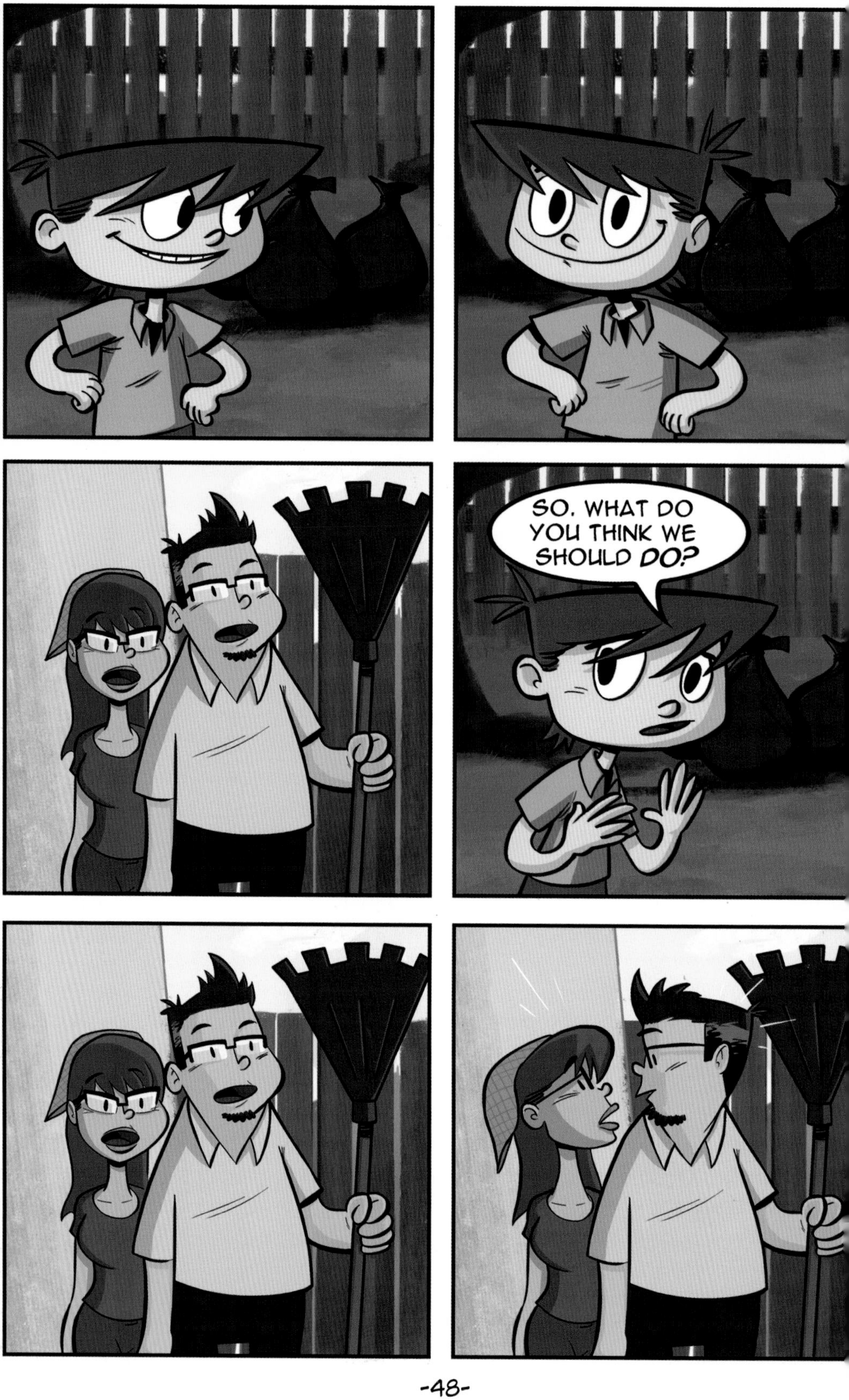
SO, WHAT DO
YOU THINK WE
SHOULD *DO?*

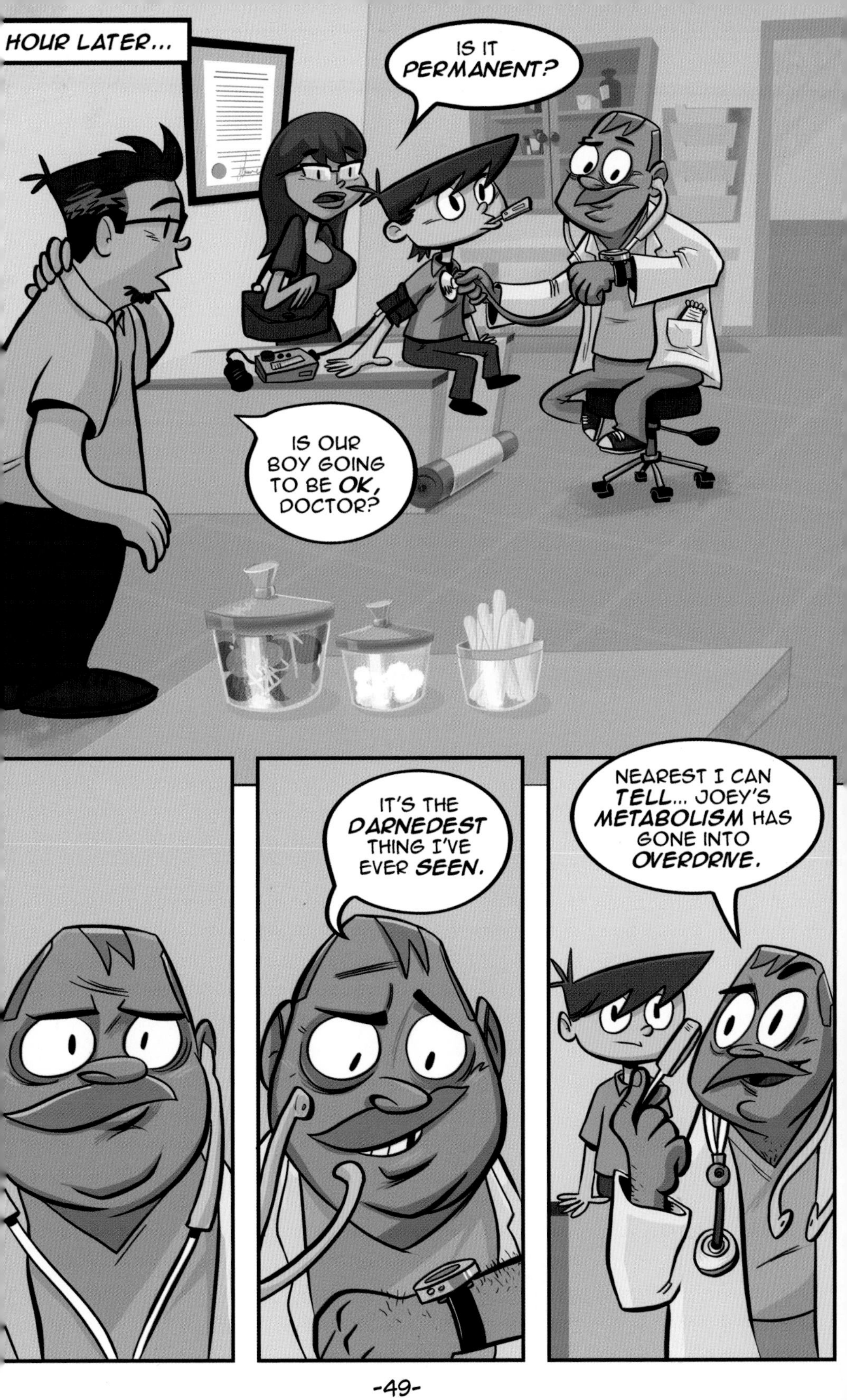
HOUR LATER...
IS IT PERMANENT?
IS OUR BOY GOING TO BE OK, DOCTOR?
IT'S THE DARNEDEST THING I'VE EVER SEEN.
NEAREST I CAN TELL... JOEY'S METABOLISM HAS GONE INTO OVERDRIVE.

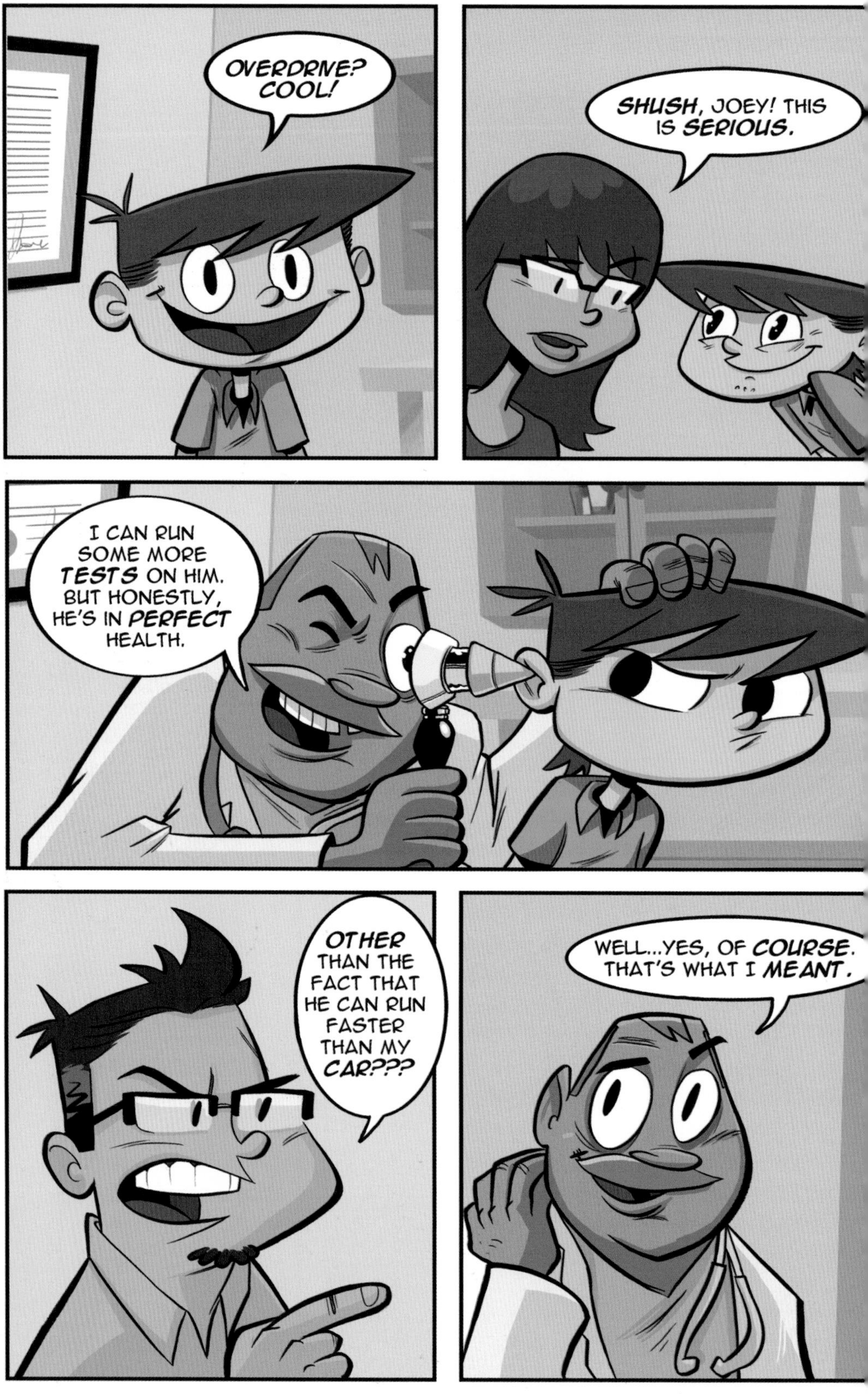

OVERDRIVE? COOL!
SHUSH, JOEY! THIS IS SERIOUS.
I CAN RUN SOME MORE TESTS ON HIM. BUT HONESTLY, HE'S IN PERFECT HEALTH.
OTHER THAN THE FACT THAT HE CAN RUN FASTER THAN MY CAR???
WELL...YES, OF COURSE. THAT'S WHAT I MEANT.

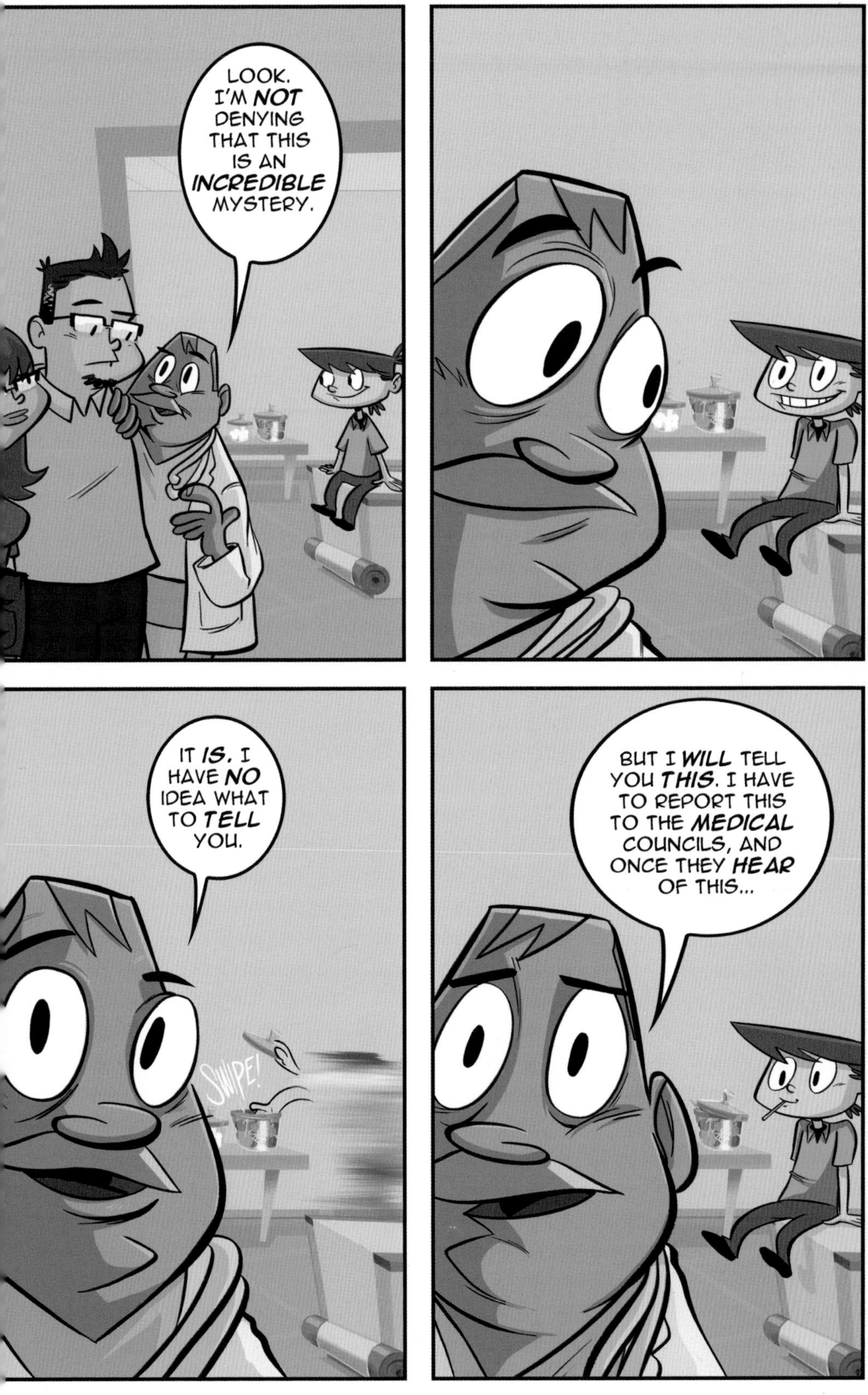
LOOK. I'M NOT DENYING THAT THIS IS AN INCREDIBLE MYSTERY.
IT IS. I HAVE NO IDEA WHAT TO TELL YOU.
SWIPE!
BUT I WILL TELL YOU THIS. I HAVE TO REPORT THIS TO THE MEDICAL COUNCILS, AND ONCE THEY HEAR OF THIS...

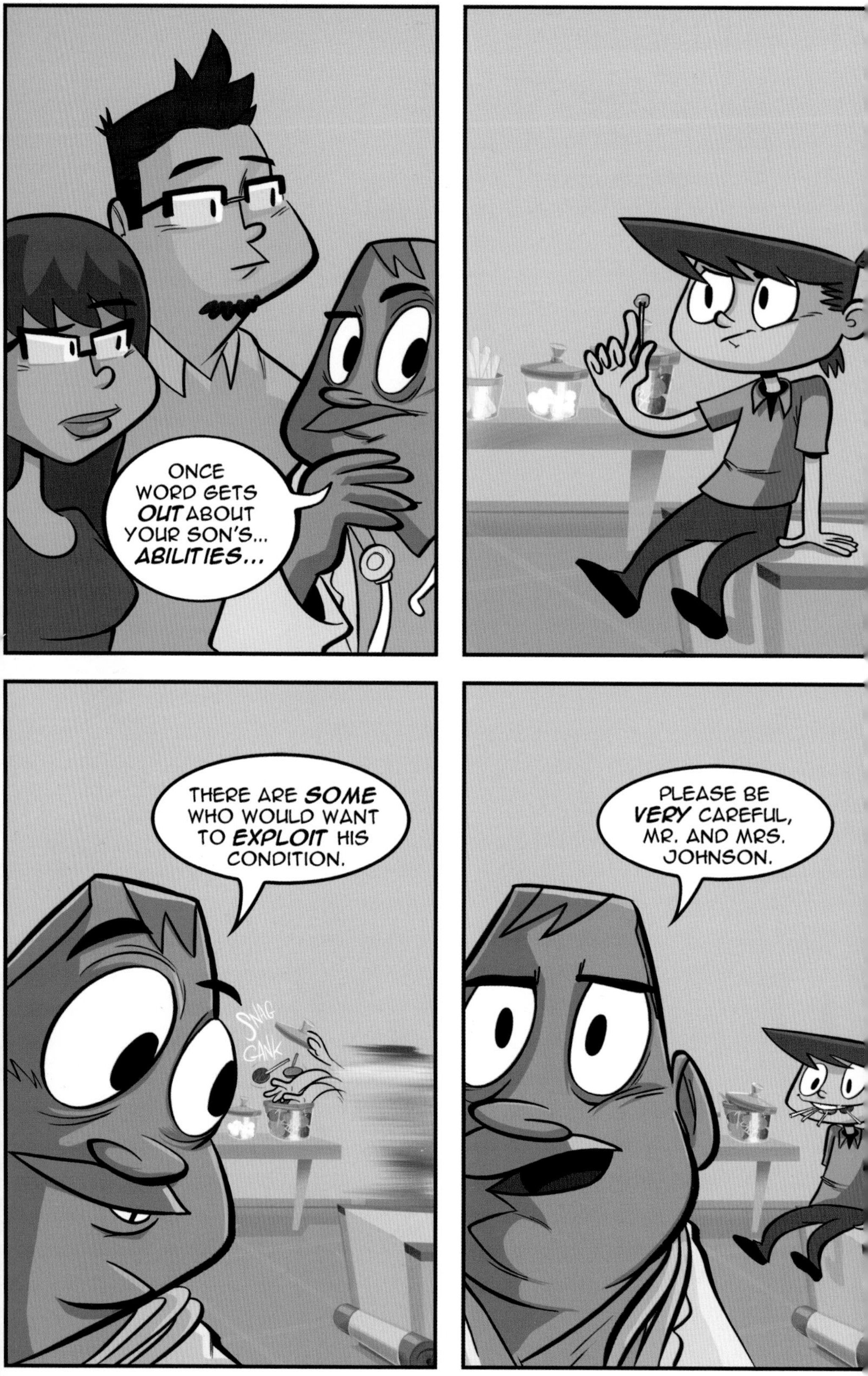
ONCE WORD GETS OUT ABOUT YOUR SON'S... ABILITIES...
THERE ARE SOME WHO WOULD WANT TO EXPLOIT HIS CONDITION.
SNAG
GANK
PLEASE BE VERY CAREFUL, MR. AND MRS. JOHNSON.

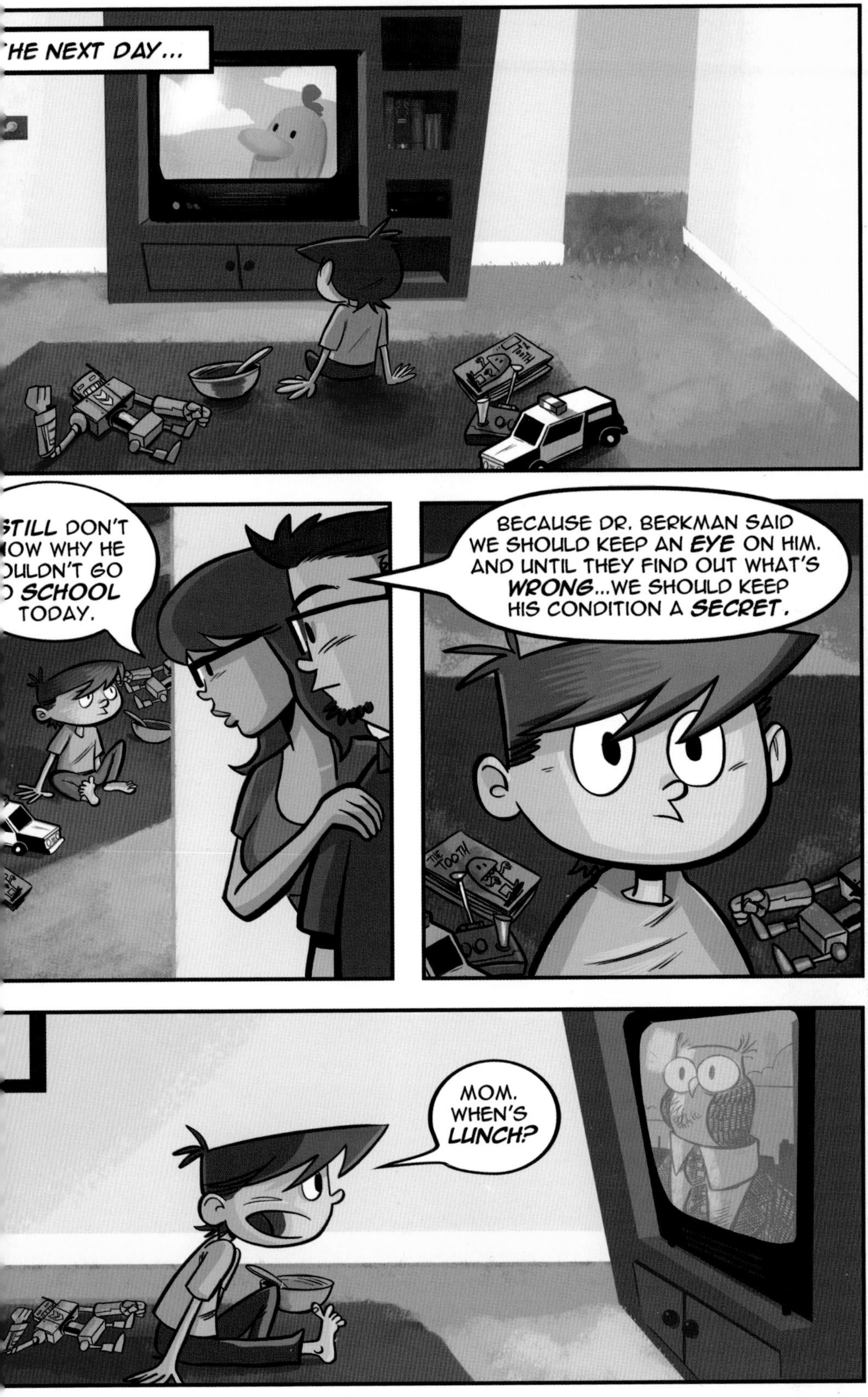

HE NEXT DAY...
TILL DON'T OW WHY HE ULDN'T GO SCHOOL TODAY.
BECAUSE DR. BERKMAN SAID WE SHOULD KEEP AN EYE ON HIM. AND UNTIL THEY FIND OUT WHAT'S WRONG...WE SHOULD KEEP HIS CONDITION A SECRET.
MOM. WHEN'S LUNCH?

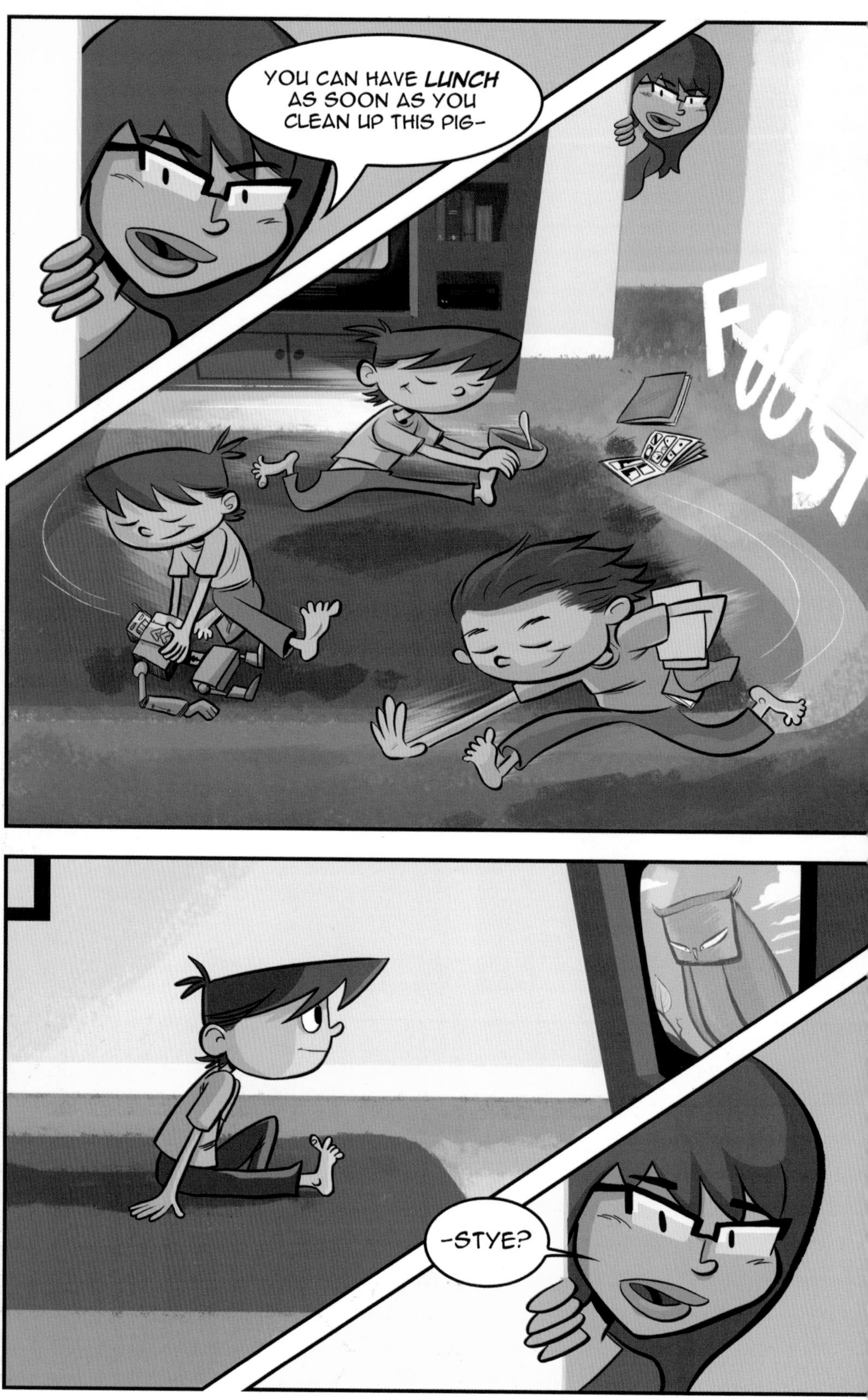
YOU CAN HAVE **LUNCH** AS SOON AS YOU CLEAN UP THIS PIG-
FOOSH
-STYE?

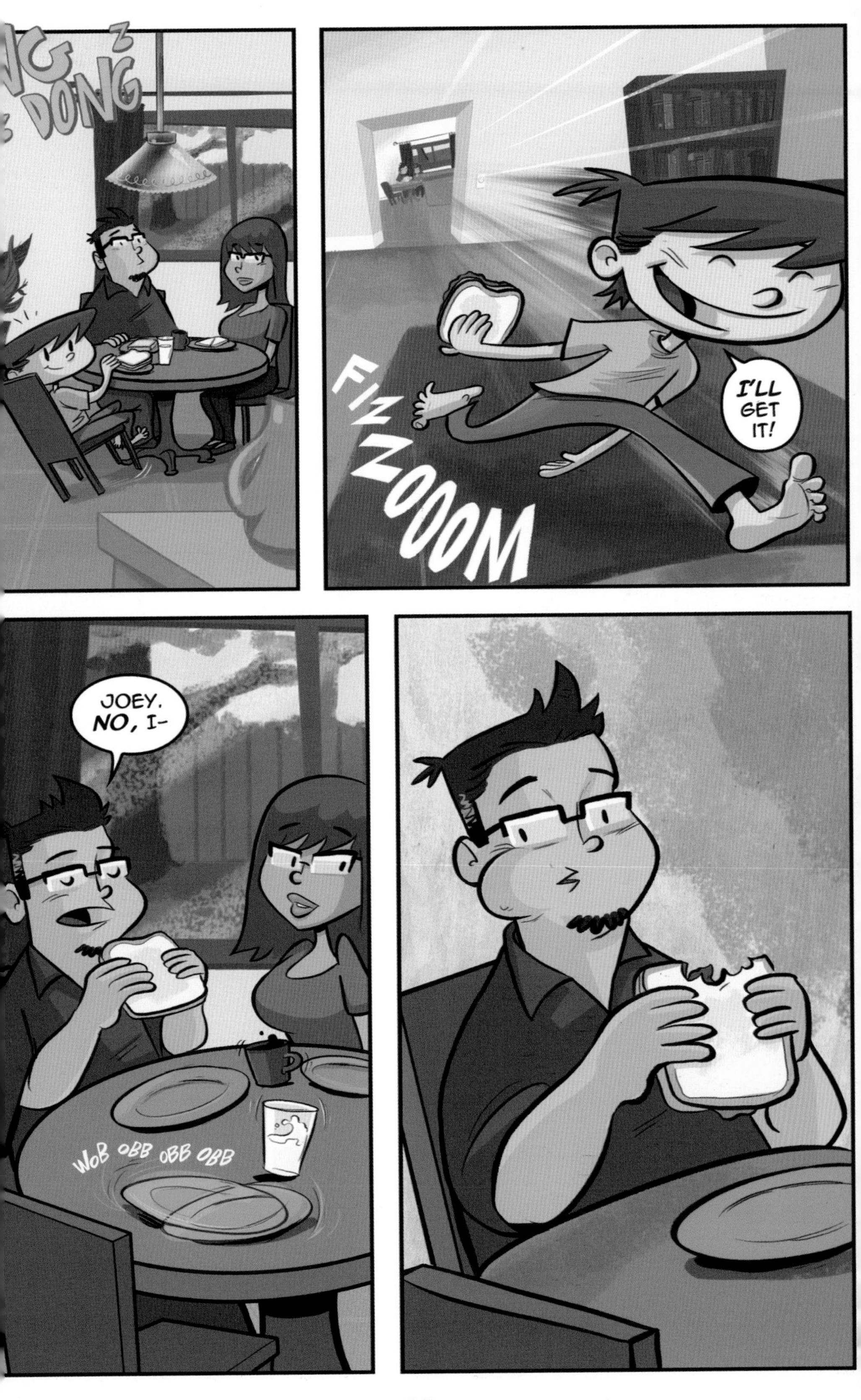

DONG
DONG
FIZZOOOM
I'LL GET IT!
JOEY. NO, I-
WoB OBB OBB OBB

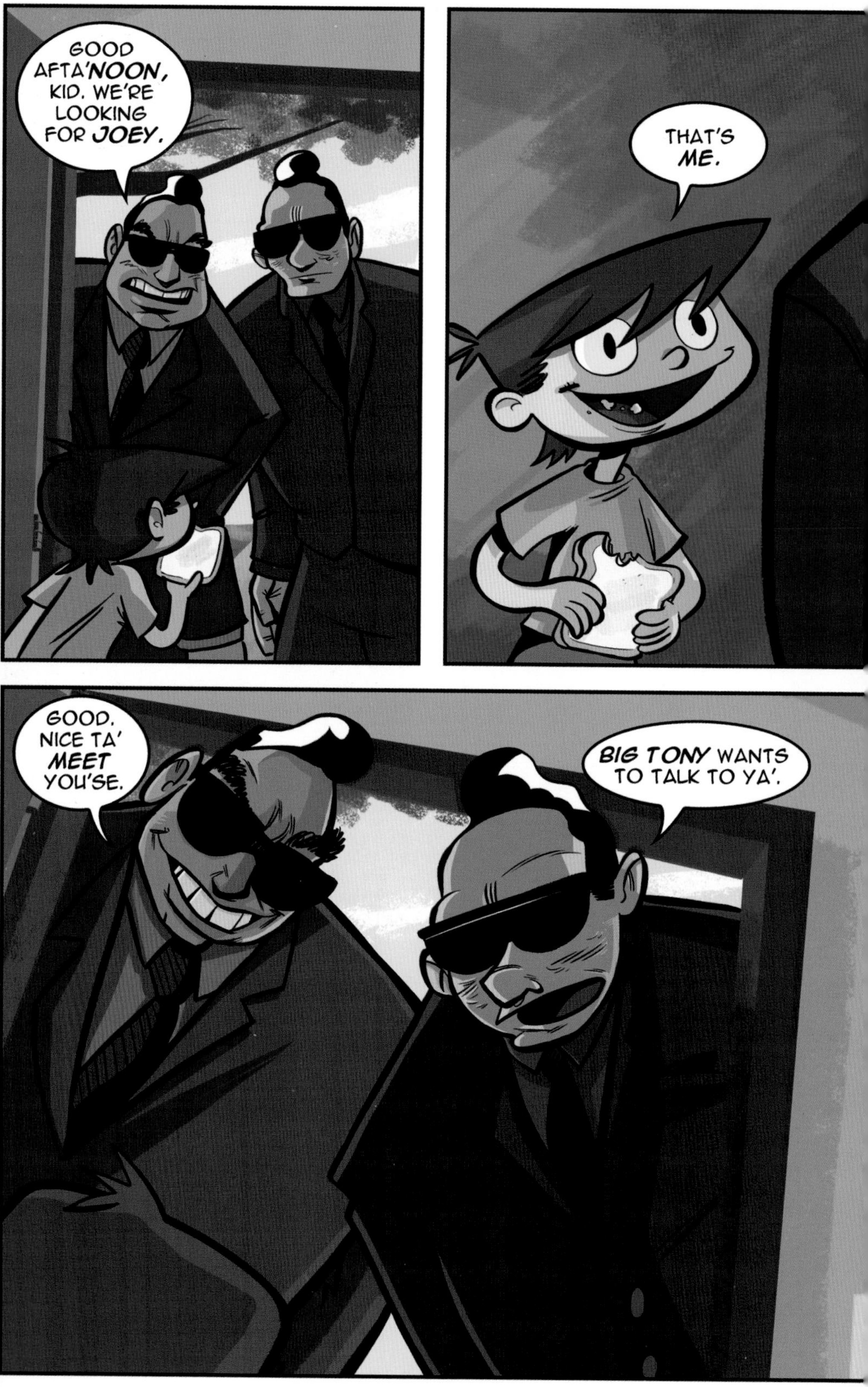
GOOD AFTA'NOON, KID. WE'RE LOOKING FOR JOEY.
THAT'S ME.
GOOD. NICE TA' MEET YOU'SE.
BIG TONY WANTS TO TALK TO YA'.

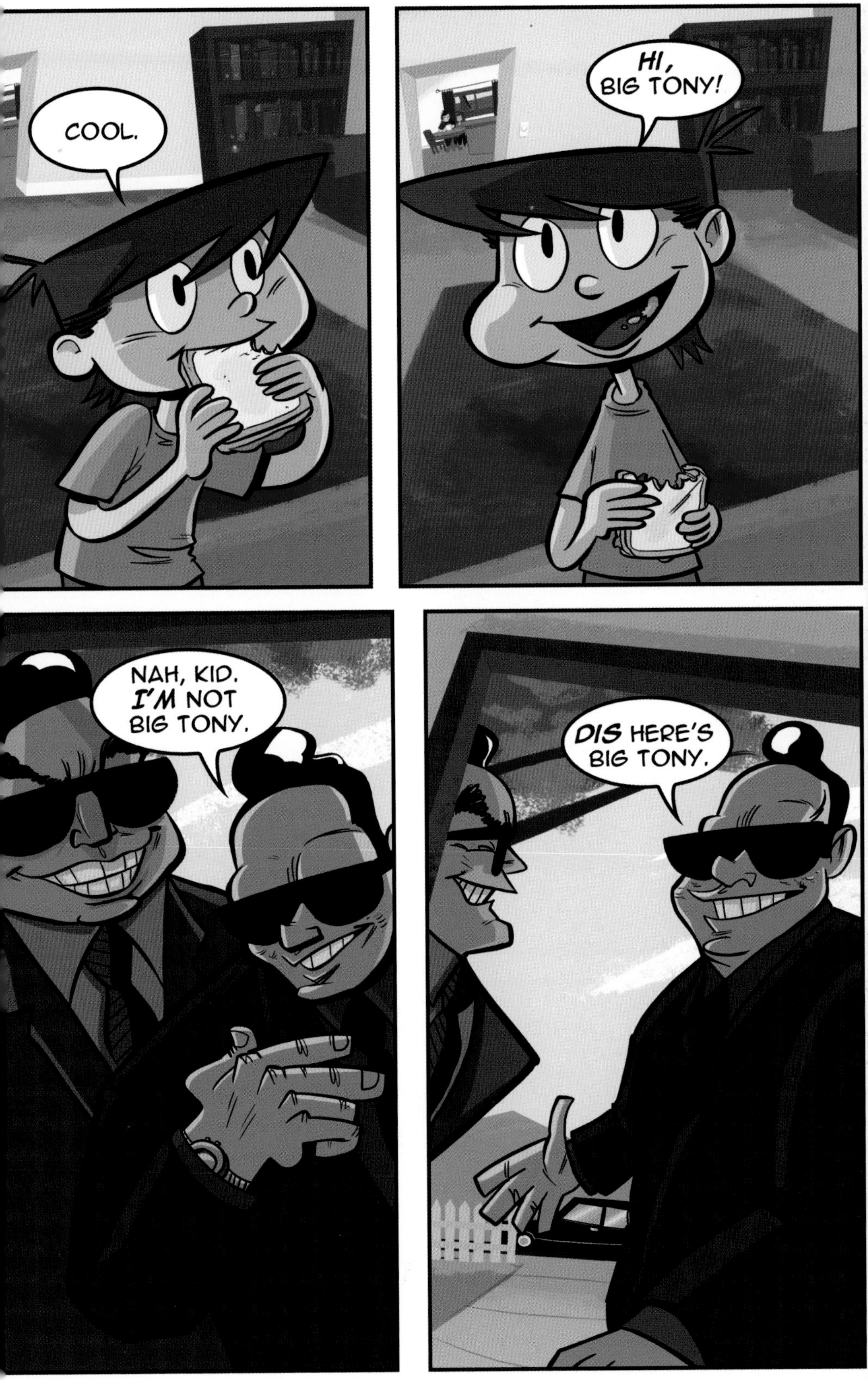
COOL.
HI, BIG TONY!
NAH, KID. I'M NOT BIG TONY.
DIS HERE'S BIG TONY.

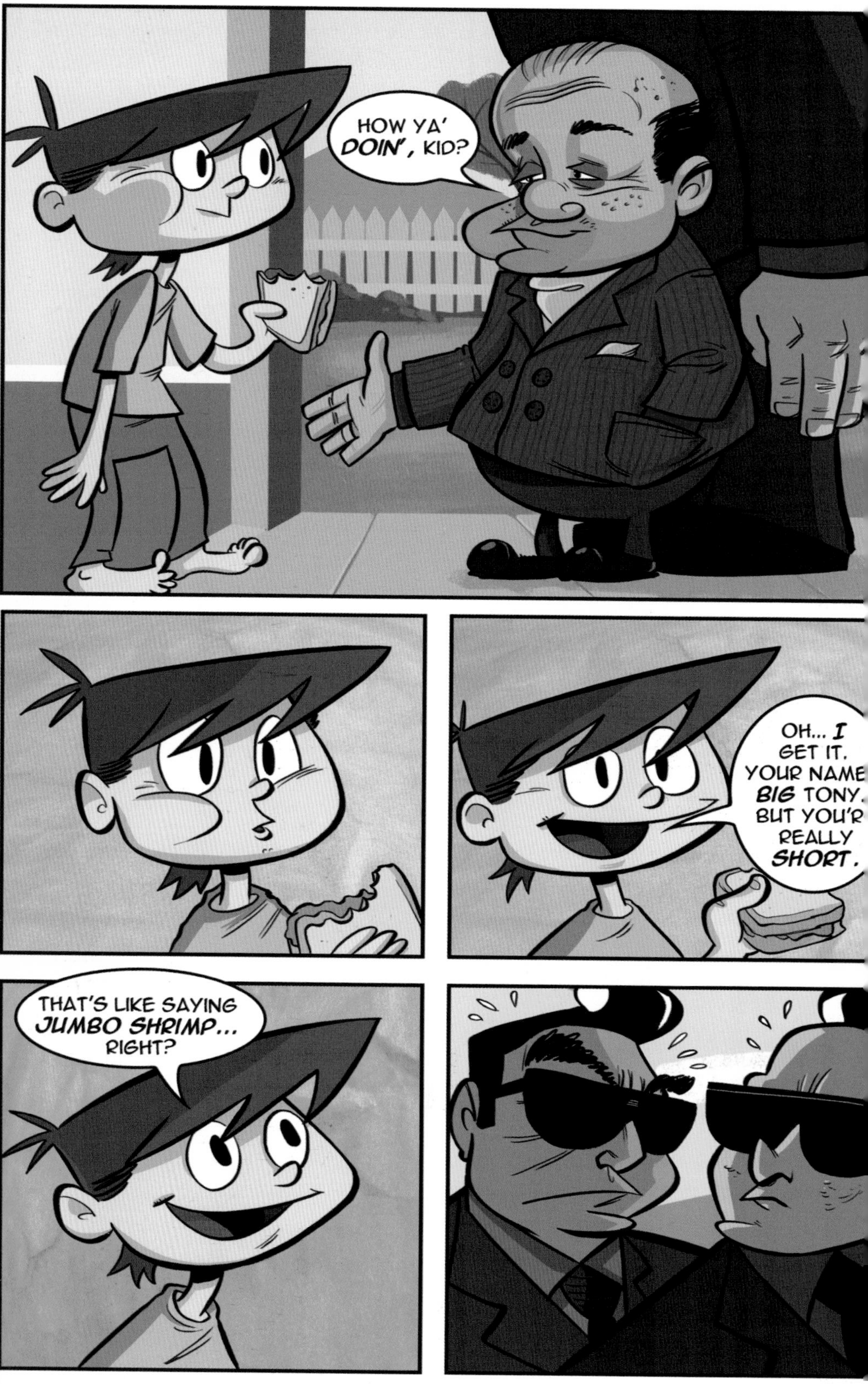
HOW YA' DOIN', KID?
OH... I GET IT. YOUR NAME BIG TONY. BUT YOU'R REALLY SHORT.
THAT'S LIKE SAYING JUMBO SHRIMP... RIGHT?

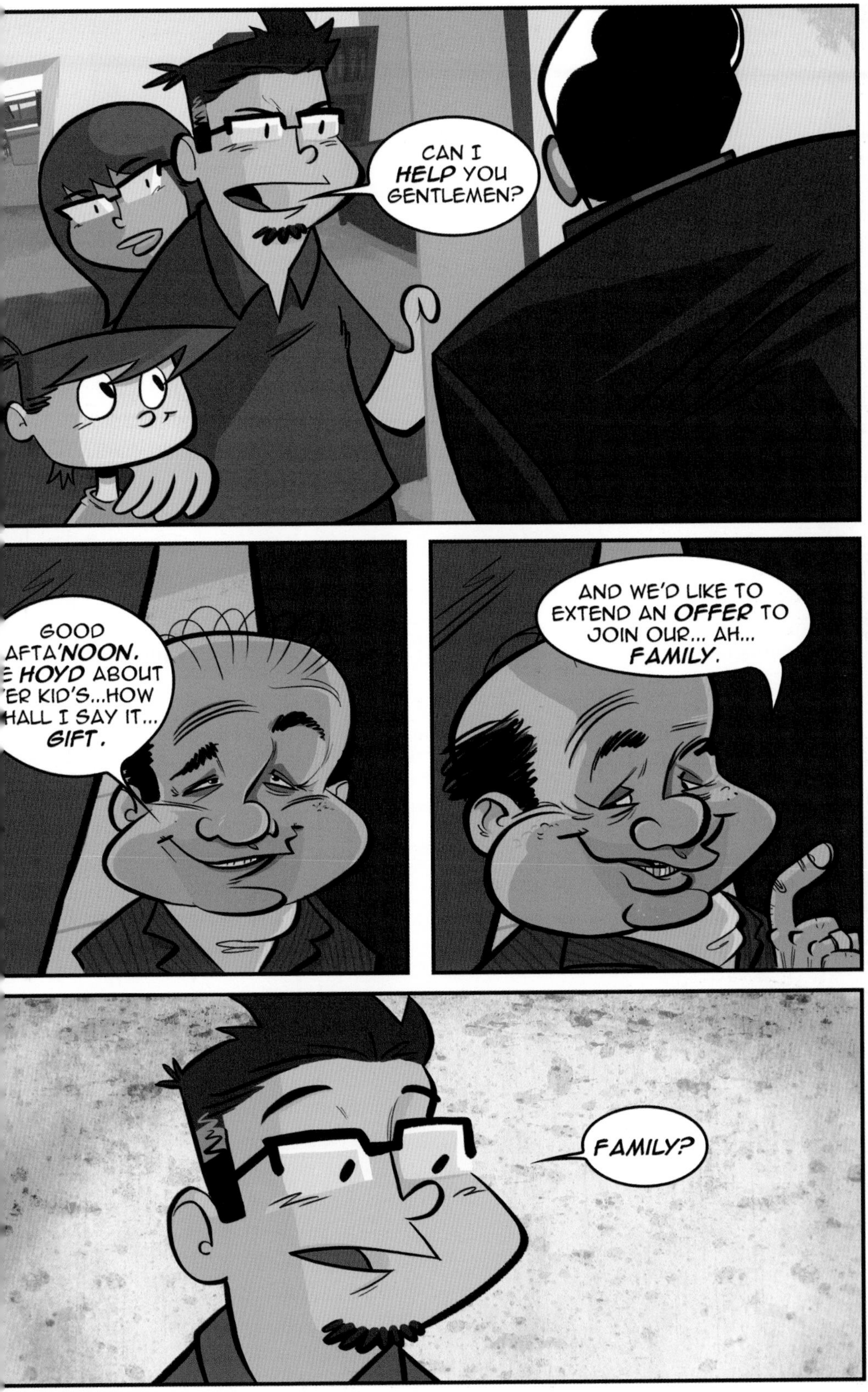
CAN I HELP YOU GENTLEMEN?
GOOD AFTA'NOON. E HOYD ABOUT 'ER KID'S...HOW HALL I SAY IT... GIFT.
AND WE'D LIKE TO EXTEND AN OFFER TO JOIN OUR... AH... FAMILY.
FAMILY?

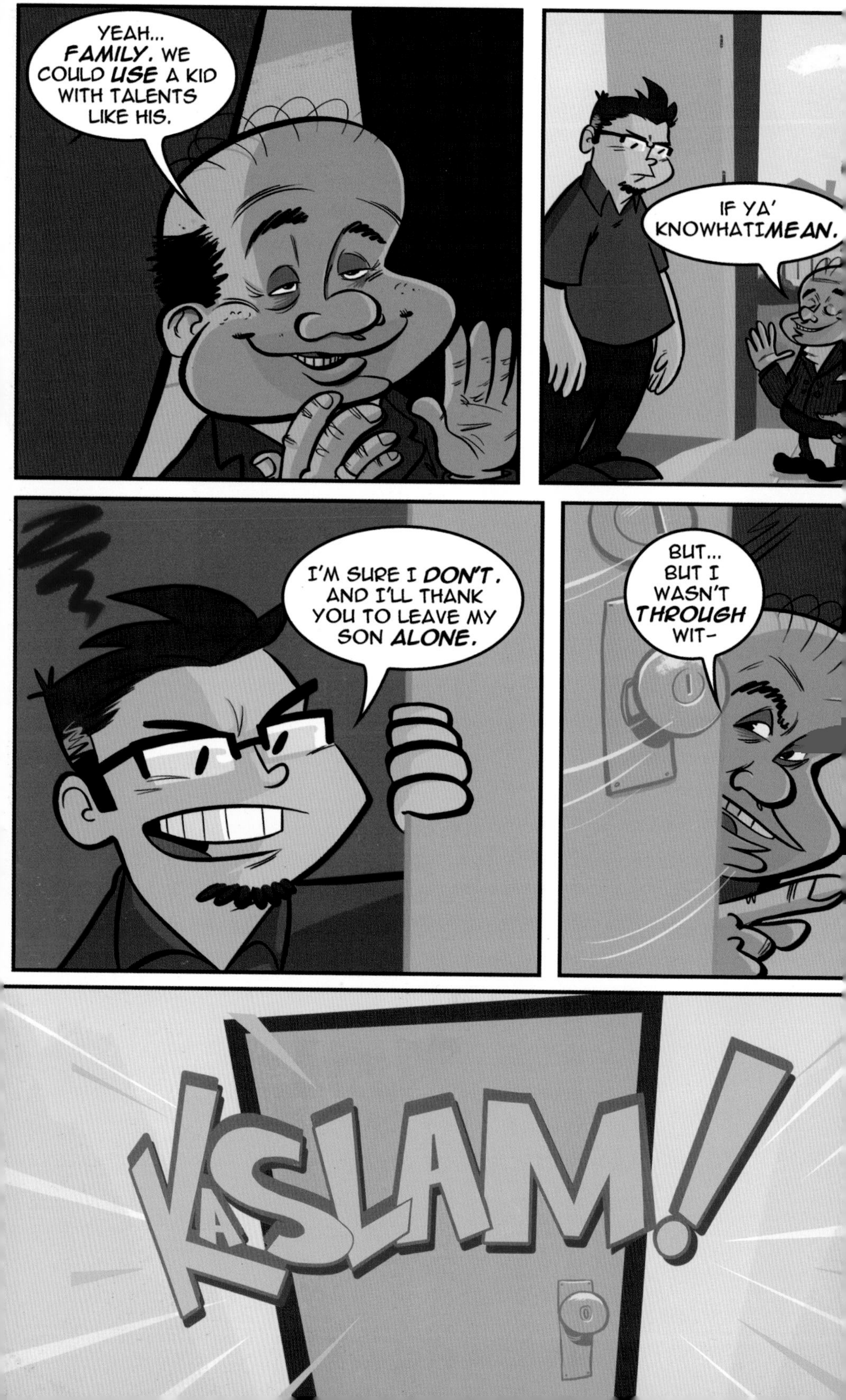
YEAH... FAMILY. WE COULD USE A KID WITH TALENTS LIKE HIS.
IF YA' KNOWHATIMEAN.
I'M SURE I DON'T. AND I'LL THANK YOU TO LEAVE MY SON ALONE.
BUT... BUT I WASN'T THROUGH WIT-
KA SLAM!

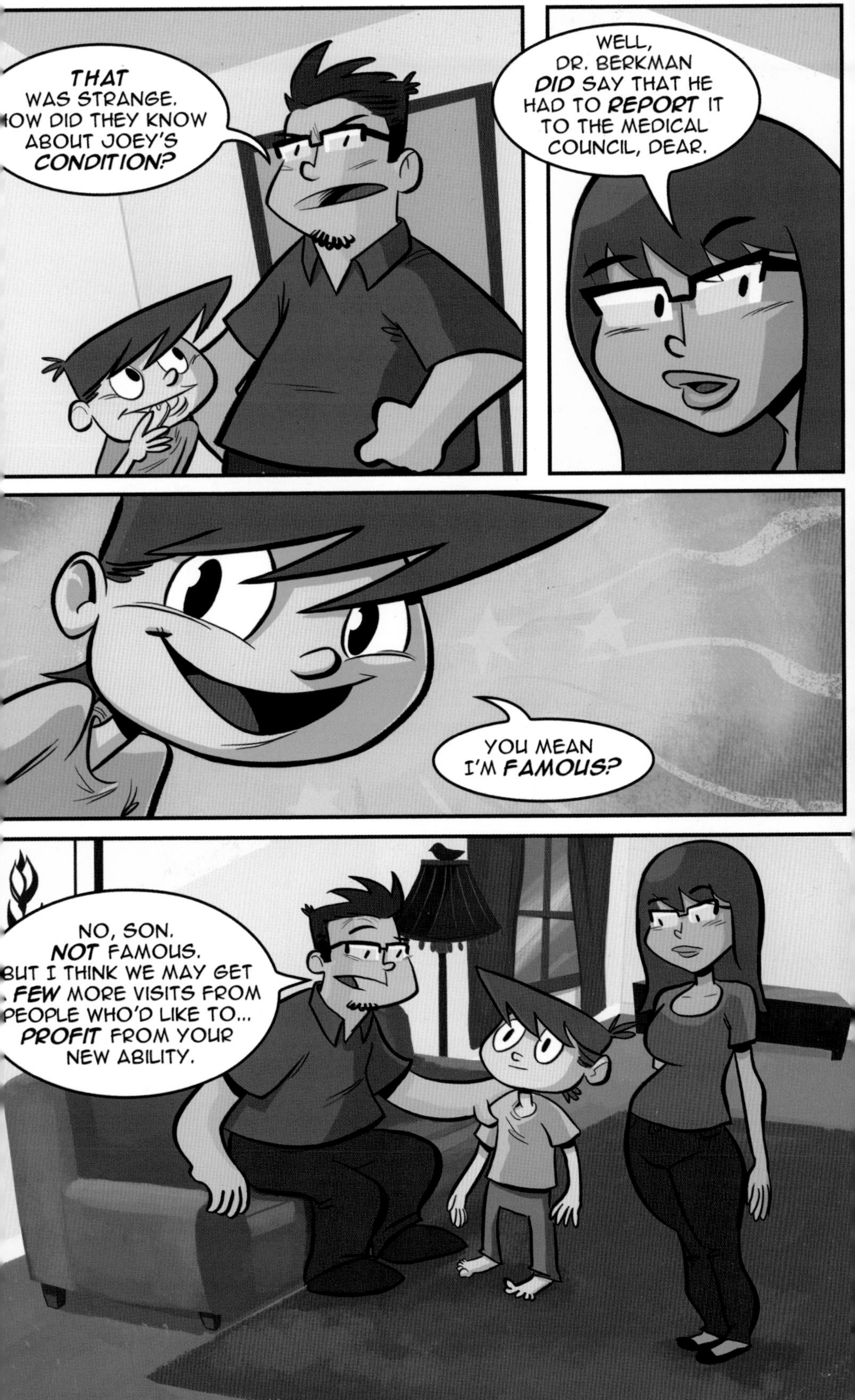

THAT WAS STRANGE. OW DID THEY KNOW ABOUT JOEY'S CONDITION?
WELL, DR. BERKMAN DID SAY THAT HE HAD TO REPORT IT TO THE MEDICAL COUNCIL, DEAR.
YOU MEAN I'M FAMOUS?
NO, SON. NOT FAMOUS. BUT I THINK WE MAY GET FEW MORE VISITS FROM PEOPLE WHO'D LIKE TO... PROFIT FROM YOUR NEW ABILITY.

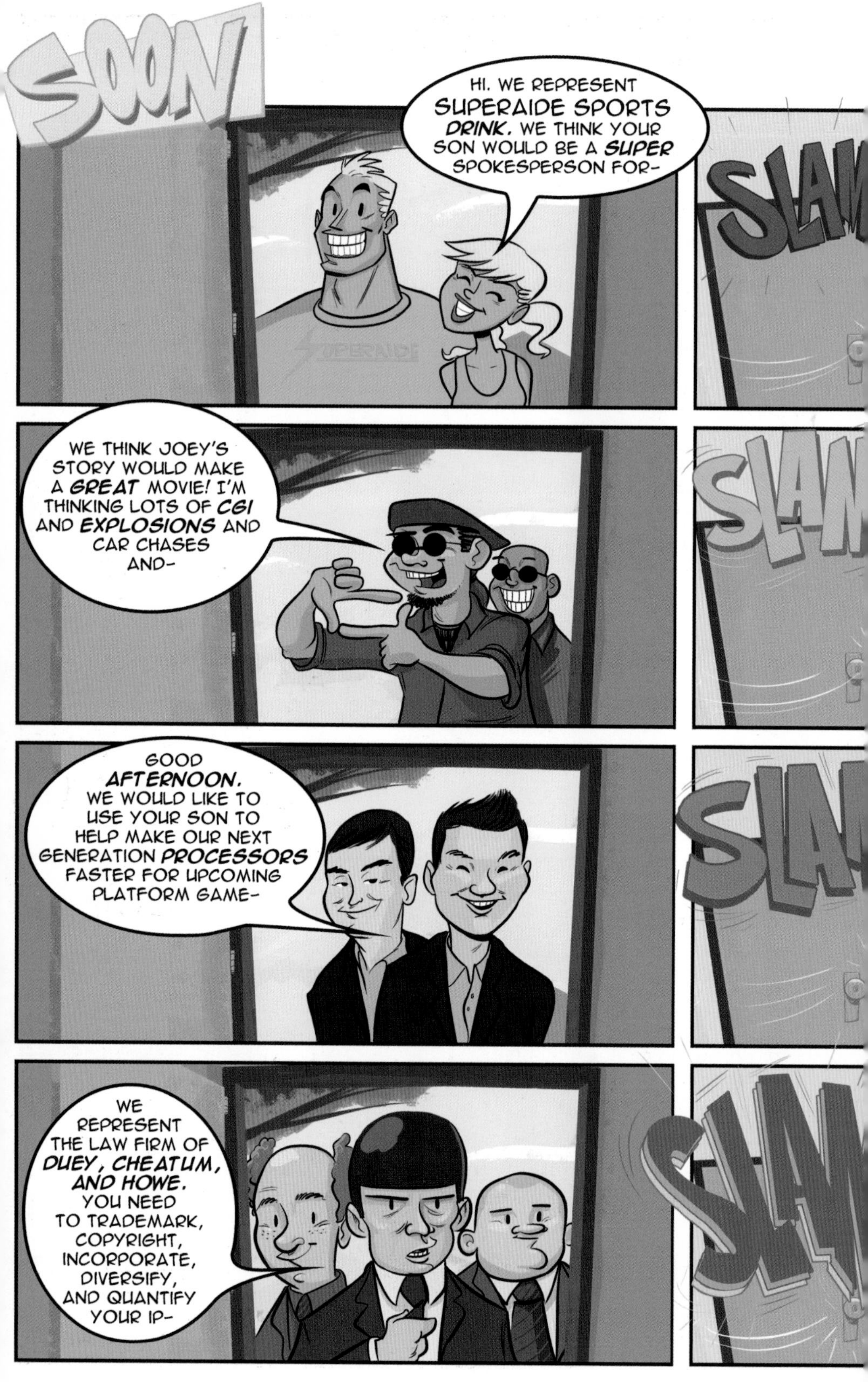
SOON
HI. WE REPRESENT SUPERAIDE SPORTS DRINK. WE THINK YOUR SON WOULD BE A SUPER SPOKESPERSON FOR-
SUPERAIDE
SLAM
WE THINK JOEY'S STORY WOULD MAKE A GREAT MOVIE! I'M THINKING LOTS OF CGI AND EXPLOSIONS AND CAR CHASES AND-
SLAM
GOOD AFTERNOON. WE WOULD LIKE TO USE YOUR SON TO HELP MAKE OUR NEXT GENERATION PROCESSORS FASTER FOR UPCOMING PLATFORM GAME-
SLAM
WE REPRESENT THE LAW FIRM OF DUEY, CHEATUM, AND HOWE. YOU NEED TO TRADEMARK, COPYRIGHT, INCORPORATE, DIVERSIFY, AND QUANTIFY YOUR IP-
SLAM

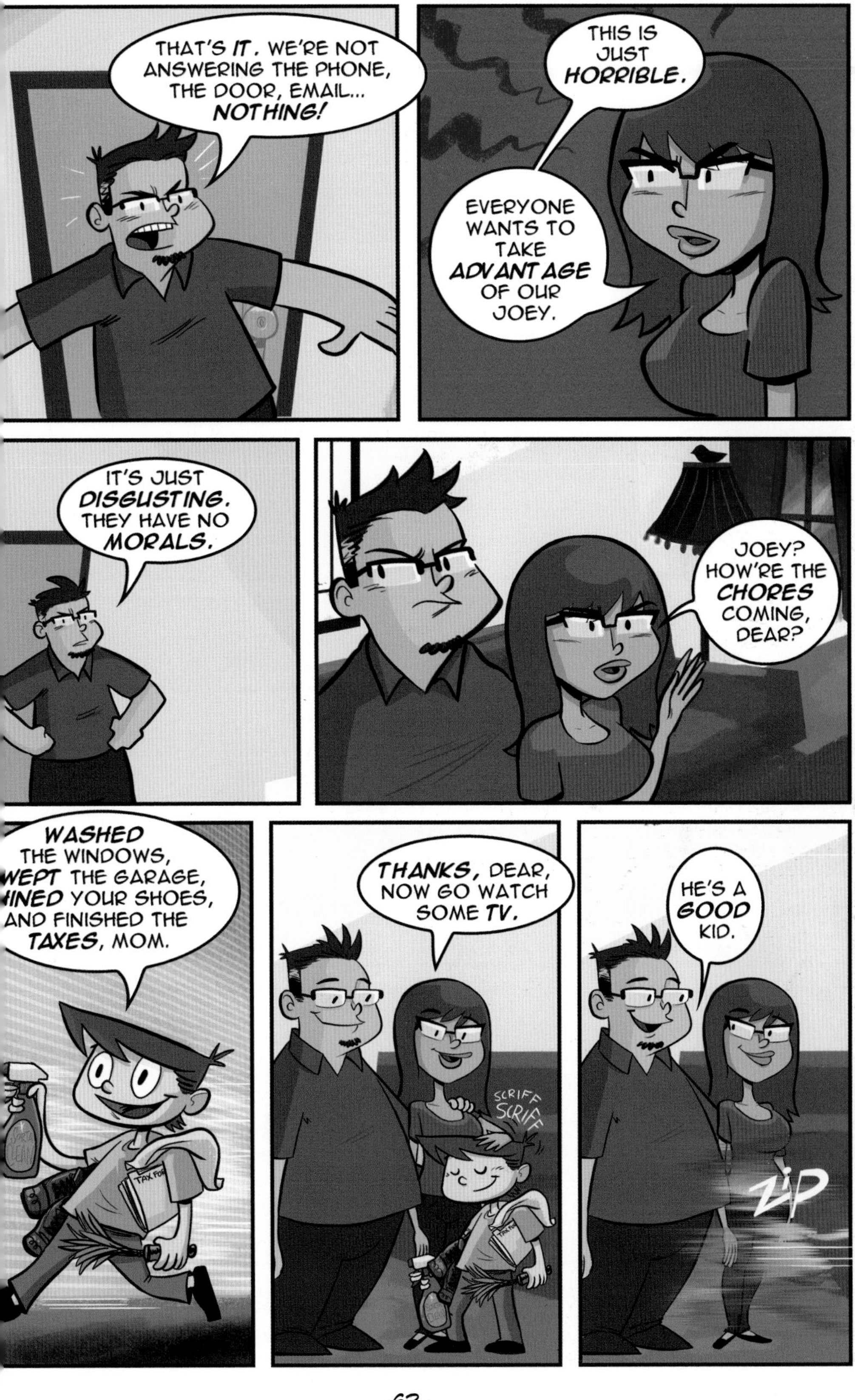
THAT'S IT. WE'RE NOT ANSWERING THE PHONE, THE DOOR, EMAIL... NOTHING!
THIS IS JUST HORRIBLE.
EVERYONE WANTS TO TAKE ADVANTAGE OF OUR JOEY.
IT'S JUST DISGUSTING. THEY HAVE NO MORALS.
JOEY? HOW'RE THE CHORES COMING, DEAR?
WASHED THE WINDOWS, WEPT THE GARAGE, INED YOUR SHOES, AND FINISHED THE TAXES, MOM.
THANKS, DEAR, NOW GO WATCH SOME TV.
SCRIFF SCRIFF
HE'S A GOOD KID.
ZIP

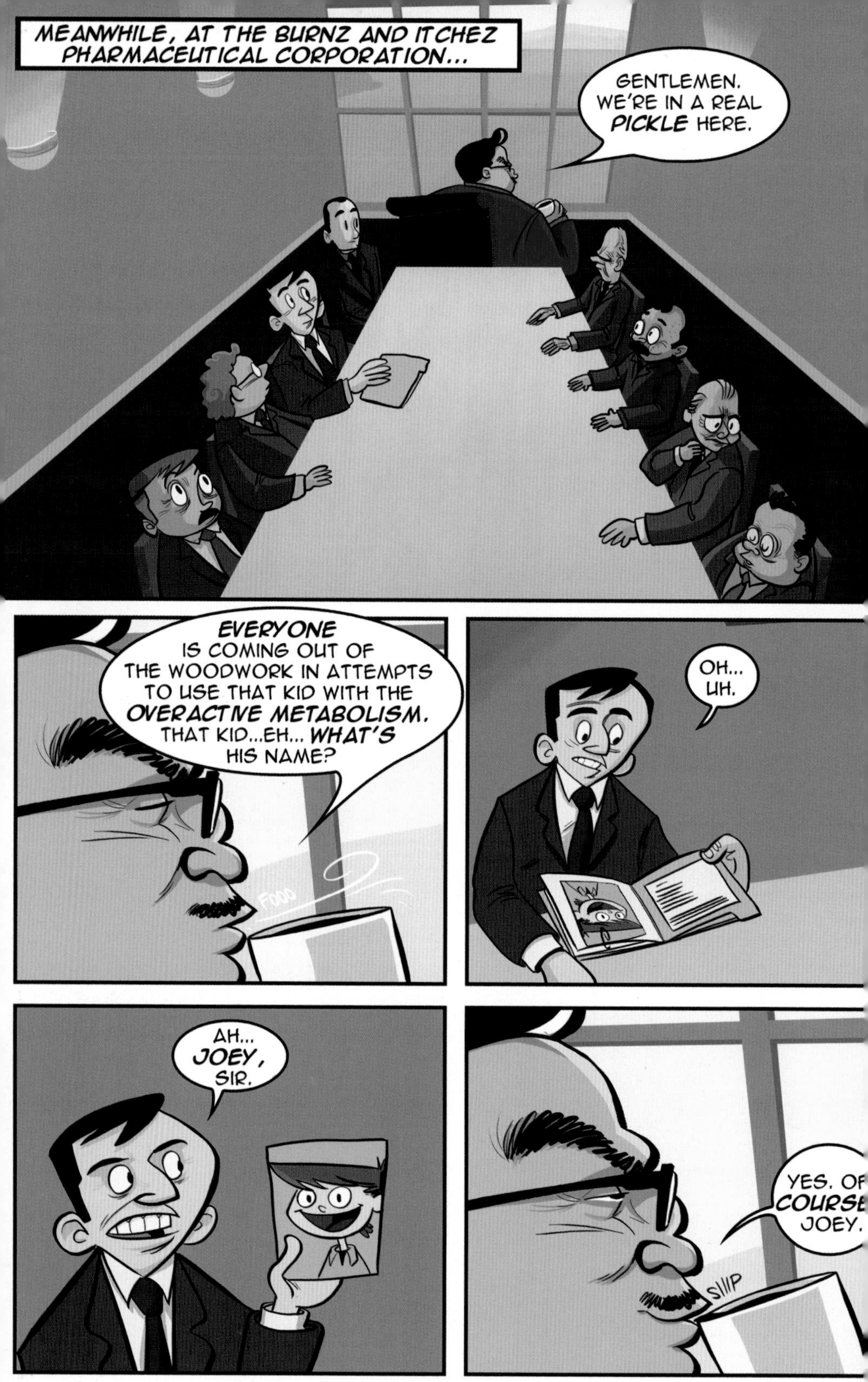
MEANWHILE, AT THE BURNZ AND ITCHEZ PHARMACEUTICAL CORPORATION...
GENTLEMEN. WE'RE IN A REAL PICKLE HERE.
EVERYONE IS COMING OUT OF THE WOODWORK IN ATTEMPTS TO USE THAT KID WITH THE OVERACTIVE METABOLISM. THAT KID...EH... WHAT'S HIS NAME?
FOOO
OH... UH.
AH... JOEY, SIR.
YES. OF COURSE JOEY.
SIIIP

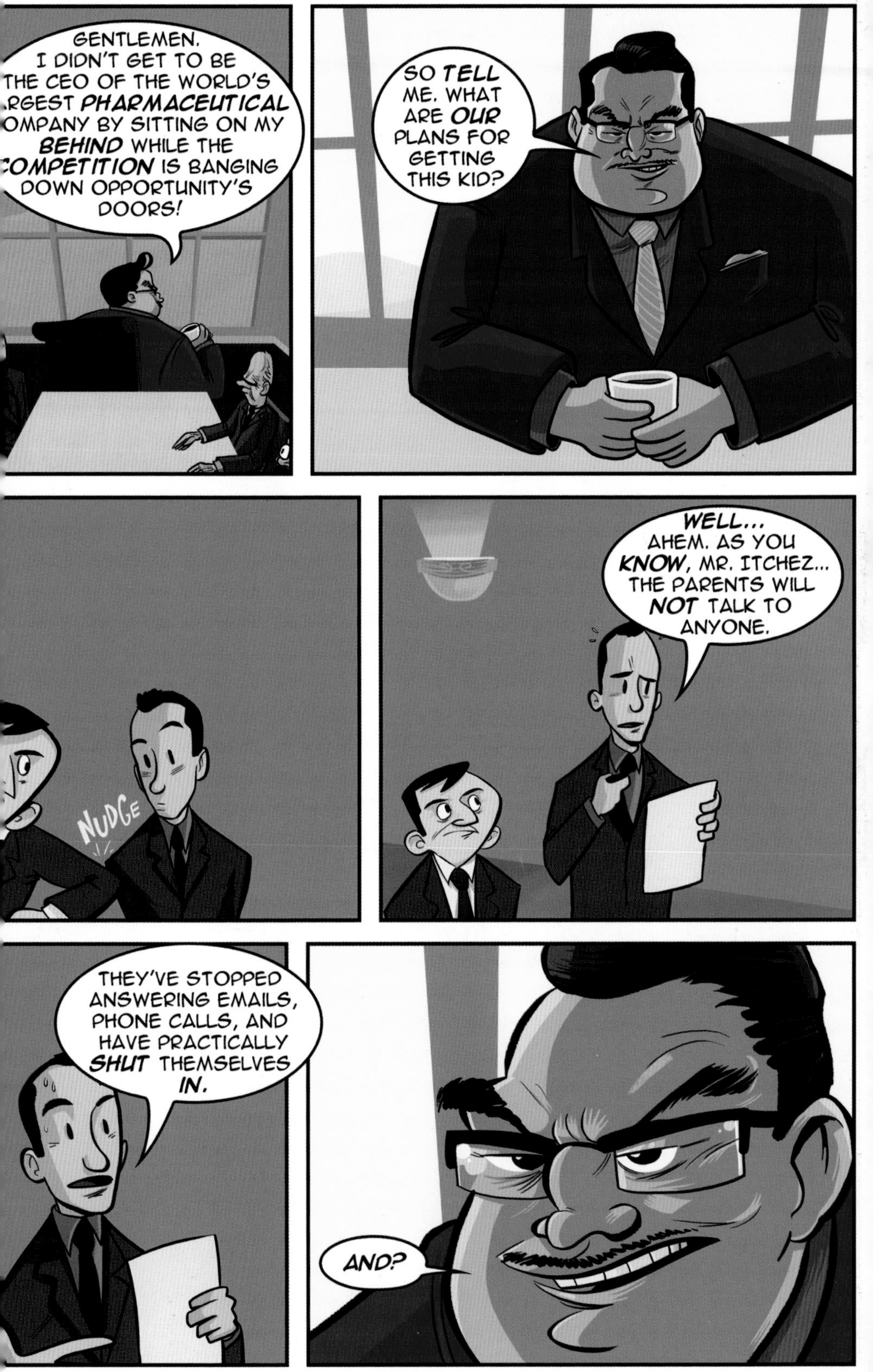
GENTLEMEN. I DIDN'T GET TO BE THE CEO OF THE WORLD'S RGEST PHARMACEUTICAL OMPANY BY SITTING ON MY BEHIND WHILE THE OMPETITION IS BANGING DOWN OPPORTUNITY'S DOORS!
SO TELL ME. WHAT ARE OUR PLANS FOR GETTING THIS KID?
NUDGE
WELL... AHEM. AS YOU KNOW, MR. ITCHEZ... THE PARENTS WILL NOT TALK TO ANYONE.
THEY'VE STOPPED ANSWERING EMAILS, PHONE CALLS, AND HAVE PRACTICALLY SHUT THEMSELVES IN.
AND?

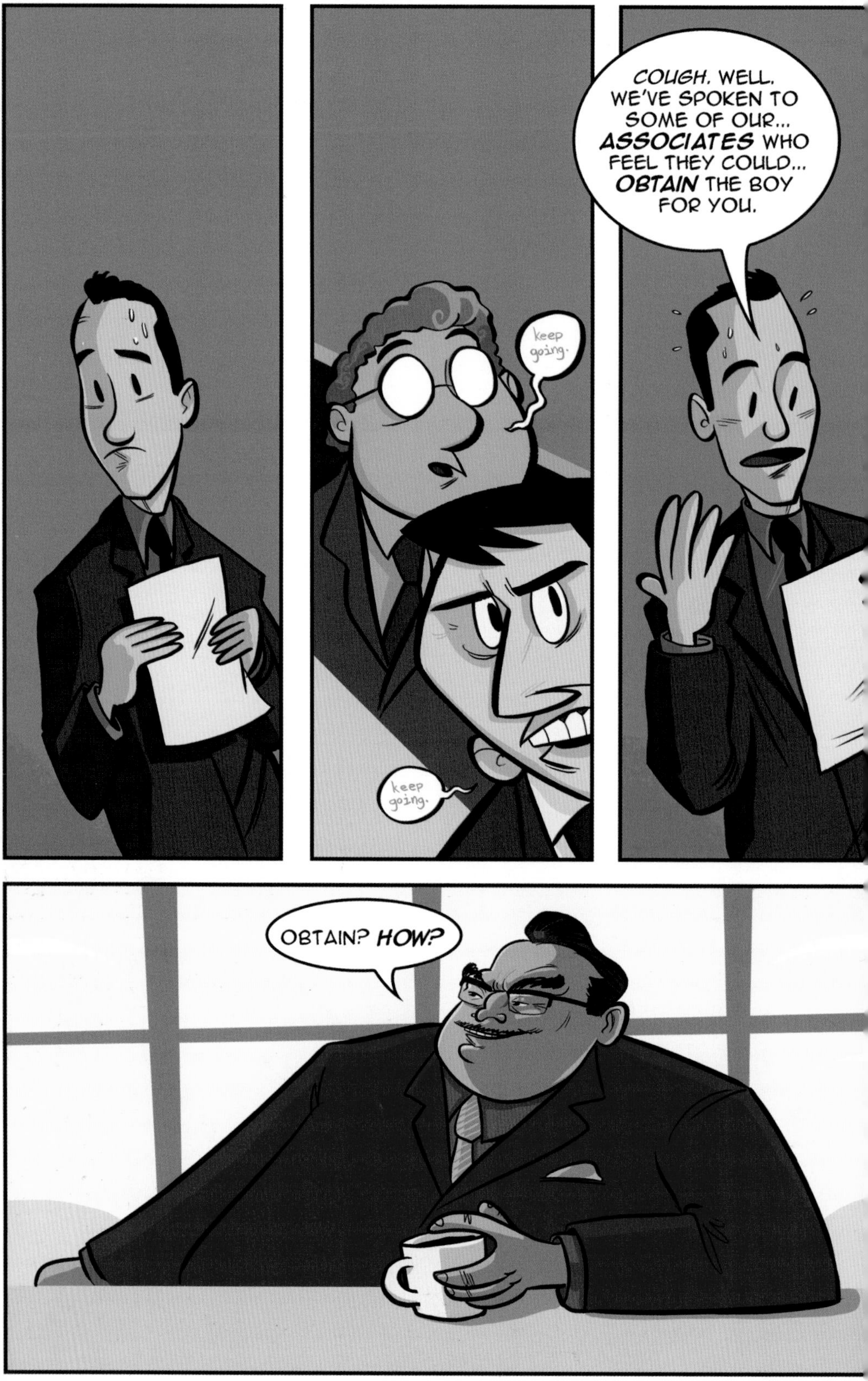
keep going.
keep going.
COUGH. WELL. WE'VE SPOKEN TO SOME OF OUR... ASSOCIATES WHO FEEL THEY COULD... OBTAIN THE BOY FOR YOU.
OBTAIN? HOW?

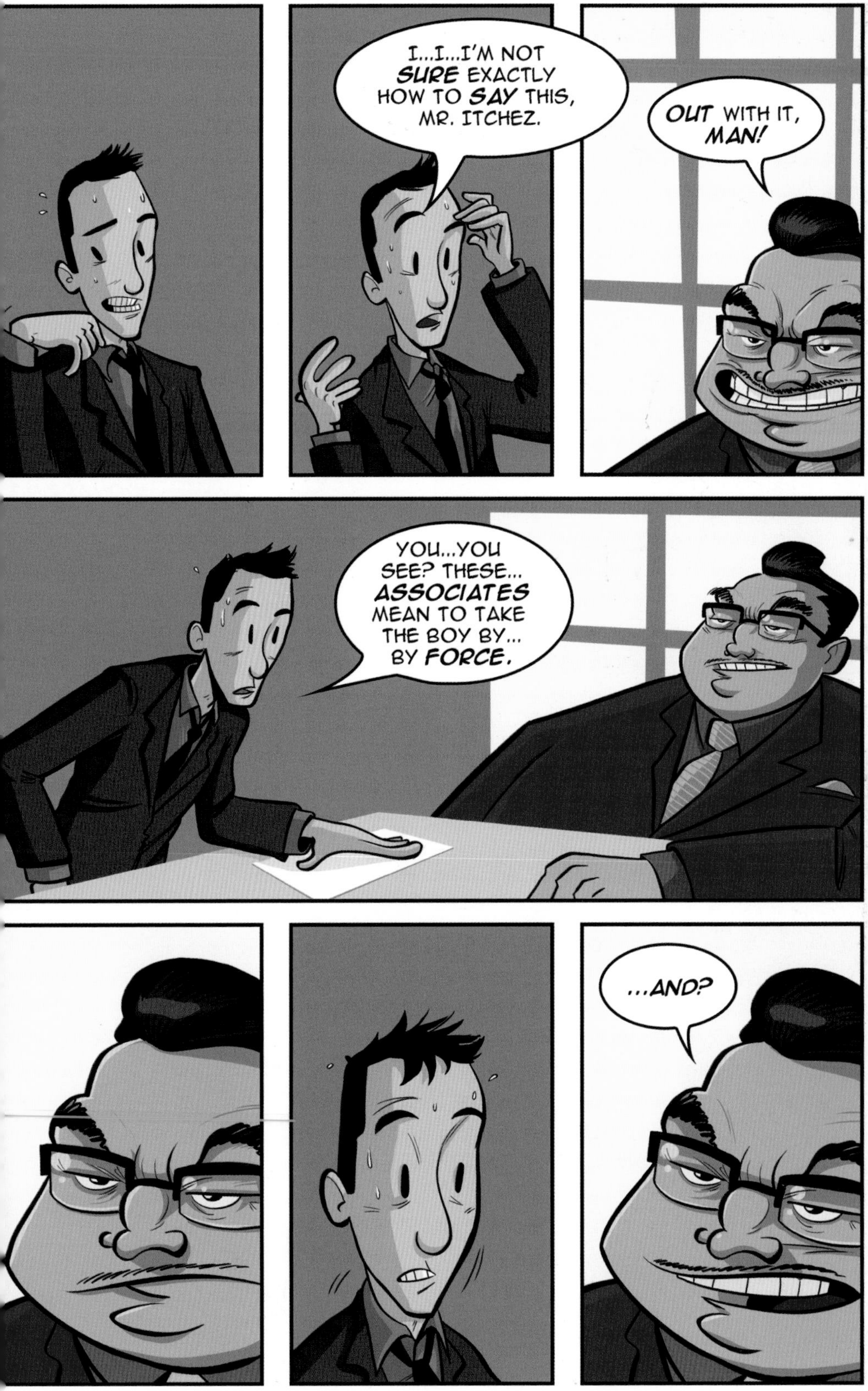
I...I...I'M NOT SURE EXACTLY HOW TO SAY THIS, MR. ITCHEZ.
OUT WITH IT, MAN!
YOU...YOU SEE? THESE... ASSOCIATES MEAN TO TAKE THE BOY BY... BY FORCE.
...AND?

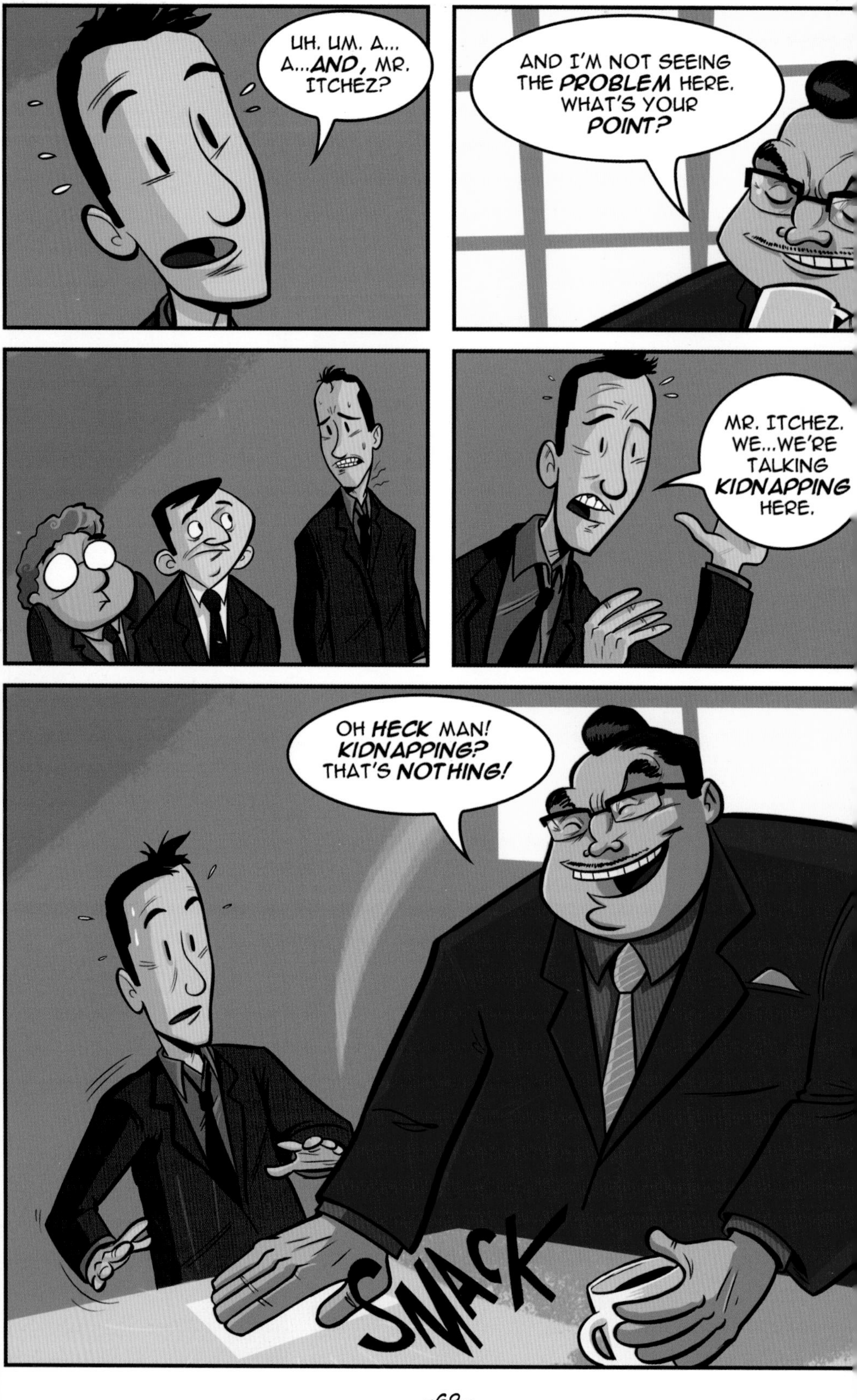
UH. UM. A... A...AND, MR. ITCHEZ?
AND I'M NOT SEEING THE PROBLEM HERE. WHAT'S YOUR POINT?
MR. ITCHEZ. WE...WE'RE TALKING KIDNAPPING HERE.
OH HECK MAN! KIDNAPPING? THAT'S NOTHING!
SMACK

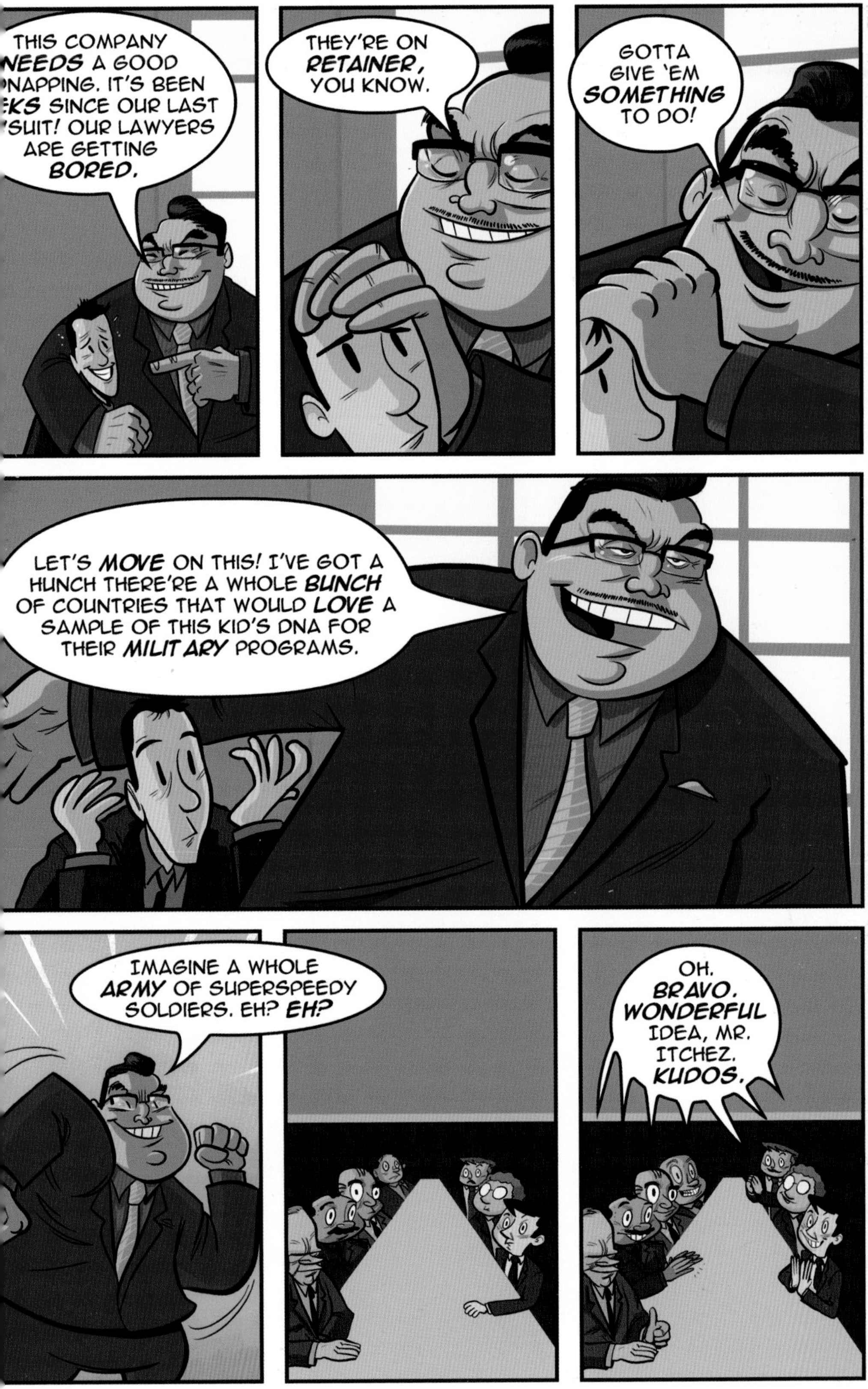

THIS COMPANY NEEDS A GOOD NAPPING. IT'S BEEN EKS SINCE OUR LAST 'SUIT! OUR LAWYERS ARE GETTING BORED.
THEY'RE ON RETAINER, YOU KNOW.
GOTTA GIVE 'EM SOMETHING TO DO!
LET'S MOVE ON THIS! I'VE GOT A HUNCH THERE'RE A WHOLE BUNCH OF COUNTRIES THAT WOULD LOVE A SAMPLE OF THIS KID'S DNA FOR THEIR MILITARY PROGRAMS.
IMAGINE A WHOLE ARMY OF SUPERSPEEDY SOLDIERS. EH? EH?
OH. BRAVO. WONDERFUL IDEA, MR. ITCHEZ. KUDOS.

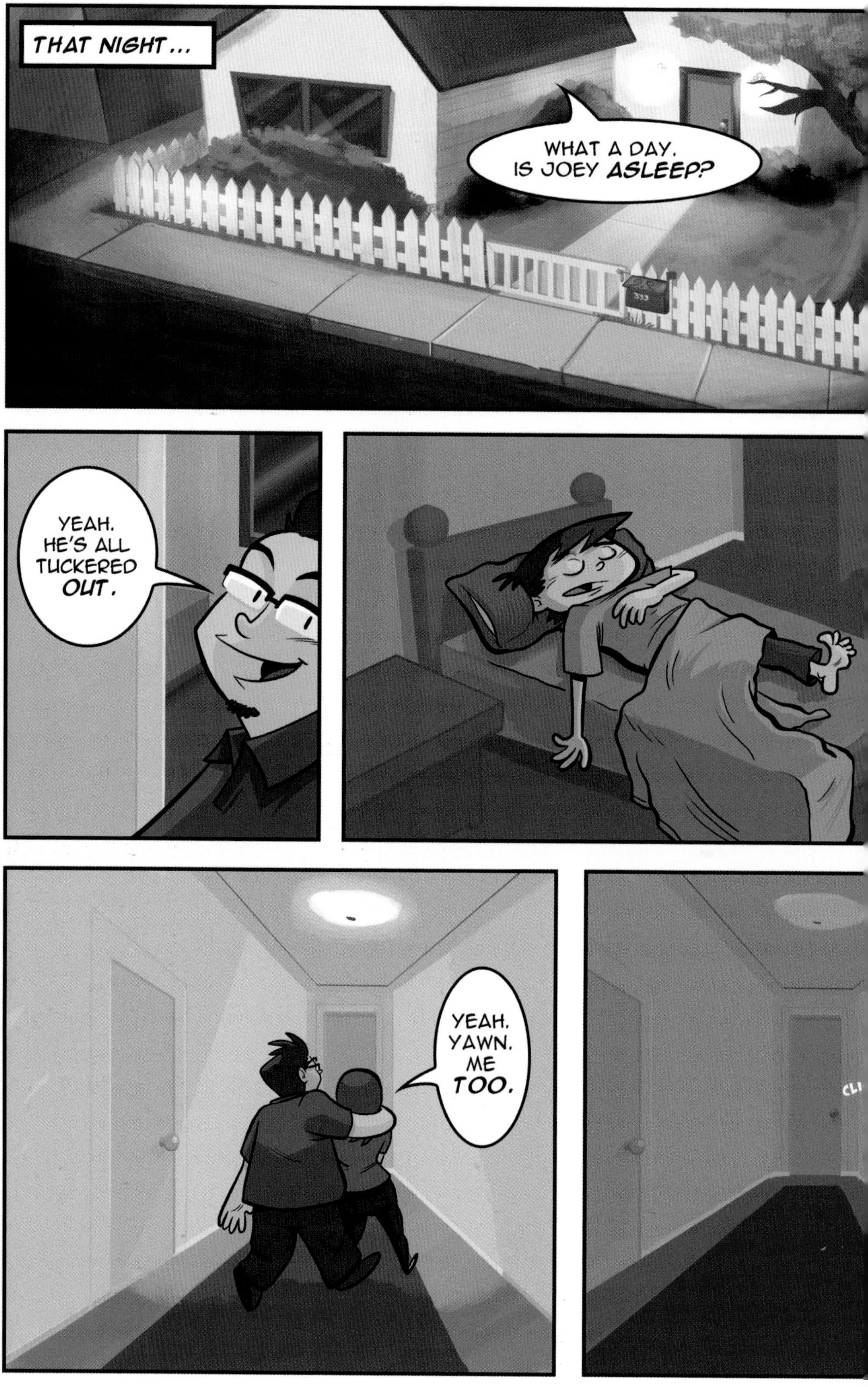
THAT NIGHT...
WHAT A DAY. IS JOEY ASLEEP?
YEAH. HE'S ALL TUCKERED OUT.
YEAH. YAWN. ME TOO.

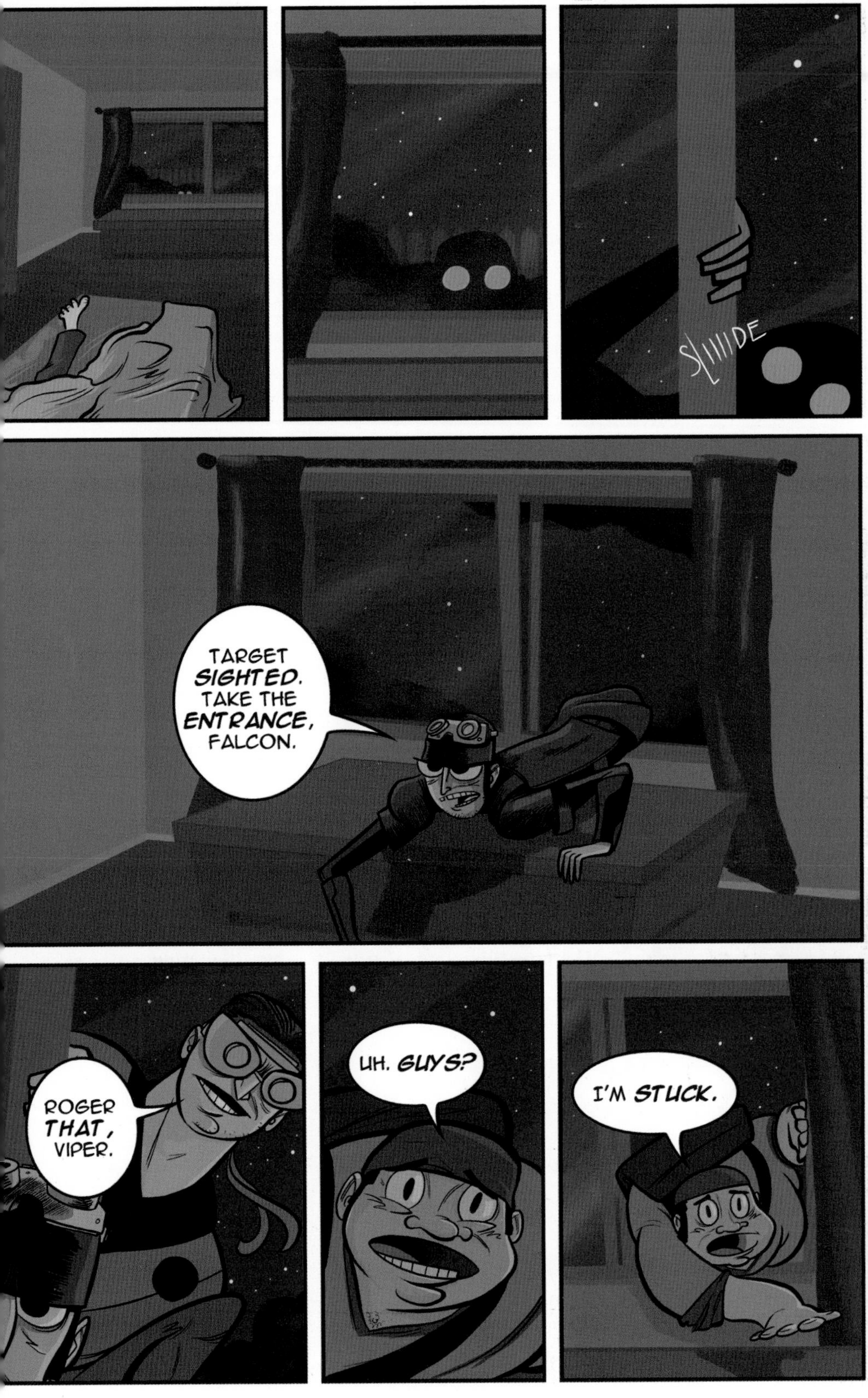
SLIIIIDE
TARGET SIGHTED. TAKE THE ENTRANCE, FALCON.
ROGER THAT, VIPER.
UH. GUYS?
I'M STUCK.

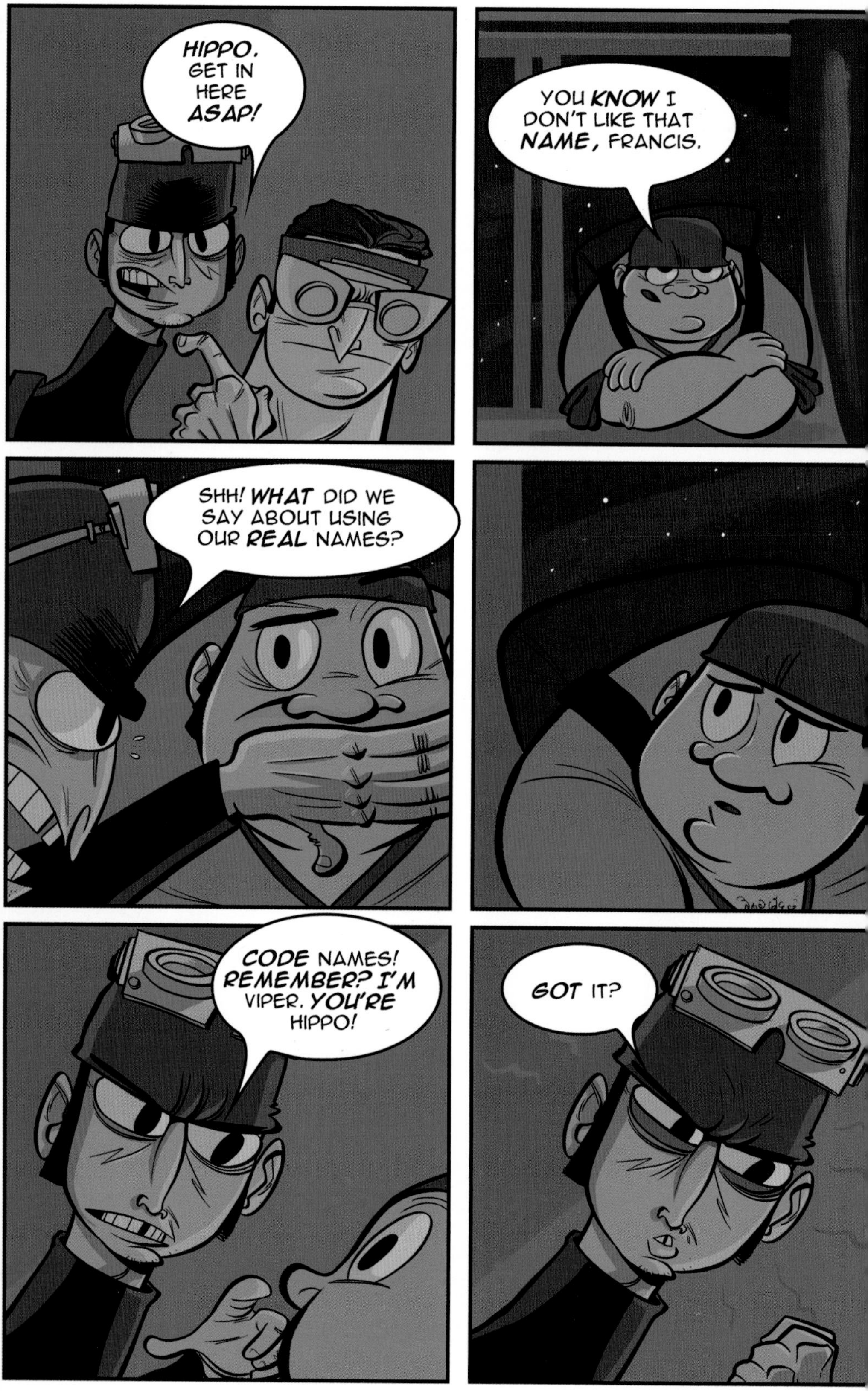
HIPPO. GET IN HERE ASAP!
YOU KNOW I DON'T LIKE THAT NAME, FRANCIS.
SHH! WHAT DID WE SAY ABOUT USING OUR REAL NAMES?
CODE NAMES! REMEMBER? I'M VIPER. YOU'RE HIPPO!
GOT IT?

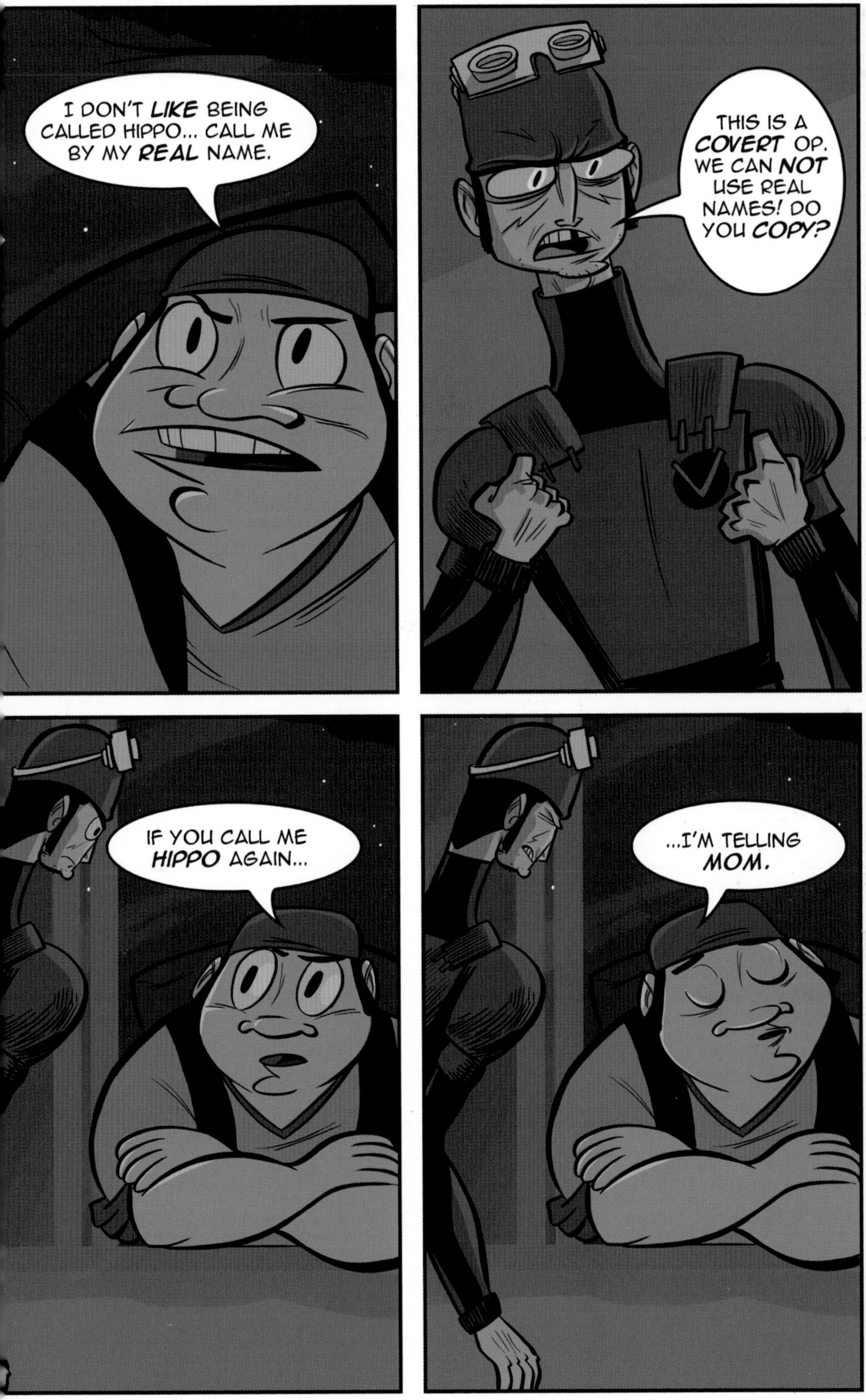
I DON'T LIKE BEING CALLED HIPPO... CALL ME BY MY REAL NAME.
THIS IS A COVERT OP. WE CAN NOT USE REAL NAMES! DO YOU COPY?
IF YOU CALL ME HIPPO AGAIN...
...I'M TELLING MOM.

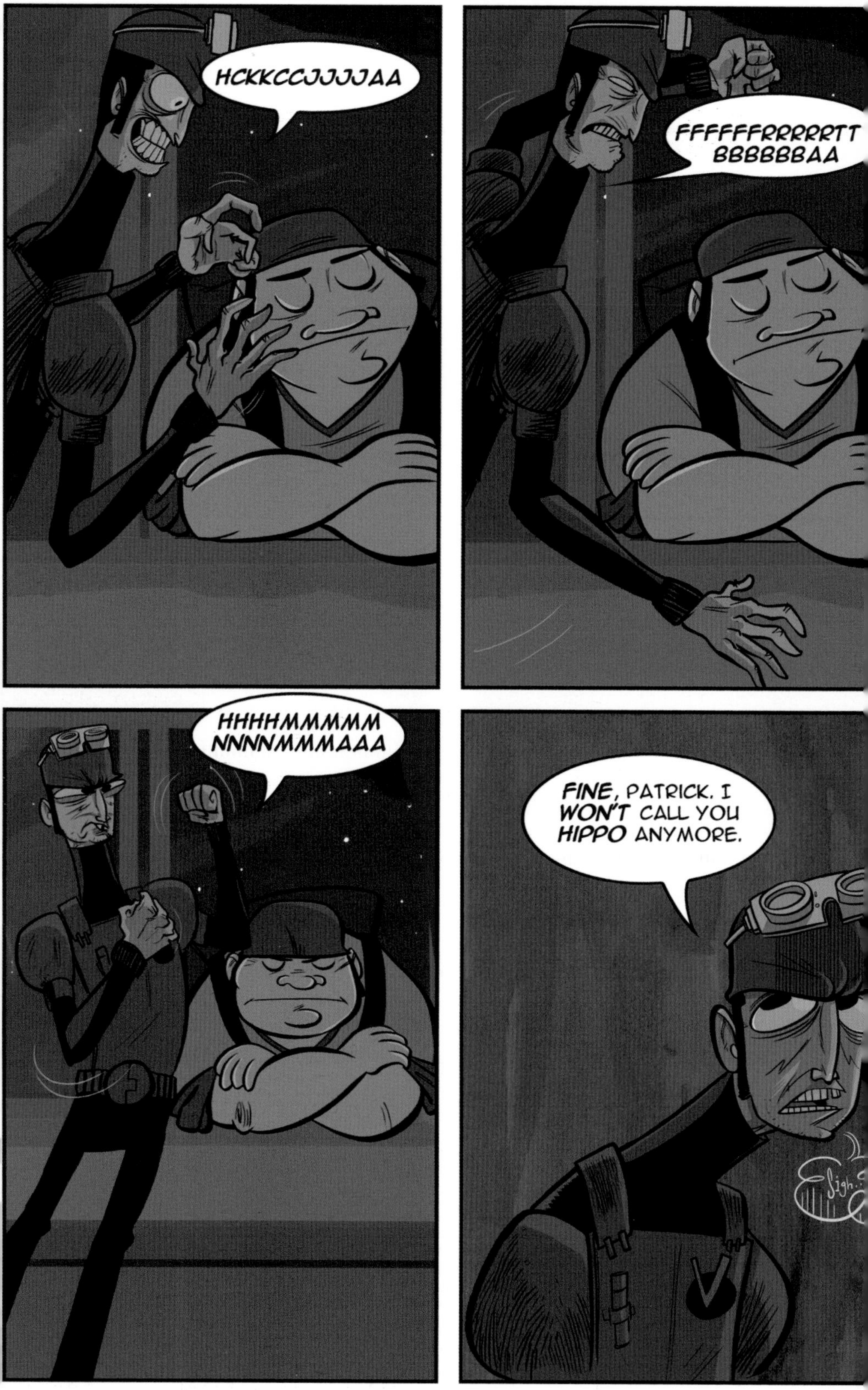
HCKKCCJJJJAA
FFFFFFRRRRRTT BBBBBBAA
HHHHMMMMM NNNNMMMAAA
FINE, PATRICK. I WON'T CALL YOU HIPPO ANYMORE.

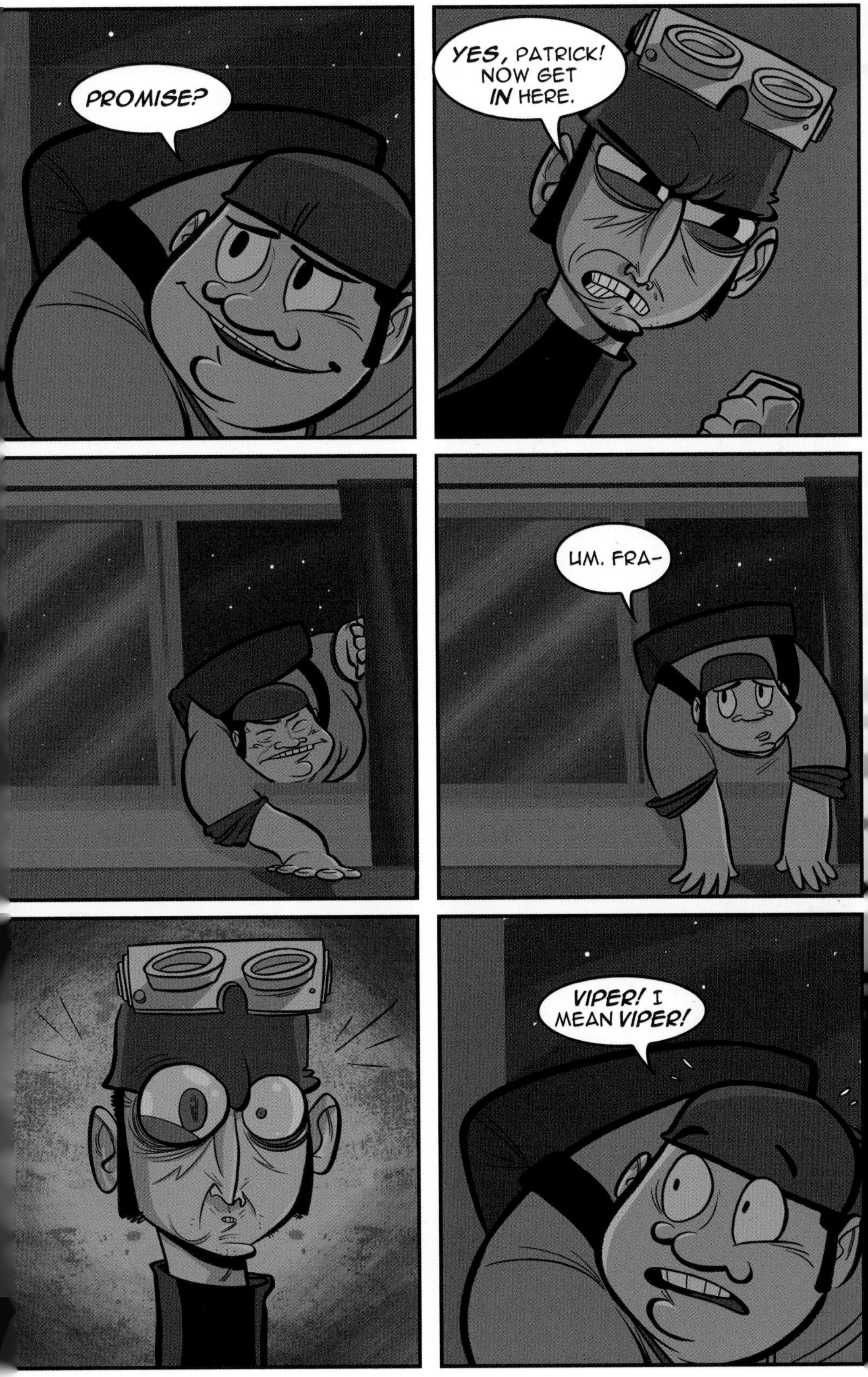
PROMISE?
YES, PATRICK! NOW GET IN HERE.
UM. FRA-
VIPER! I MEAN VIPER!

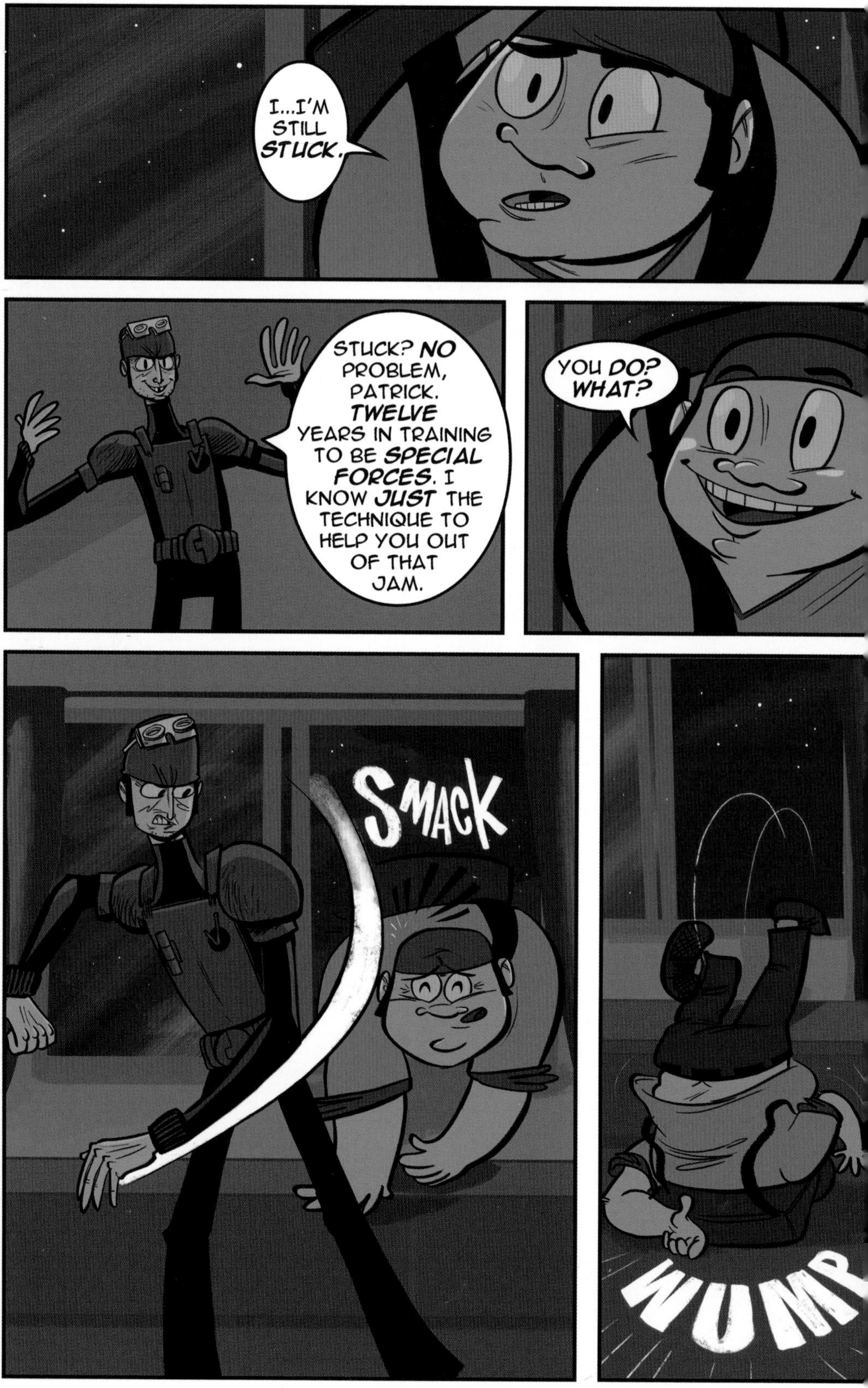

I...I'M STILL STUCK.
STUCK? NO PROBLEM, PATRICK. TWELVE YEARS IN TRAINING TO BE SPECIAL FORCES. I KNOW JUST THE TECHNIQUE TO HELP YOU OUT OF THAT JAM.
YOU DO? WHAT?
SMACK
WUMP

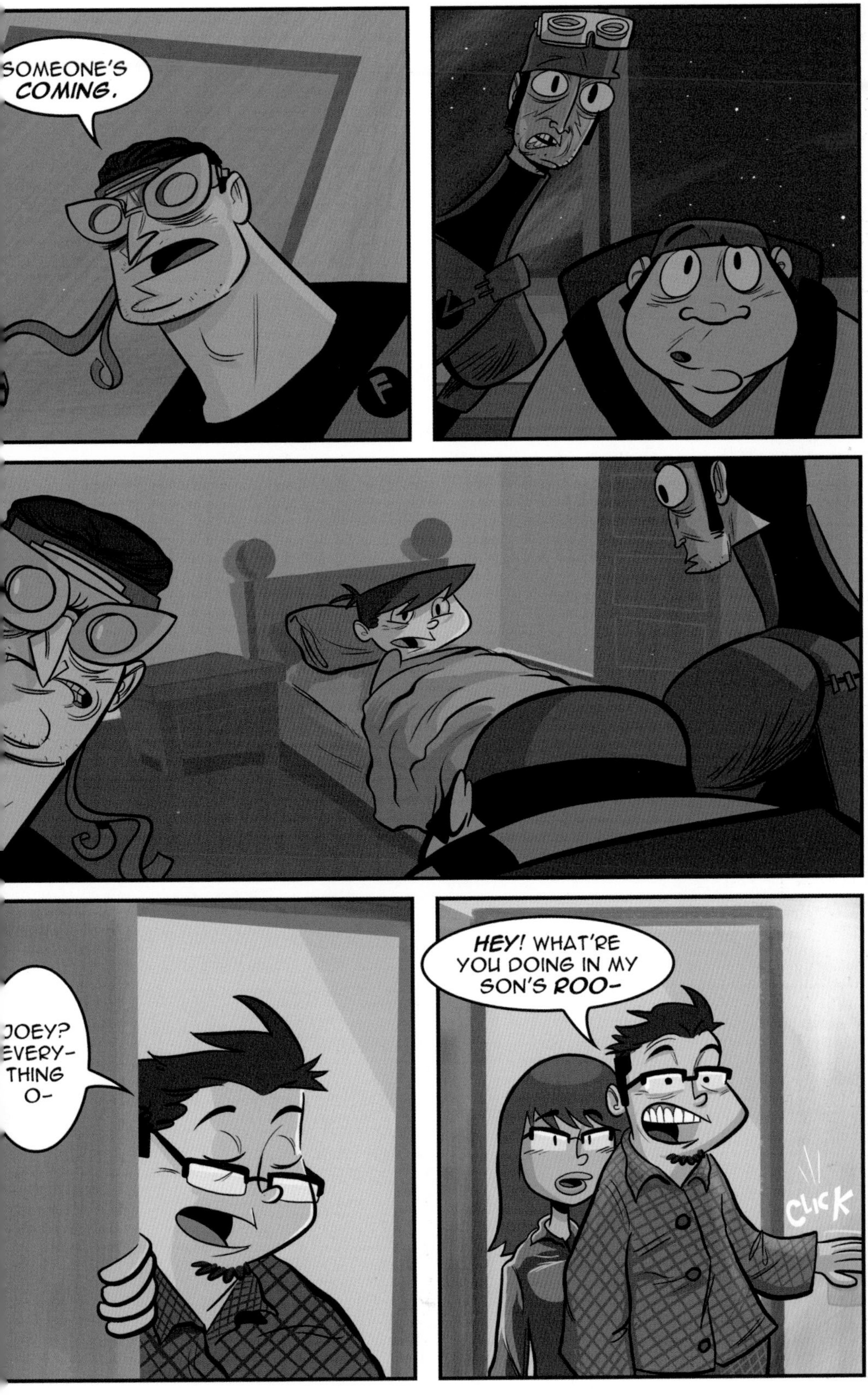
SOMEONE'S COMING.
JOEY? EVERY- THING O-
HEY! WHAT'RE YOU DOING IN MY SON'S ROO-
CLICK

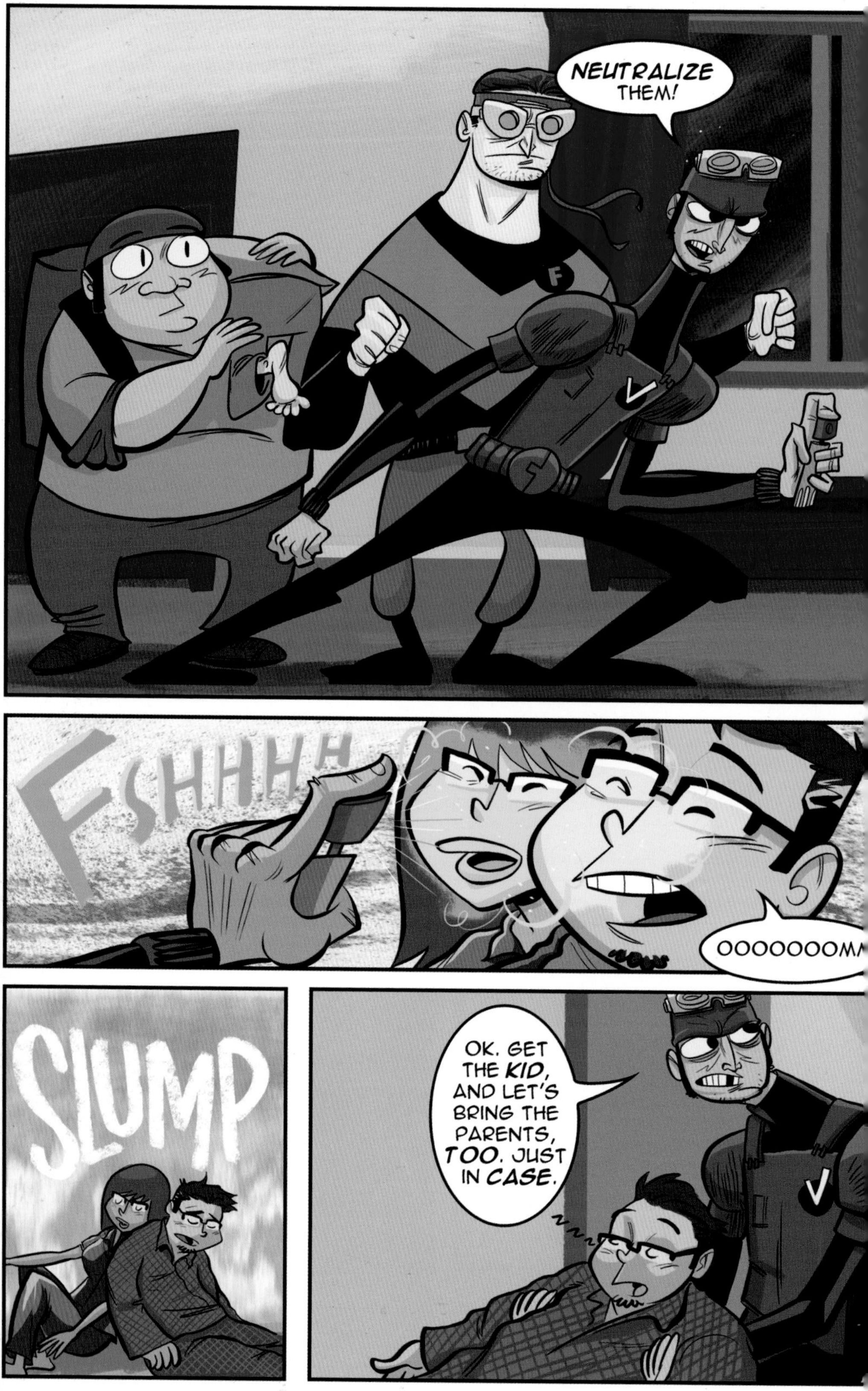
NEUTRALIZE THEM!
FSHHHH
OOOOOOOMA
SLUMP
OK. GET THE KID, AND LET'S BRING THE PARENTS, TOO. JUST IN CASE.

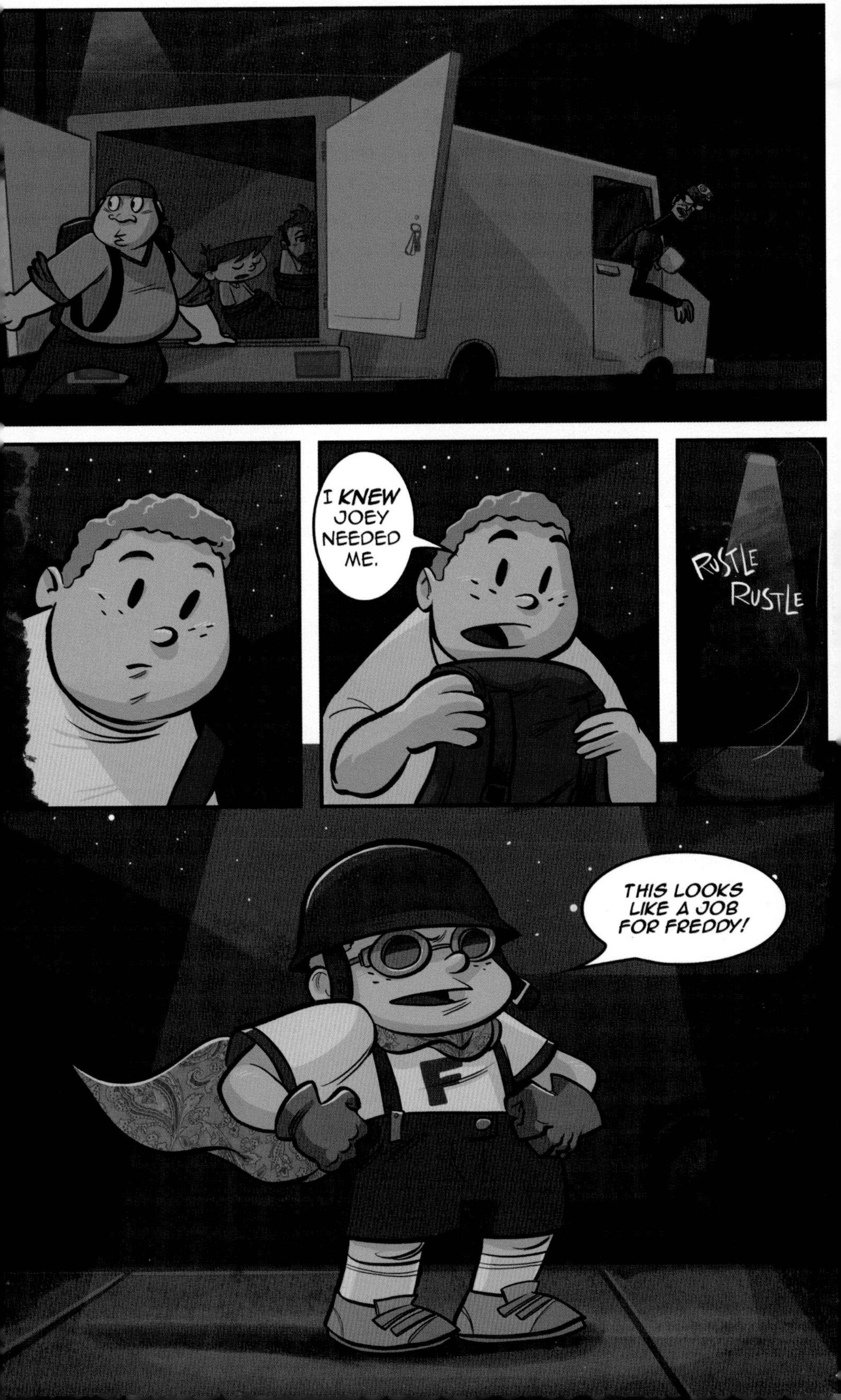
I KNEW JOEY NEEDED ME.
RUSTLE RUSTLE
THIS LOOKS LIKE A JOB FOR FREDDY!

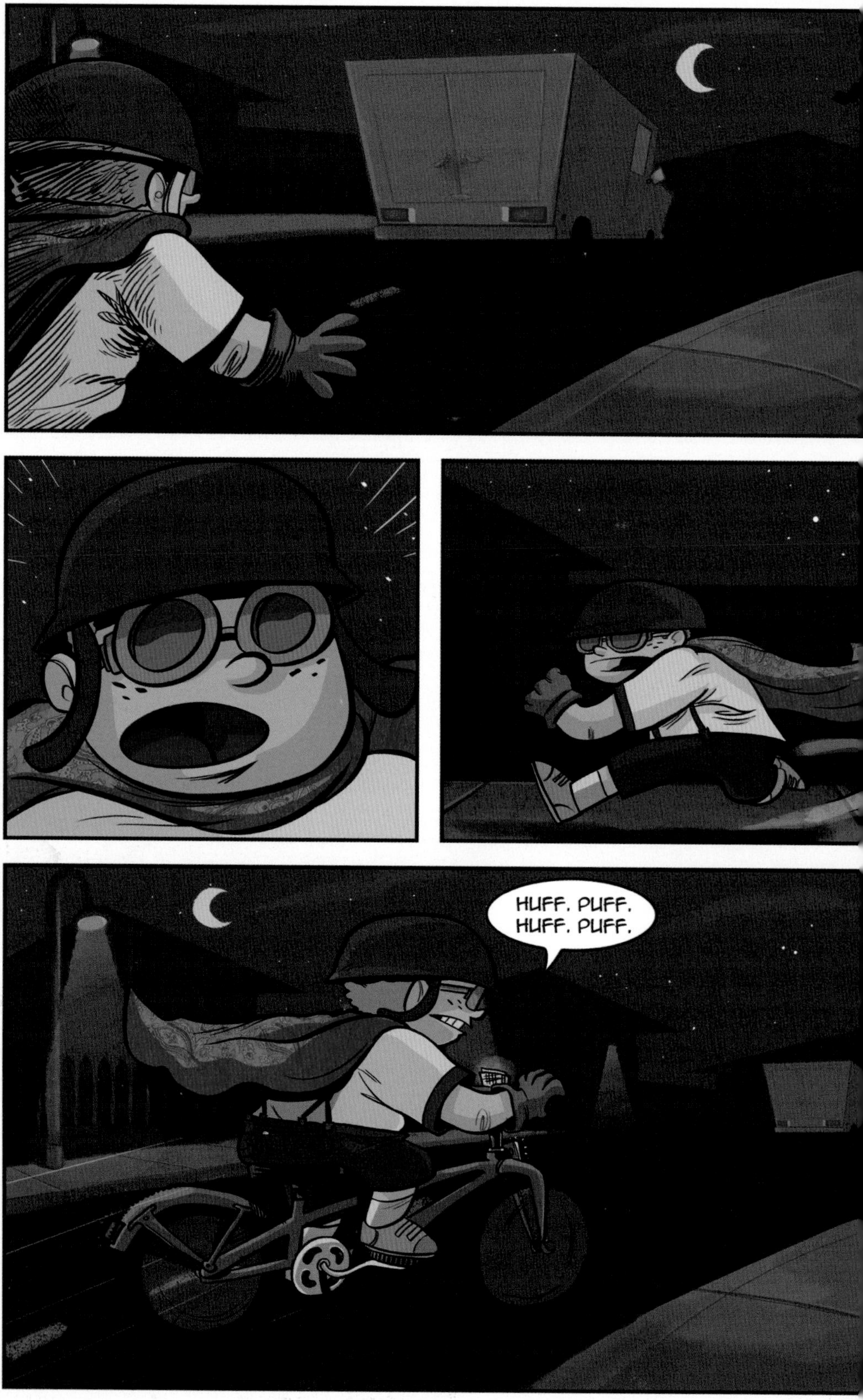
HUFF. PUFF.
HUFF. PUFF.

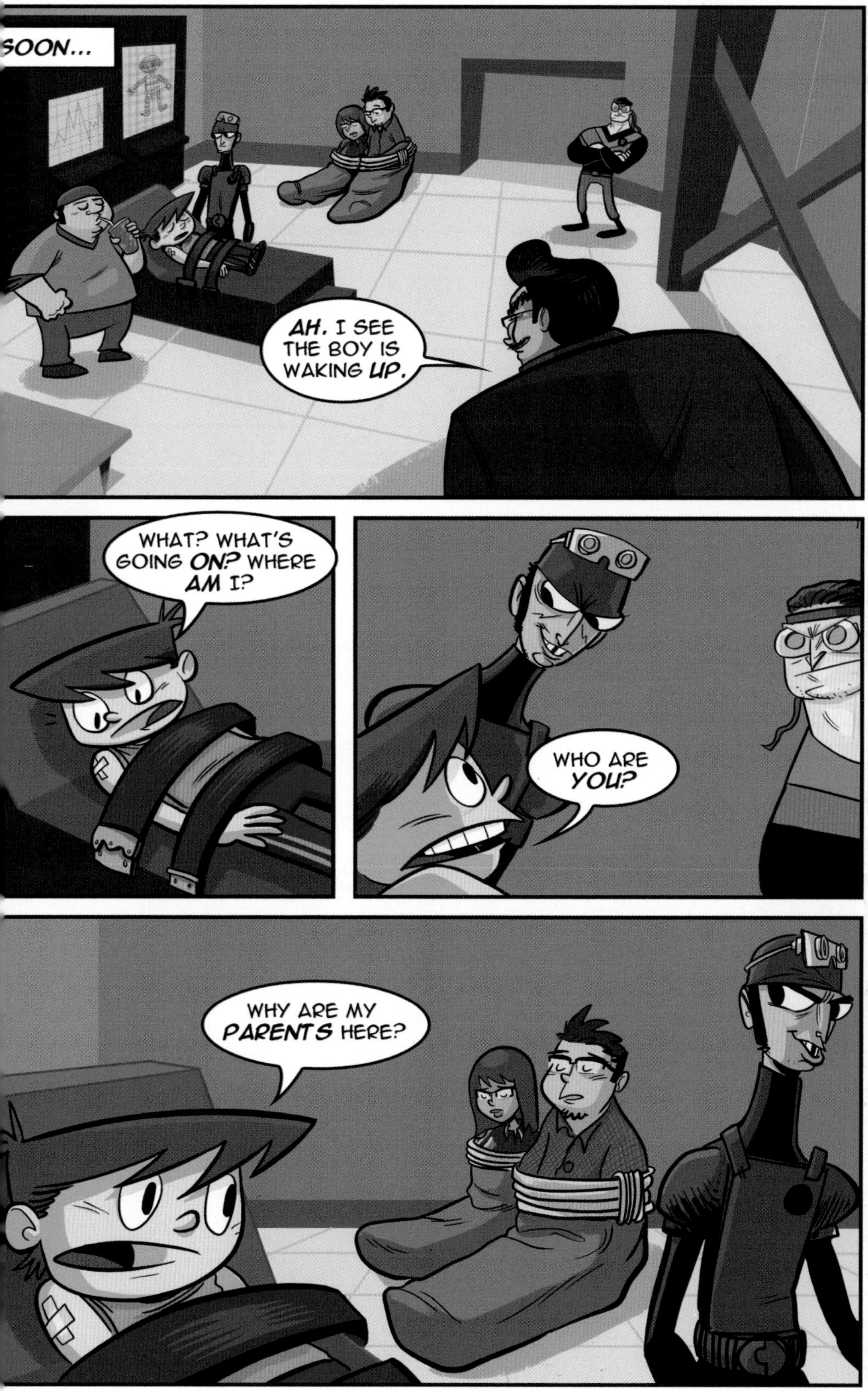
SOON...
AH. I SEE THE BOY IS WAKING UP.
WHAT? WHAT'S GOING ON? WHERE AM I?
WHO ARE YOU?
WHY ARE MY PARENTS HERE?

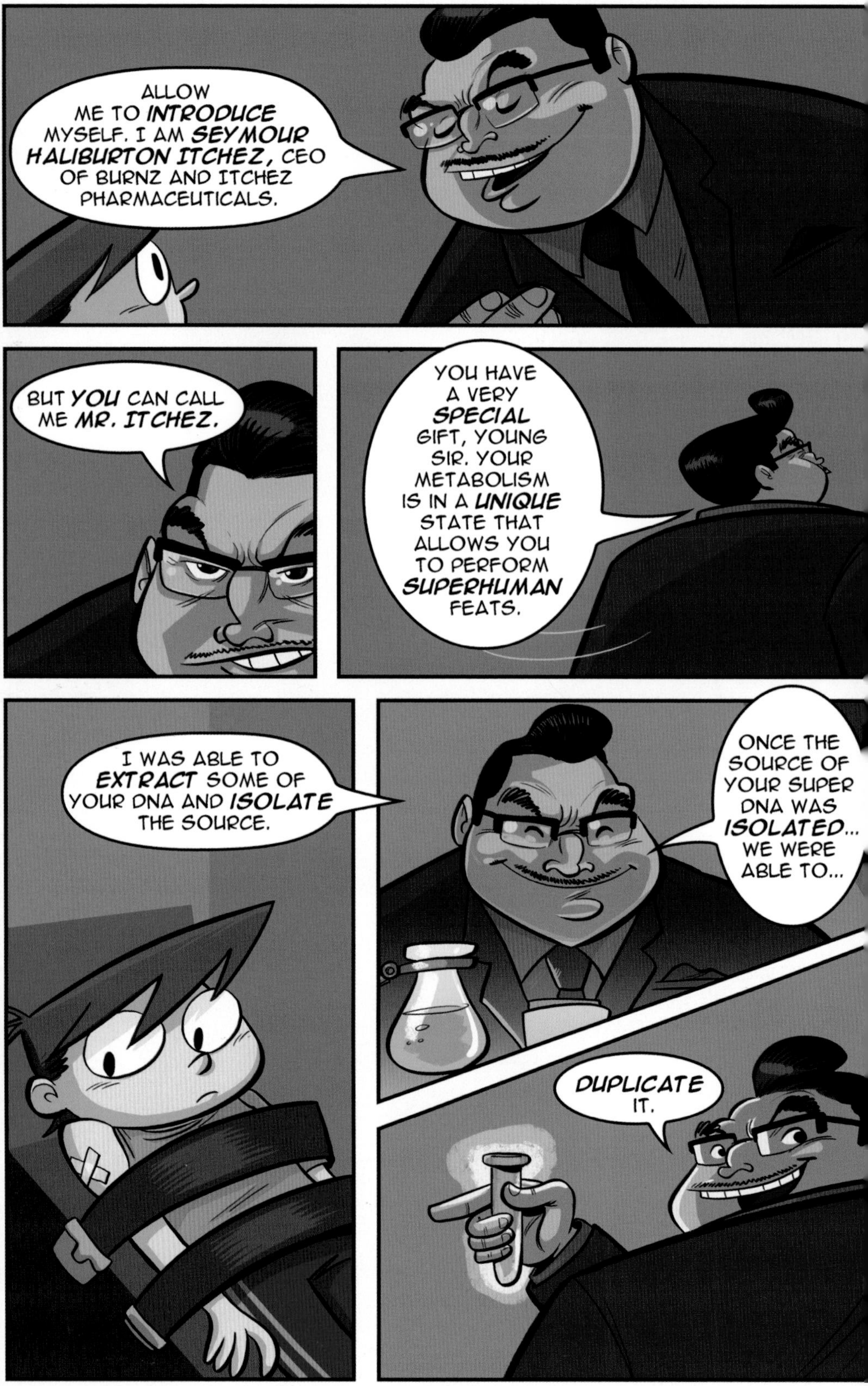
ALLOW ME TO INTRODUCE MYSELF. I AM SEYMOUR HALIBURTON ITCHEZ, CEO OF BURNZ AND ITCHEZ PHARMACEUTICALS.
BUT YOU CAN CALL ME MR. ITCHEZ.
YOU HAVE A VERY SPECIAL GIFT, YOUNG SIR. YOUR METABOLISM IS IN A UNIQUE STATE THAT ALLOWS YOU TO PERFORM SUPERHUMAN FEATS.
I WAS ABLE TO EXTRACT SOME OF YOUR DNA AND ISOLATE THE SOURCE.
ONCE THE SOURCE OF YOUR SUPER DNA WAS ISOLATED... WE WERE ABLE TO...
DUPLICATE IT.

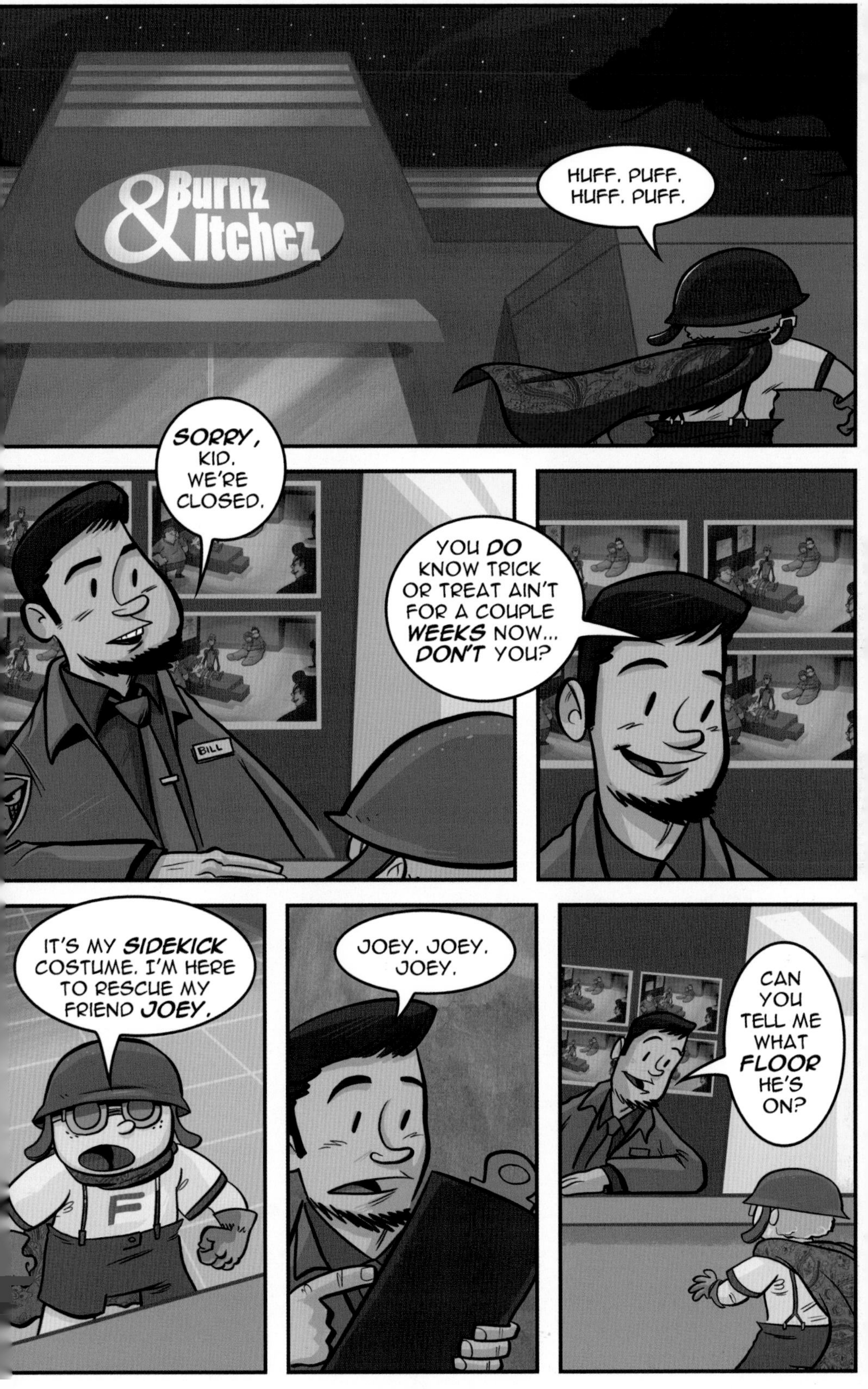
Burnz & Itchez
HUFF. PUFF. HUFF. PUFF.
SORRY, KID. WE'RE CLOSED.
BILL
YOU DO KNOW TRICK OR TREAT AIN'T FOR A COUPLE WEEKS NOW... DON'T YOU?
IT'S MY SIDEKICK COSTUME. I'M HERE TO RESCUE MY FRIEND JOEY.
F
JOEY. JOEY. JOEY.
CAN YOU TELL ME WHAT FLOOR HE'S ON?

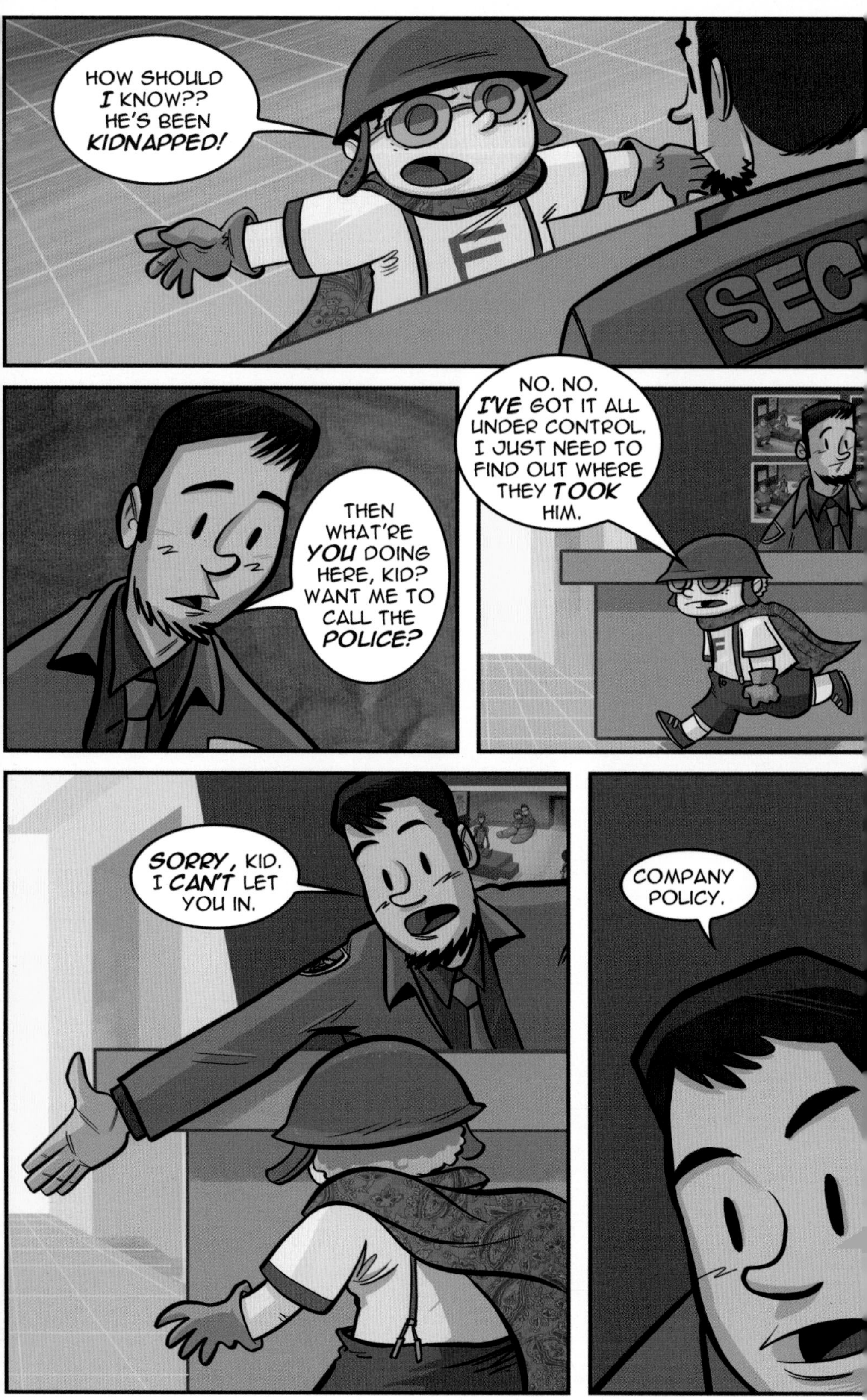

HOW SHOULD I KNOW?? HE'S BEEN KIDNAPPED!
THEN WHAT'RE YOU DOING HERE, KID? WANT ME TO CALL THE POLICE?
NO. NO. I'VE GOT IT ALL UNDER CONTROL. I JUST NEED TO FIND OUT WHERE THEY TOOK HIM.
SORRY, KID. I CAN'T LET YOU IN.
COMPANY POLICY.

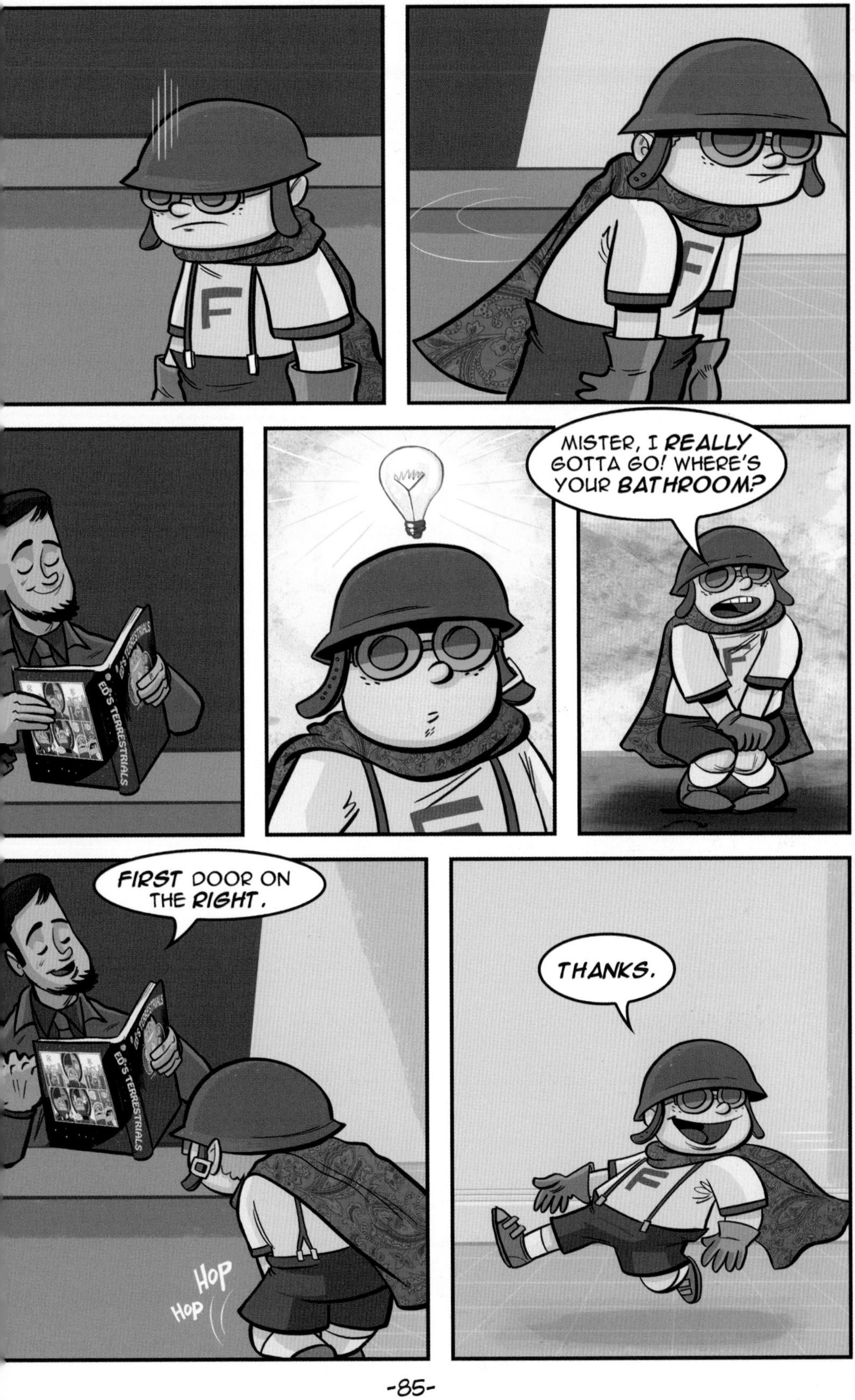

MISTER, I REALLY GOTTA GO! WHERE'S YOUR BATHROOM?
ED'S TERRESTRIALS
FIRST DOOR ON THE RIGHT.
HOP HOP
THANKS.

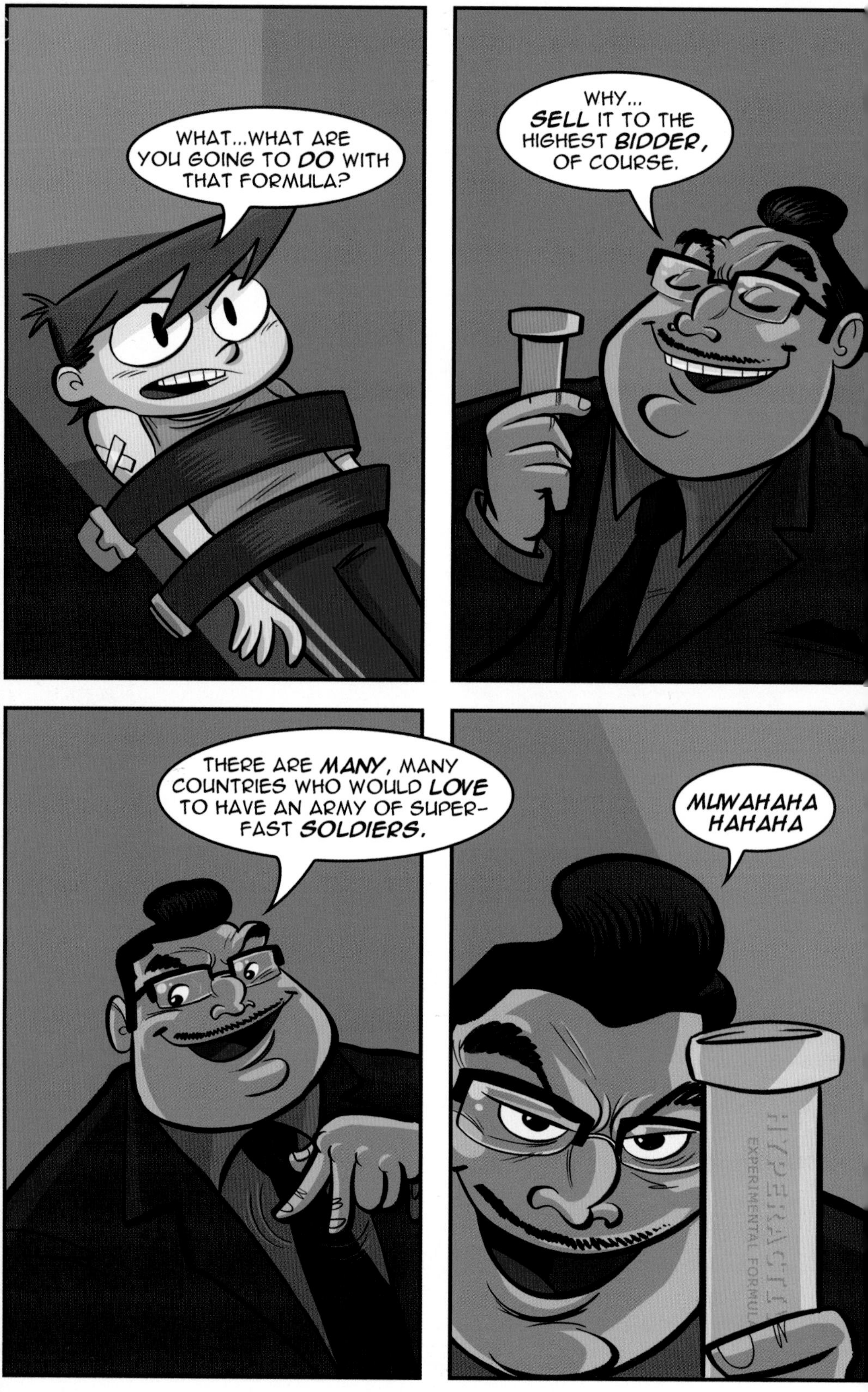
WHAT...WHAT ARE YOU GOING TO DO WITH THAT FORMULA?
WHY... SELL IT TO THE HIGHEST BIDDER, OF COURSE.
THERE ARE MANY, MANY COUNTRIES WHO WOULD LOVE TO HAVE AN ARMY OF SUPER-FAST SOLDIERS.
MUWAHAHA HAHAHA

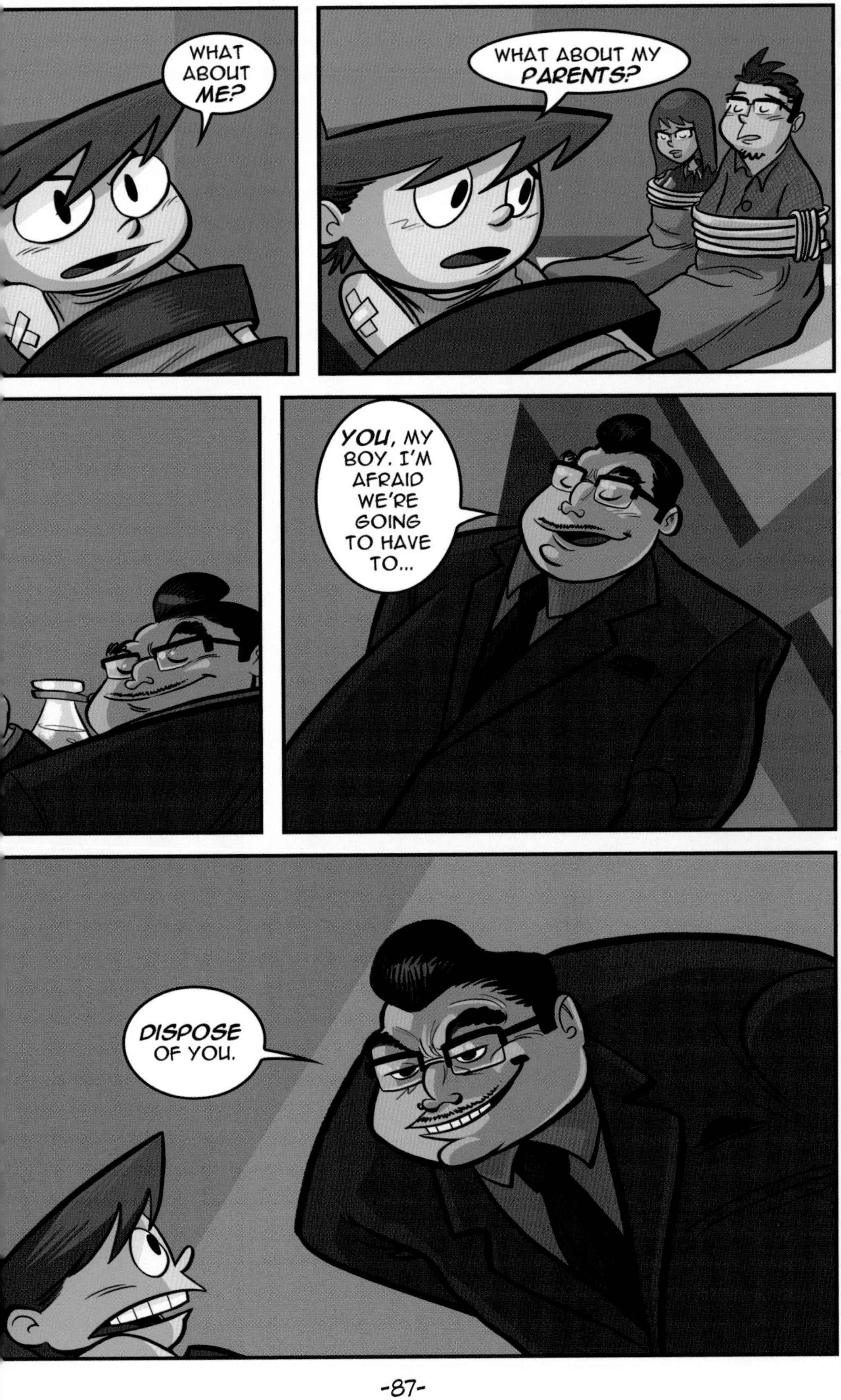
WHAT ABOUT ME?
WHAT ABOUT MY PARENTS?
YOU, MY BOY. I'M AFRAID WE'RE GOING TO HAVE TO...
DISPOSE OF YOU.

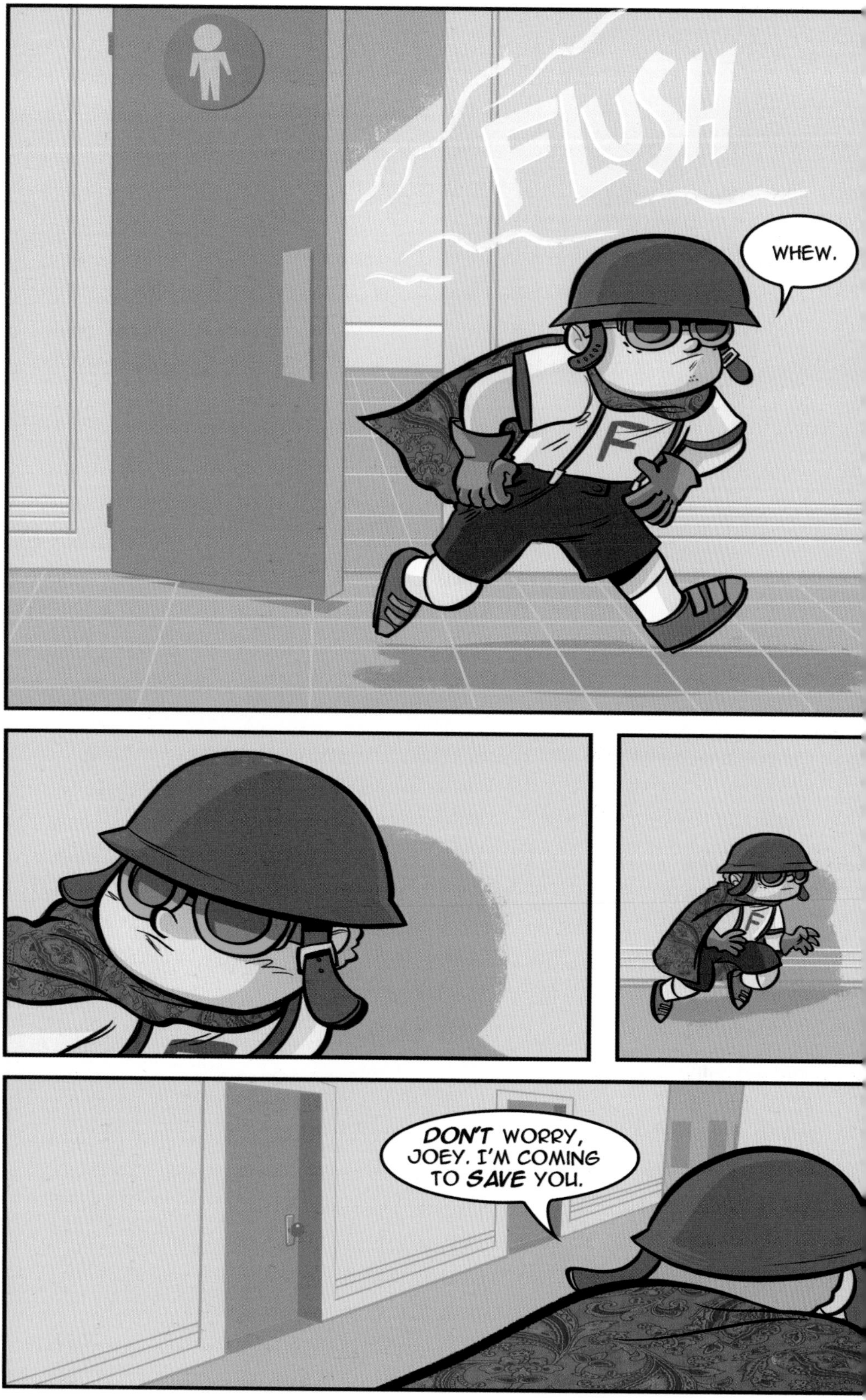
FLUSH
WHEW.
DON'T WORRY, JOEY. I'M COMING TO SAVE YOU.

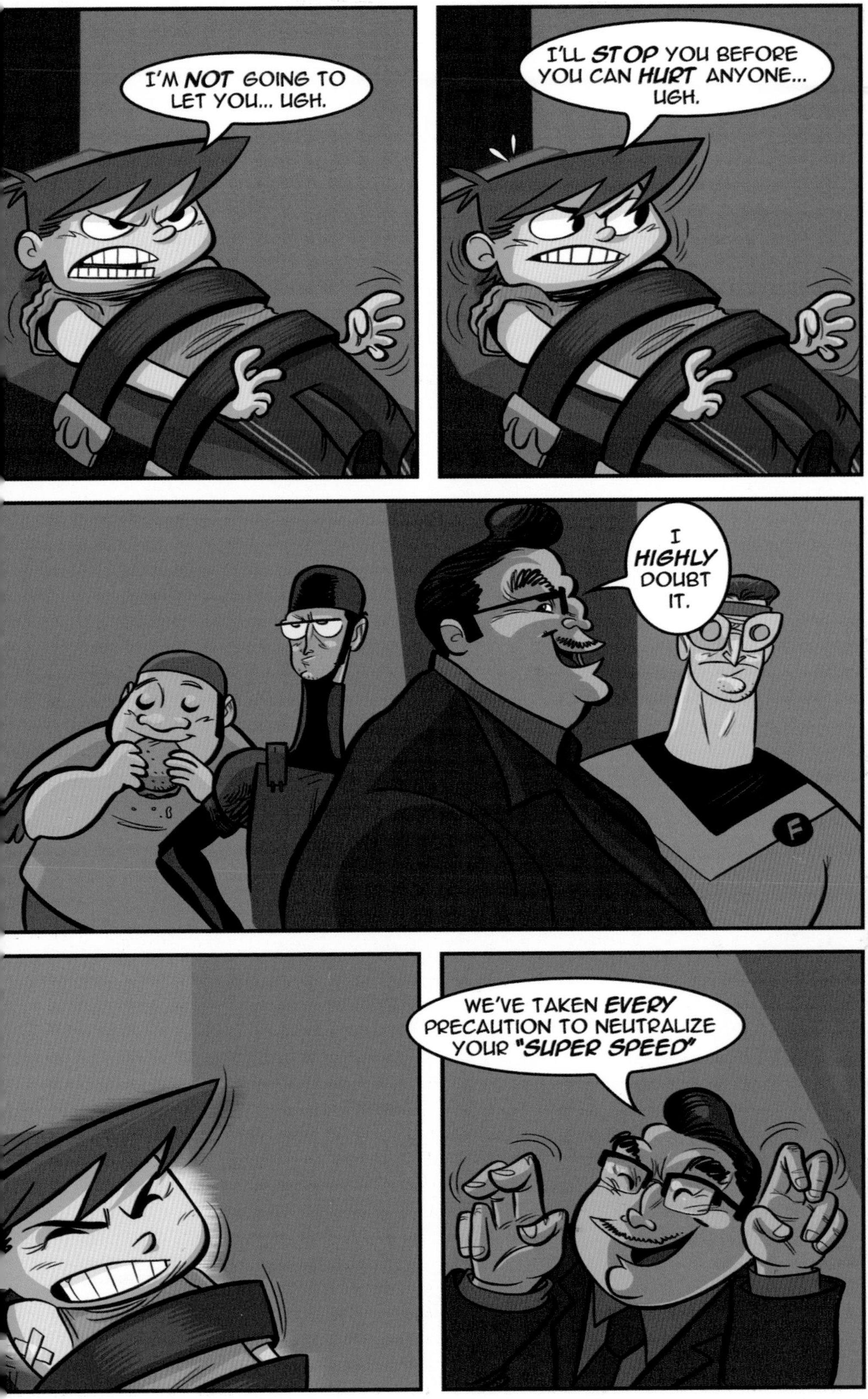

I'M NOT GOING TO LET YOU... UGH.
I'LL STOP YOU BEFORE YOU CAN HURT ANYONE... UGH.
I HIGHLY DOUBT IT.
F
WE'VE TAKEN EVERY PRECAUTION TO NEUTRALIZE YOUR "SUPER SPEED"

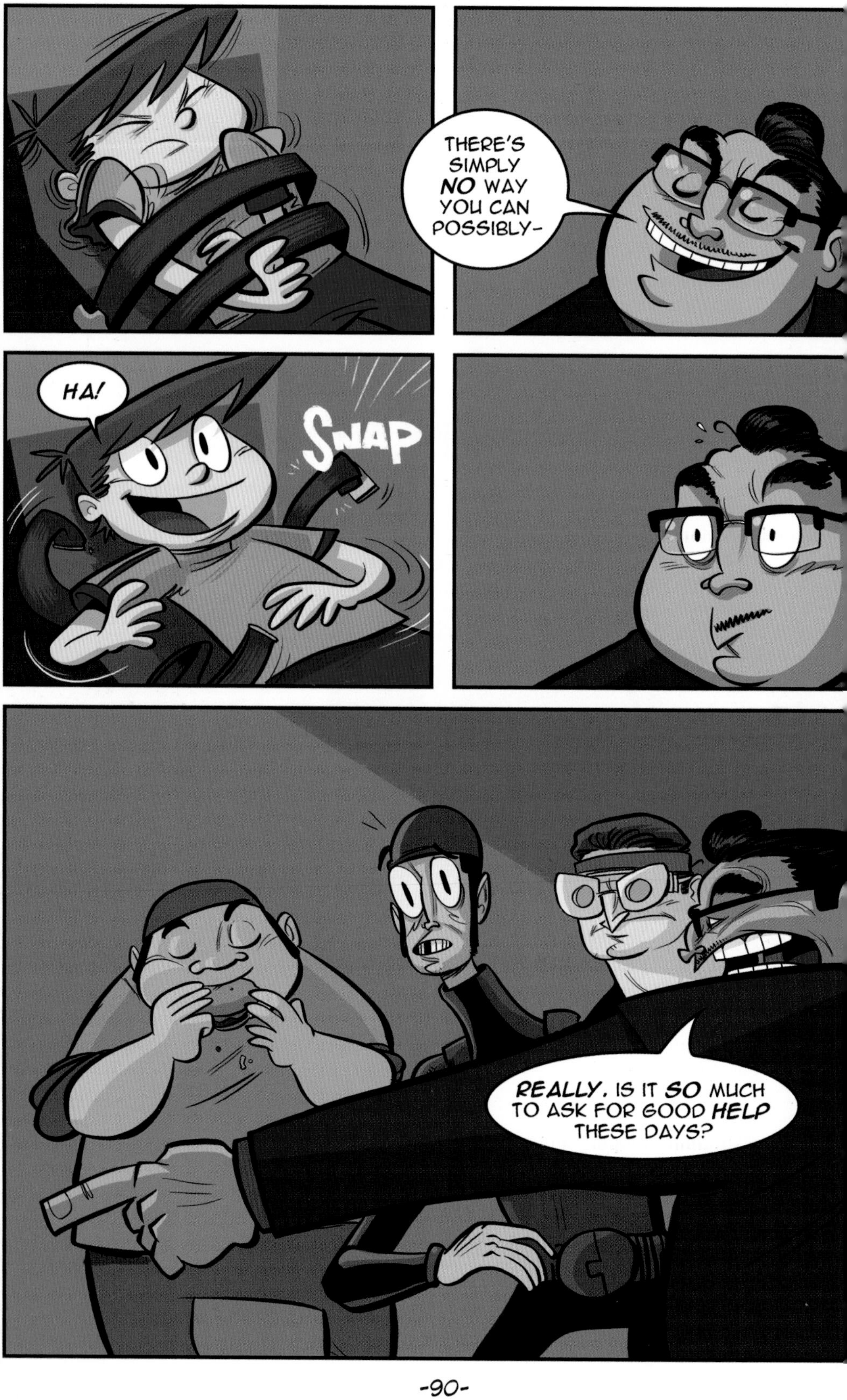
THERE'S SIMPLY NO WAY YOU CAN POSSIBLY-
HA!
SNAP
REALLY. IS IT SO MUCH TO ASK FOR GOOD HELP THESE DAYS?

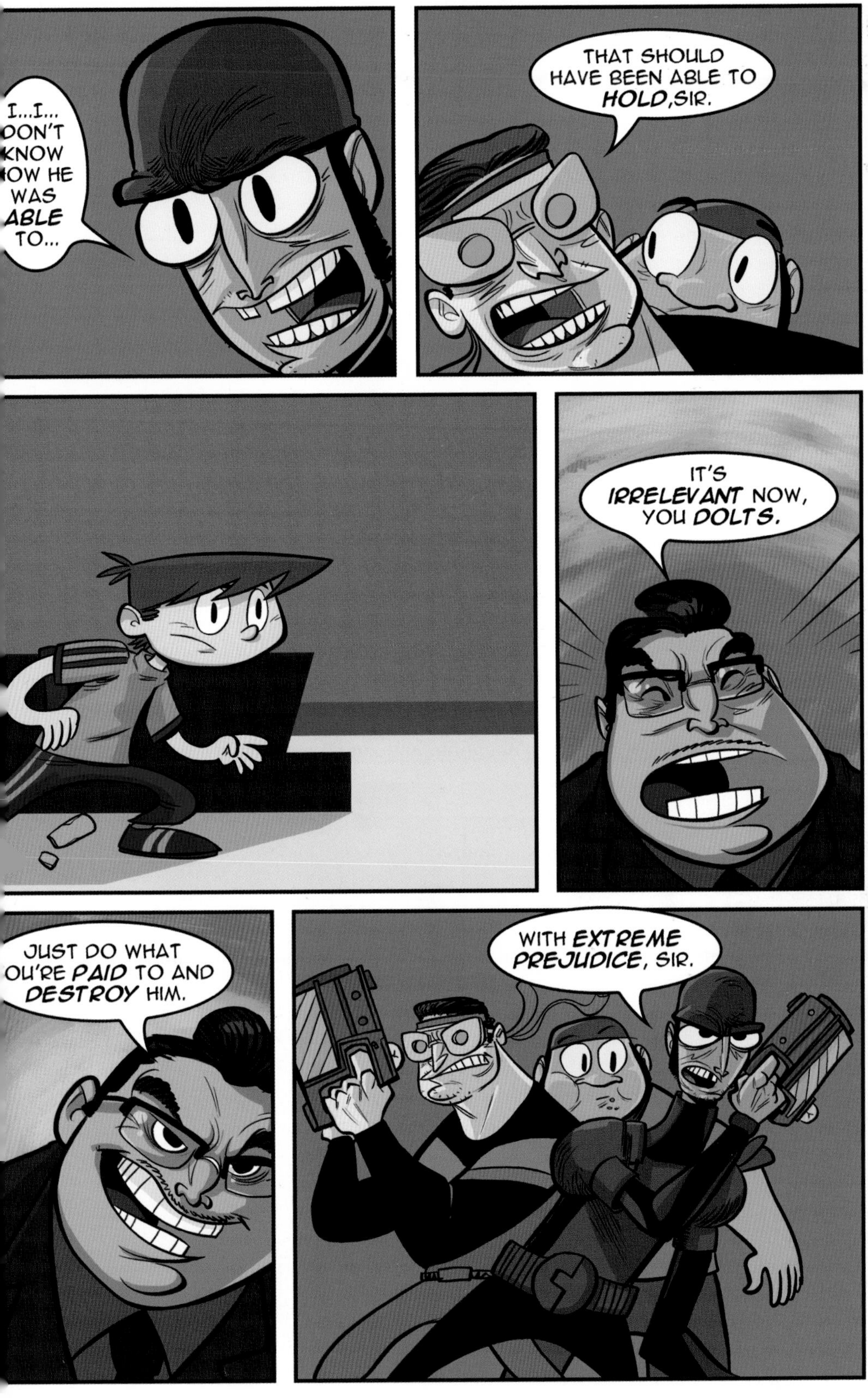
I...I... DON'T KNOW OW HE WAS ABLE TO...
THAT SHOULD HAVE BEEN ABLE TO HOLD, SIR.
IT'S IRRELEVANT NOW, YOU DOLTS.
JUST DO WHAT OU'RE PAID TO AND DESTROY HIM.
WITH EXTREME PREJUDICE, SIR.

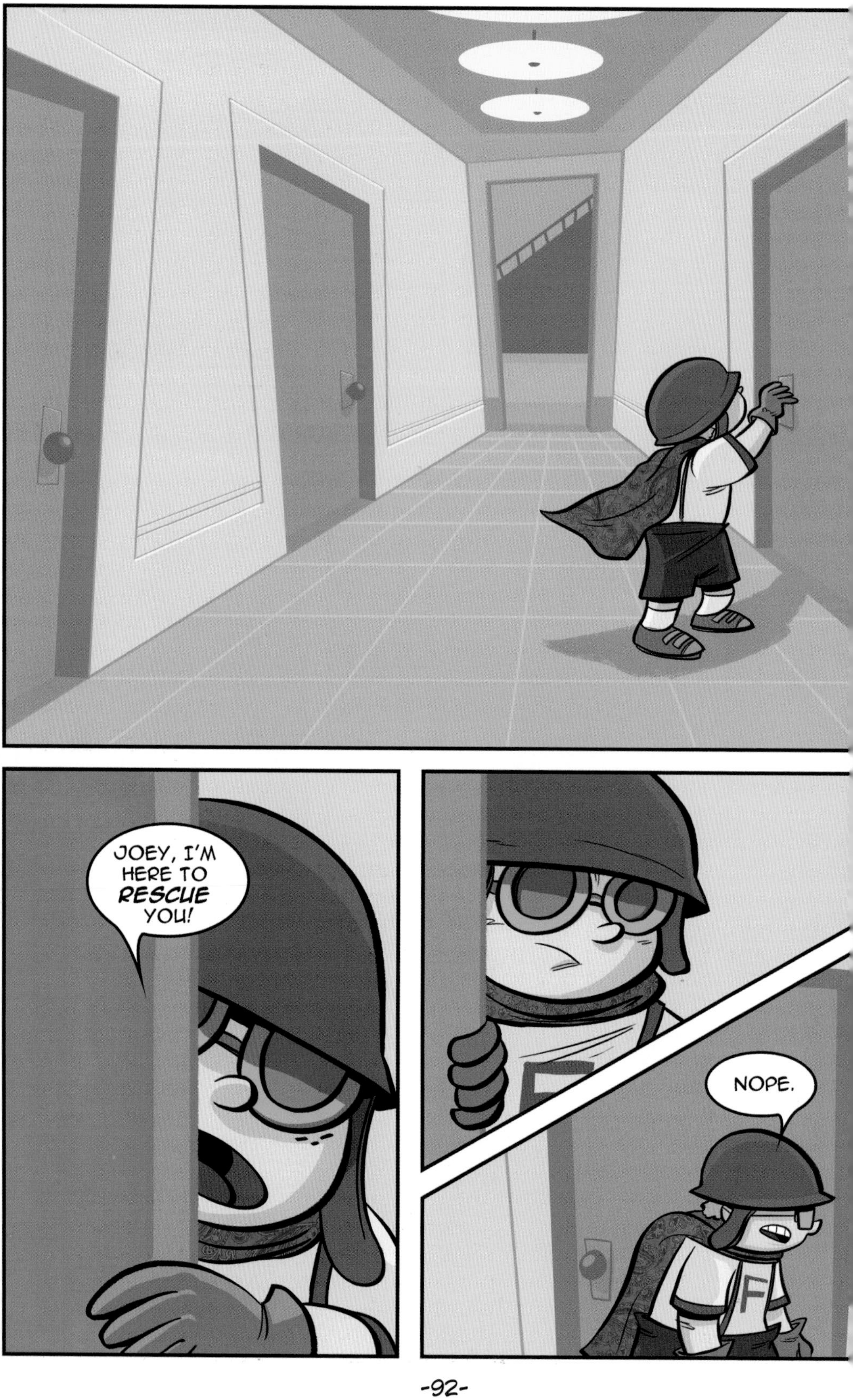
JOEY, I'M HERE TO *RESCUE* YOU!
NOPE.

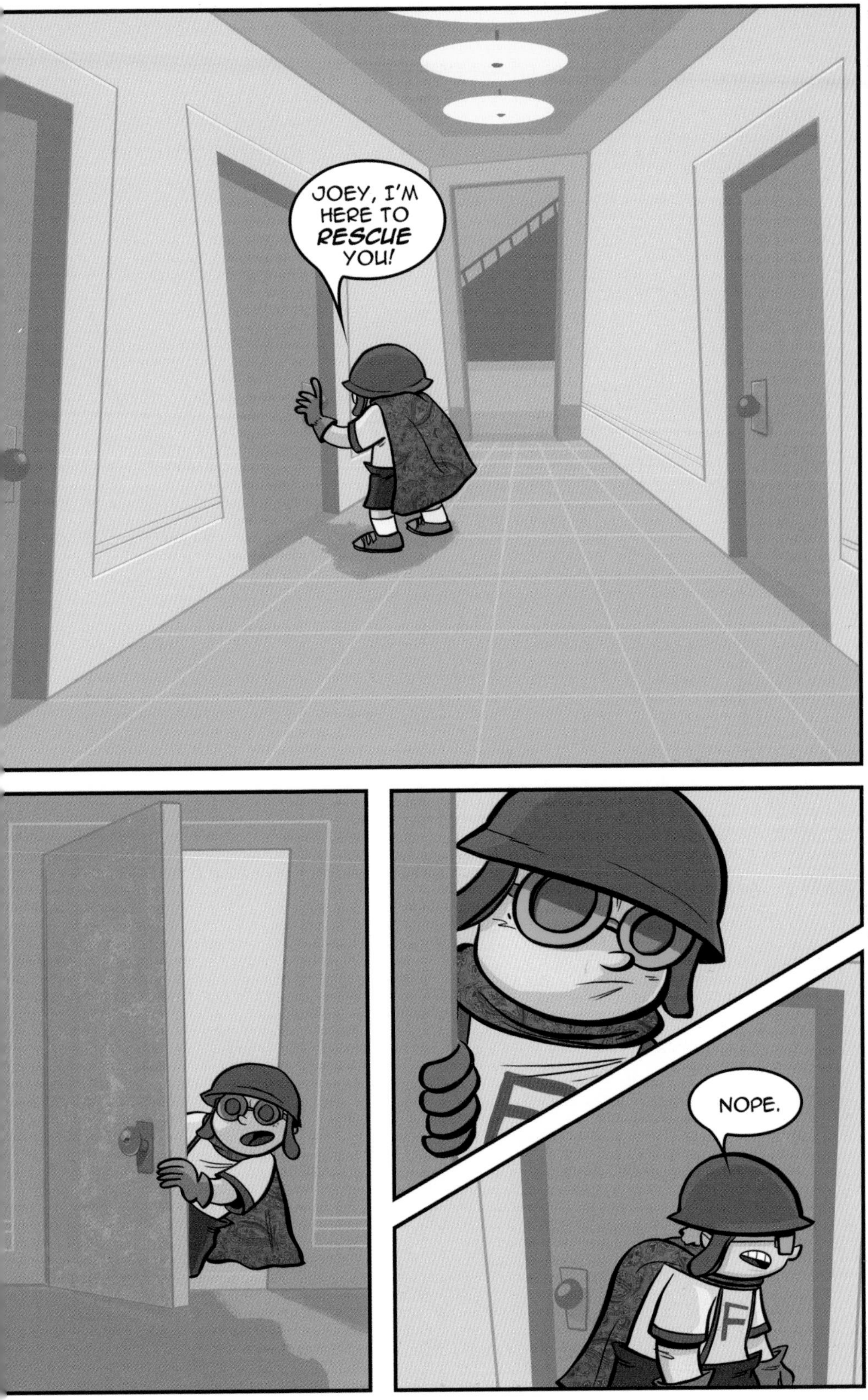
JOEY, I'M HERE TO *RESCUE* YOU!
NOPE.

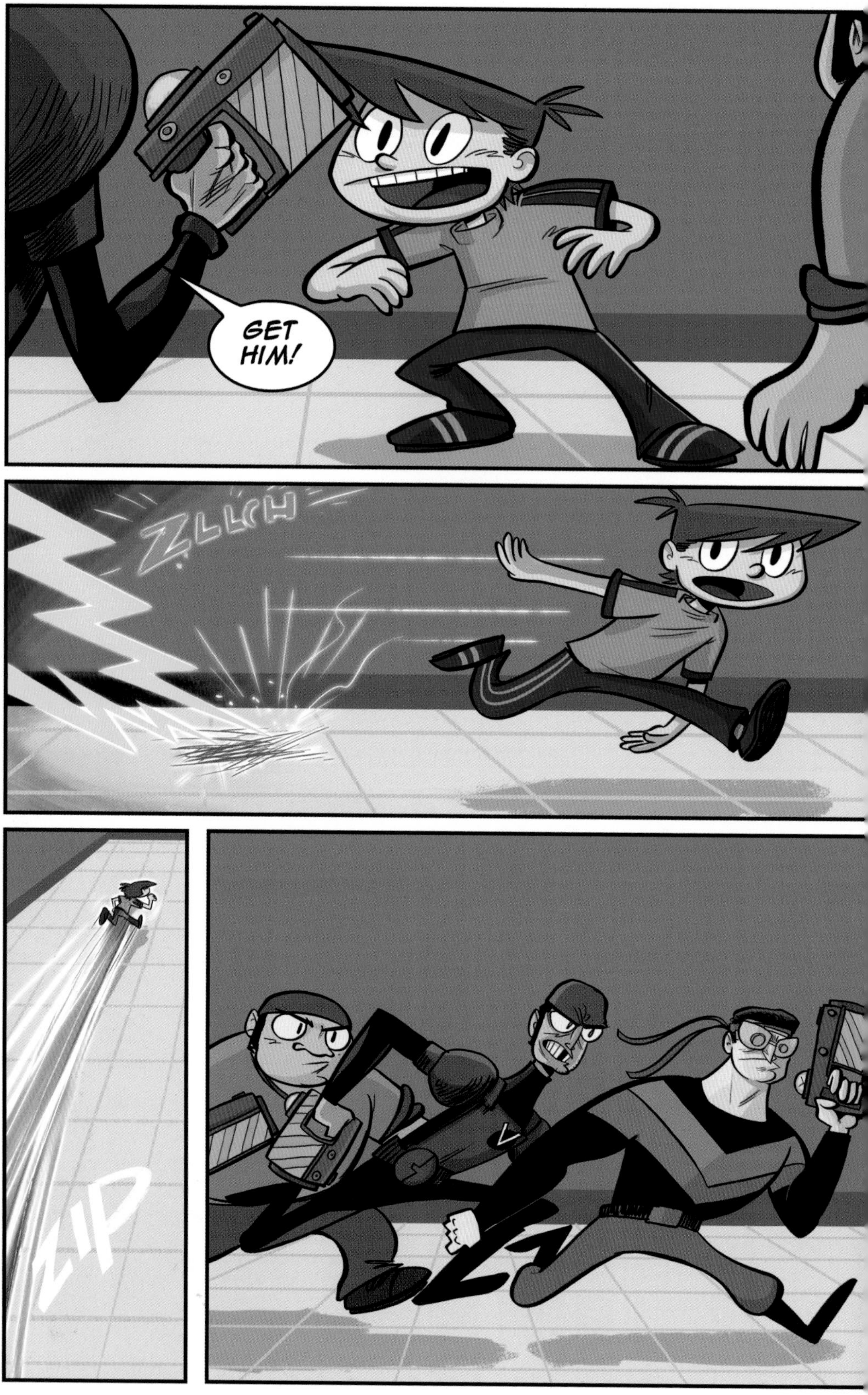
GET HIM!
ZLLCH
ZIP

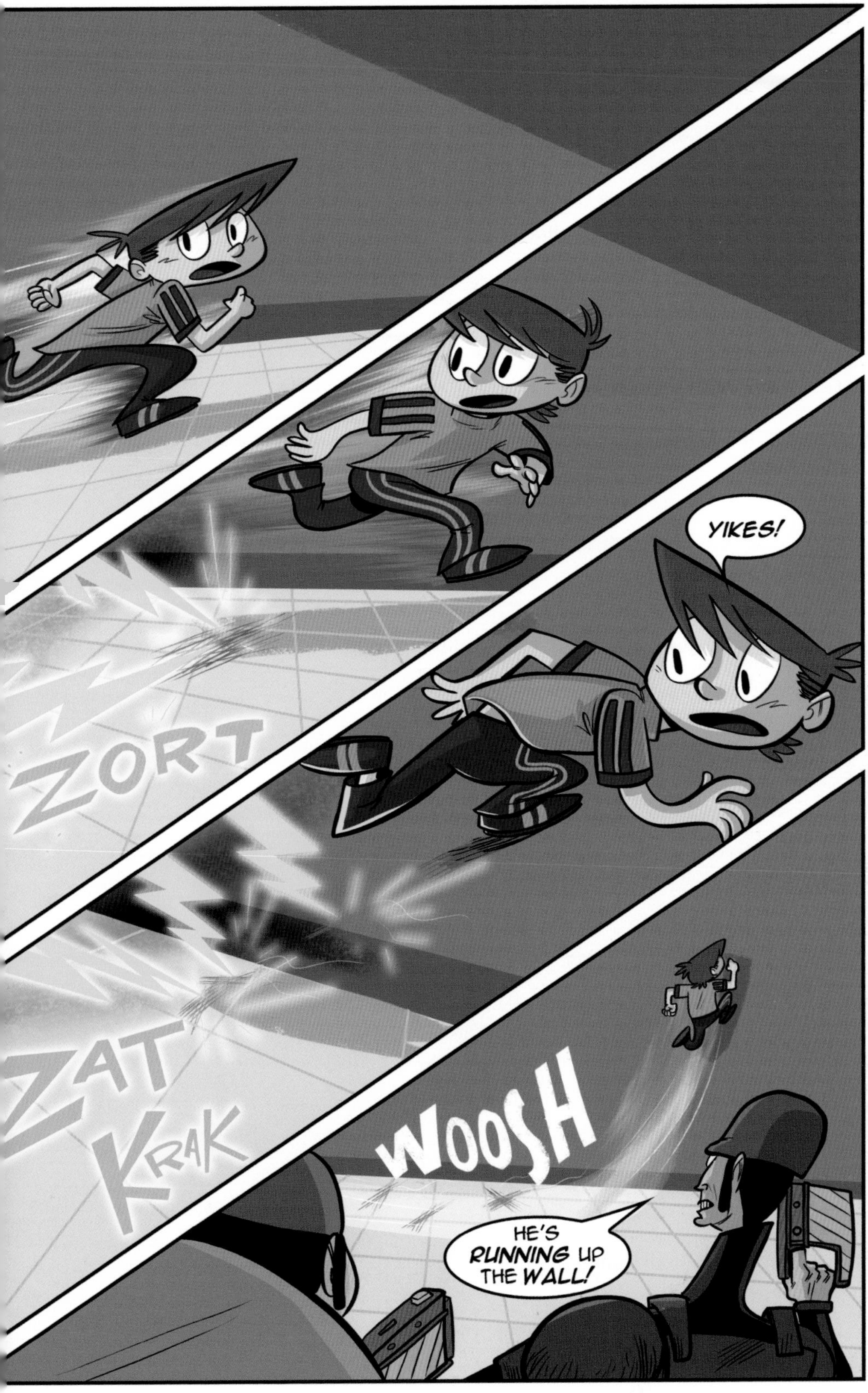
YIKES!
ZORT
ZAT
KRAK
WOOSH
HE'S RUNNING UP THE WALL!

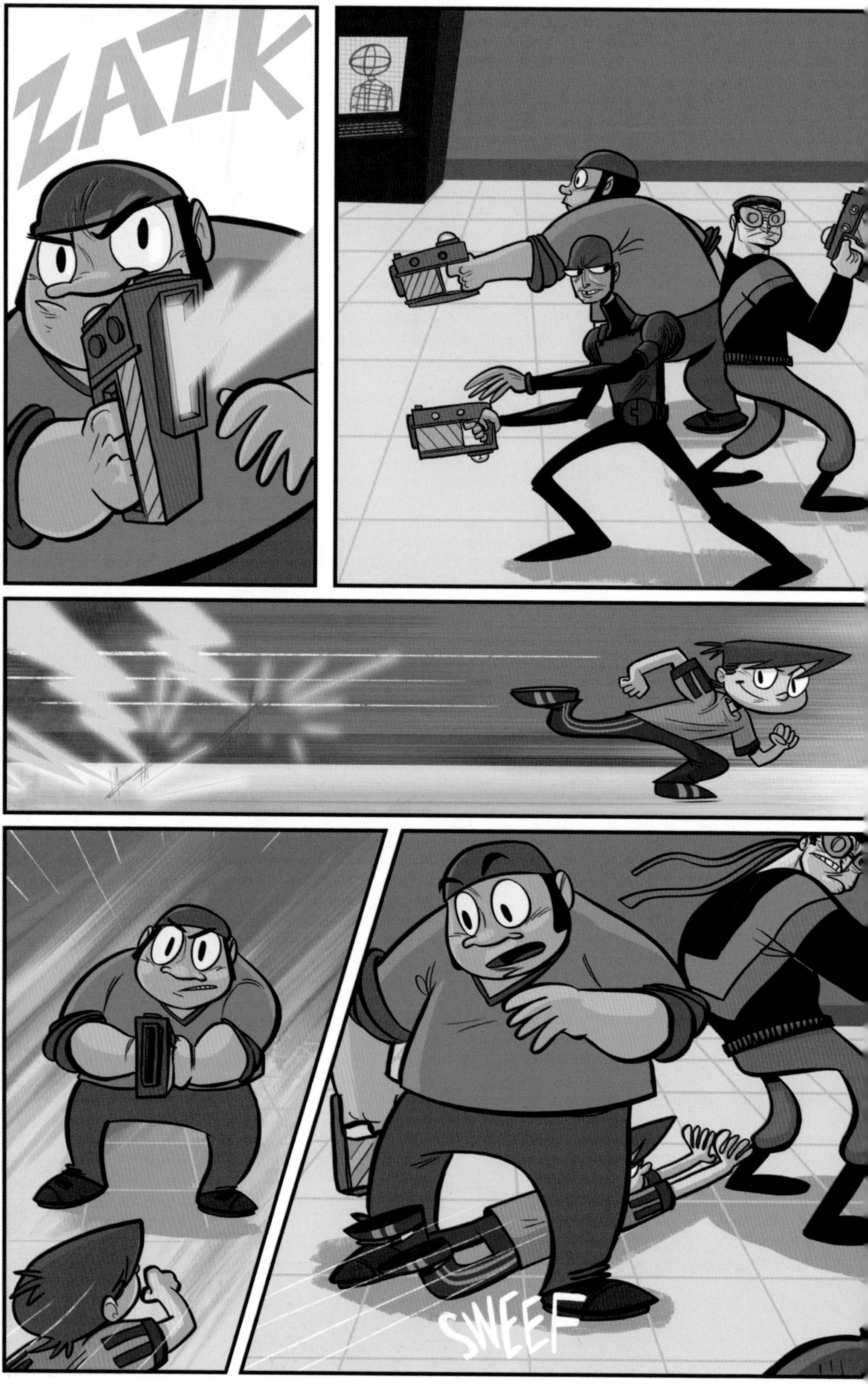
ZAZK
SWEEF

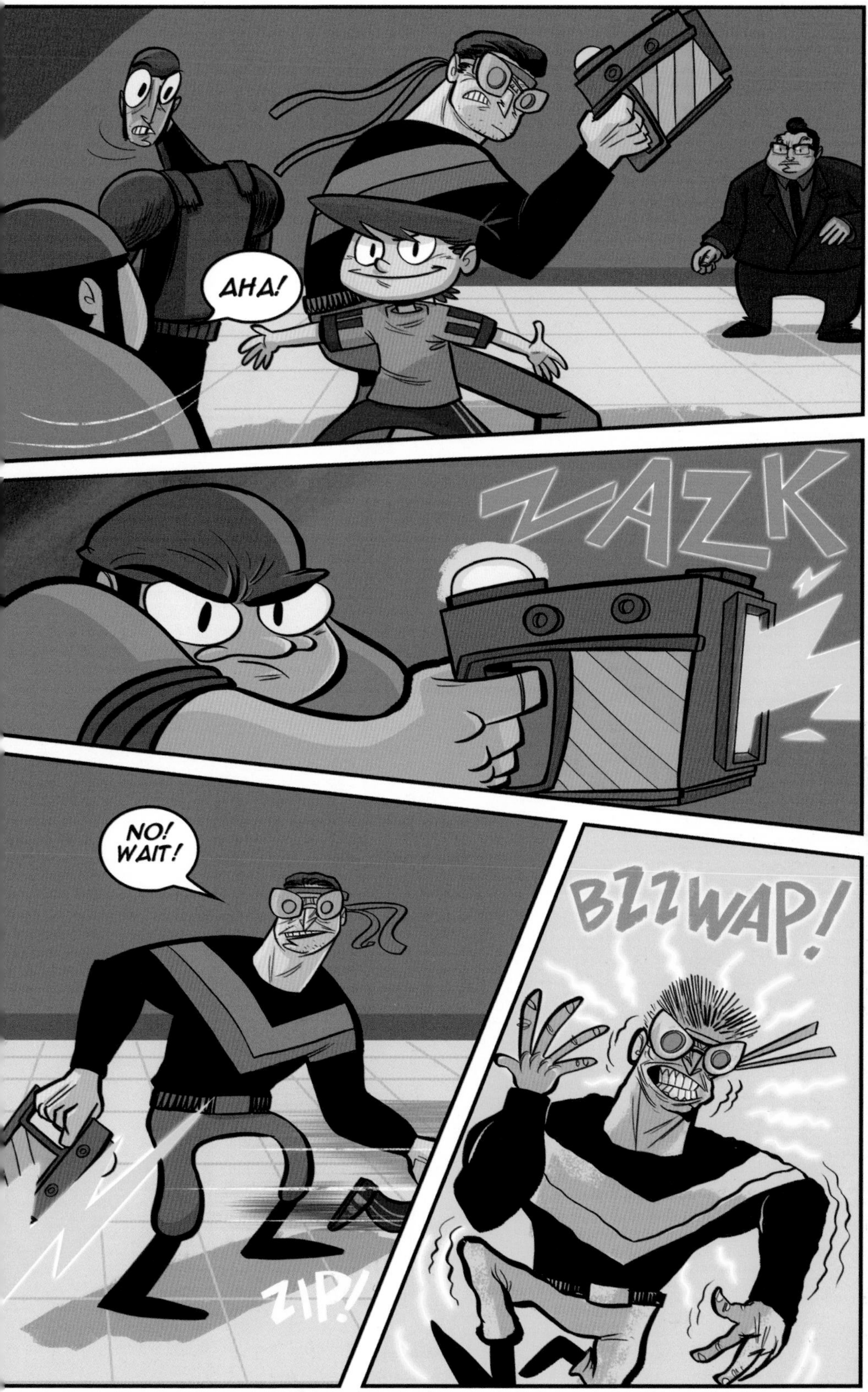
AHA!
ZAZK
NO! WAIT!
ZIP!
BZZWAP!

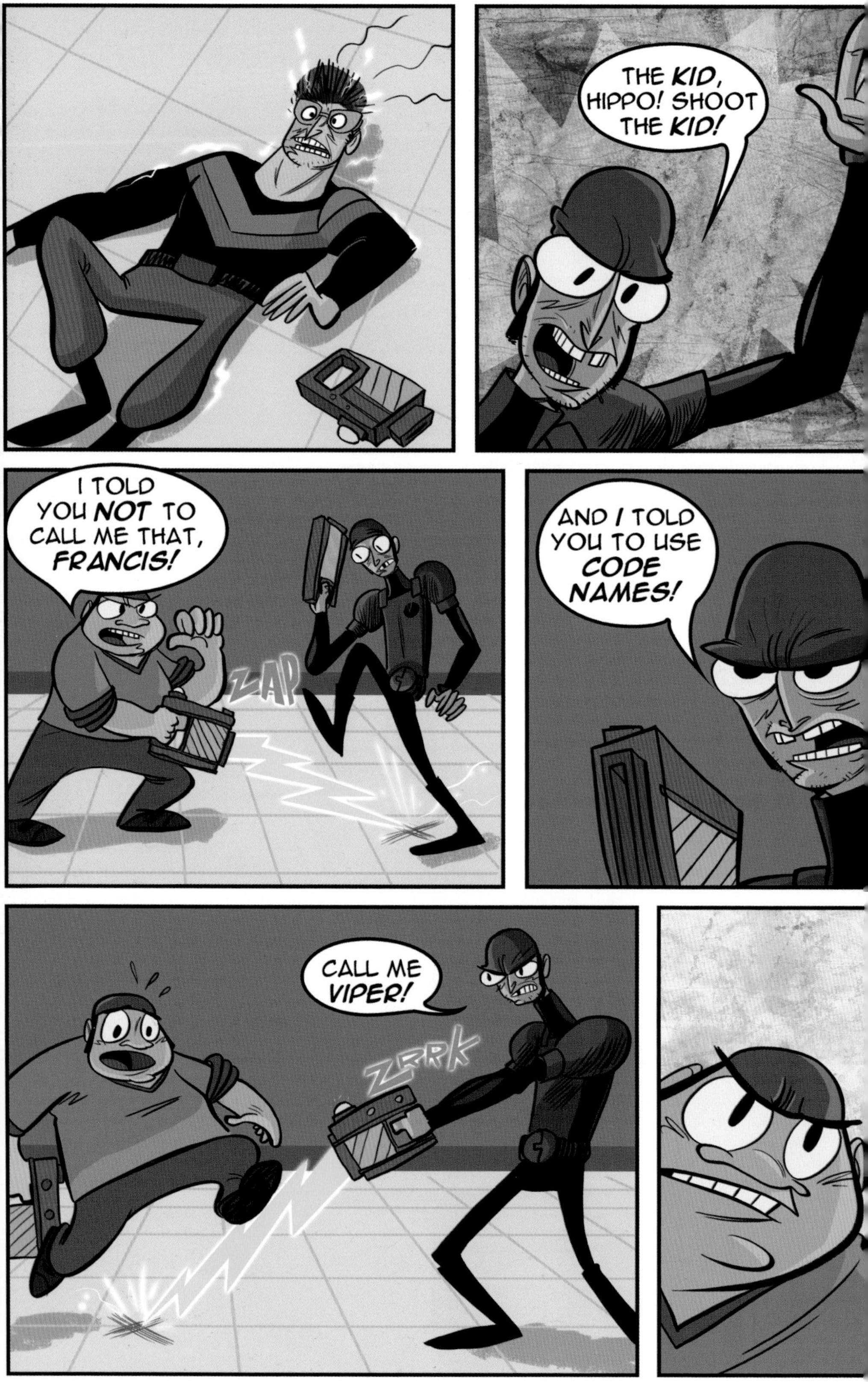

THE KID, HIPPO! SHOOT THE KID!
I TOLD YOU NOT TO CALL ME THAT, FRANCIS!
ZAP
AND I TOLD YOU TO USE CODE NAMES!
CALL ME VIPER!
ZRRK

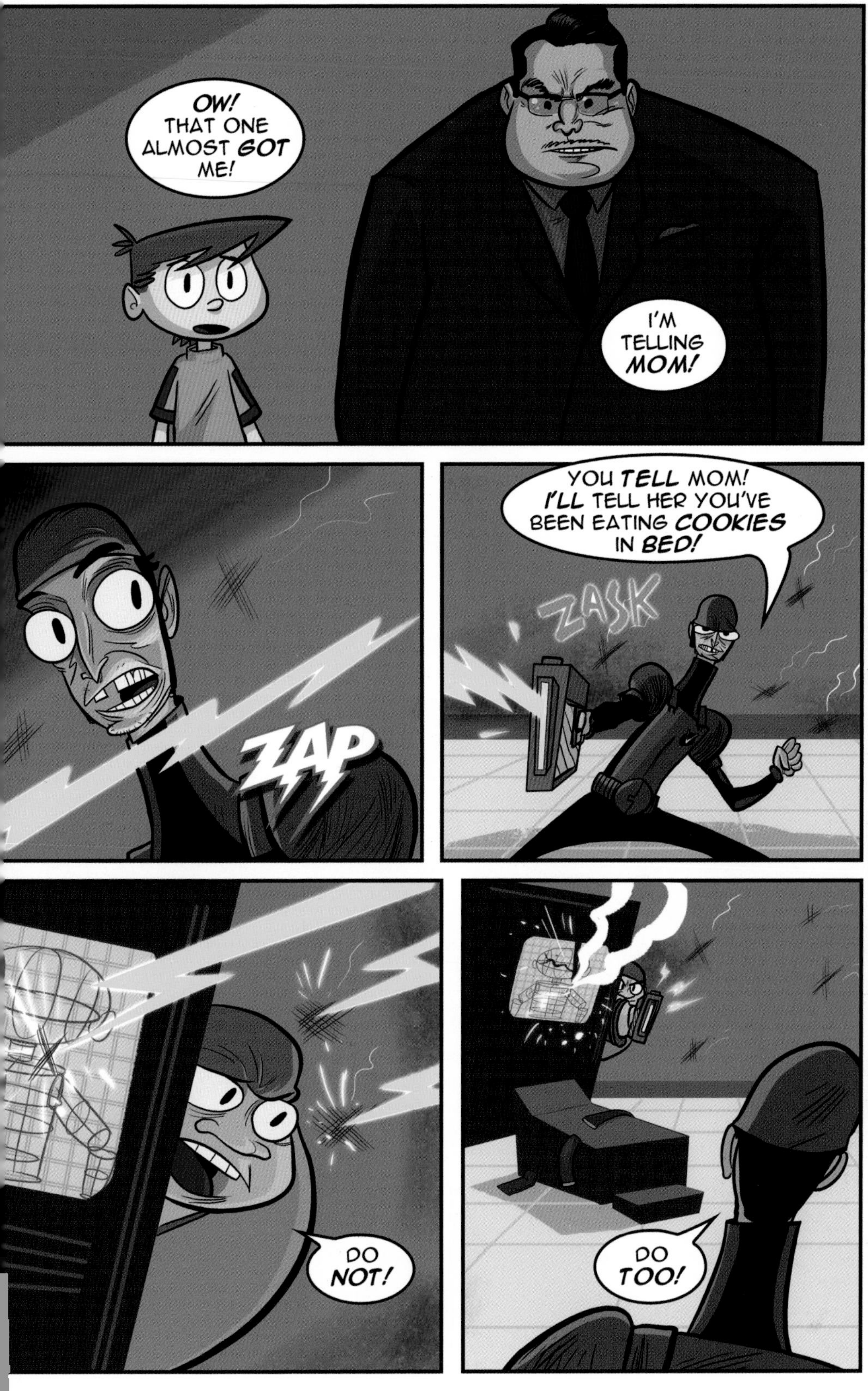
OW! THAT ONE ALMOST GOT ME!
I'M TELLING MOM!
ZAP
YOU TELL MOM! I'LL TELL HER YOU'VE BEEN EATING COOKIES IN BED!
ZASK
DO NOT!
DO TOO!

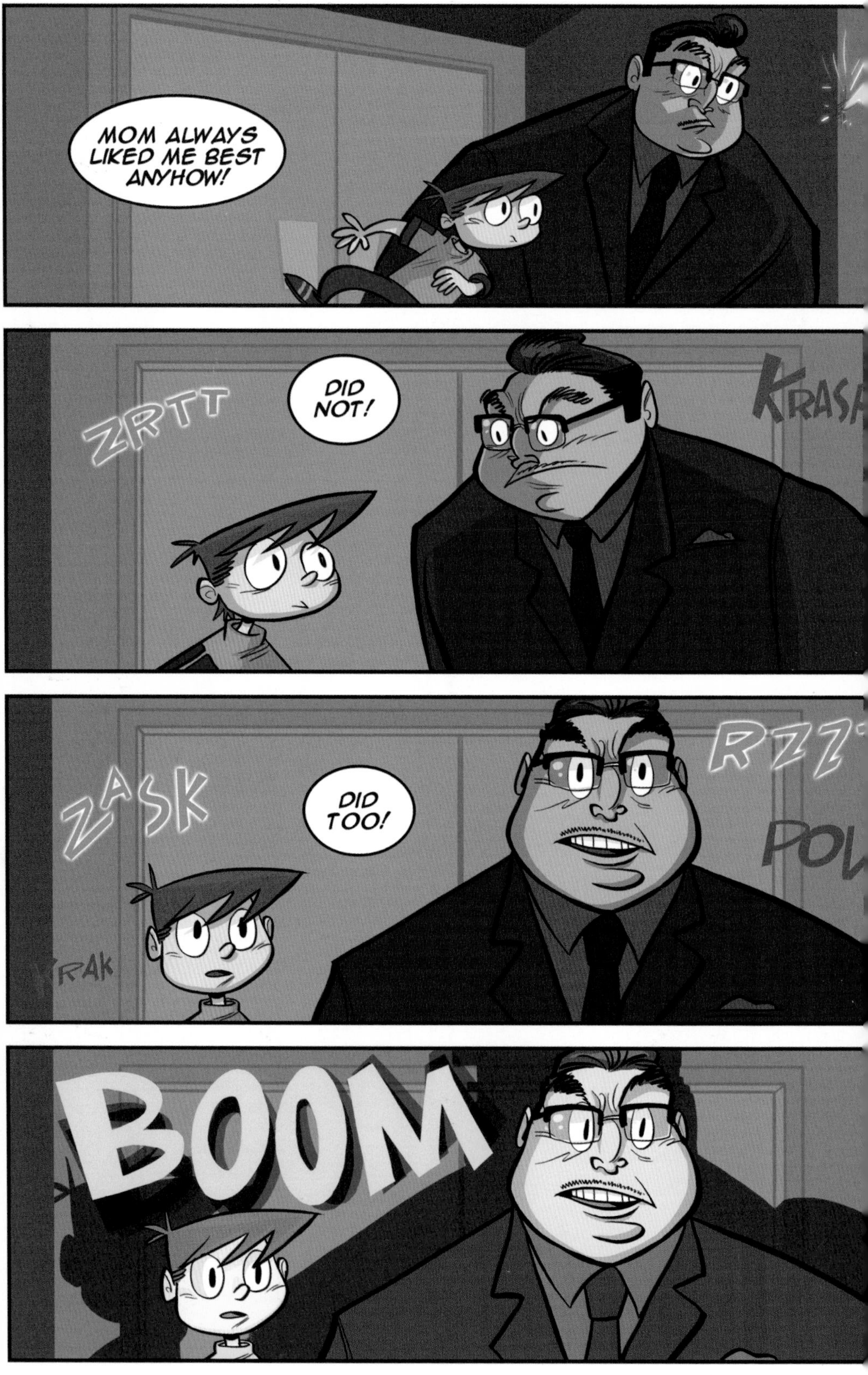
MOM ALWAYS LIKED ME BEST ANYHOW!
ZRTT
DID NOT!
ZASK
DID TOO!
RAK
POW
BOOM

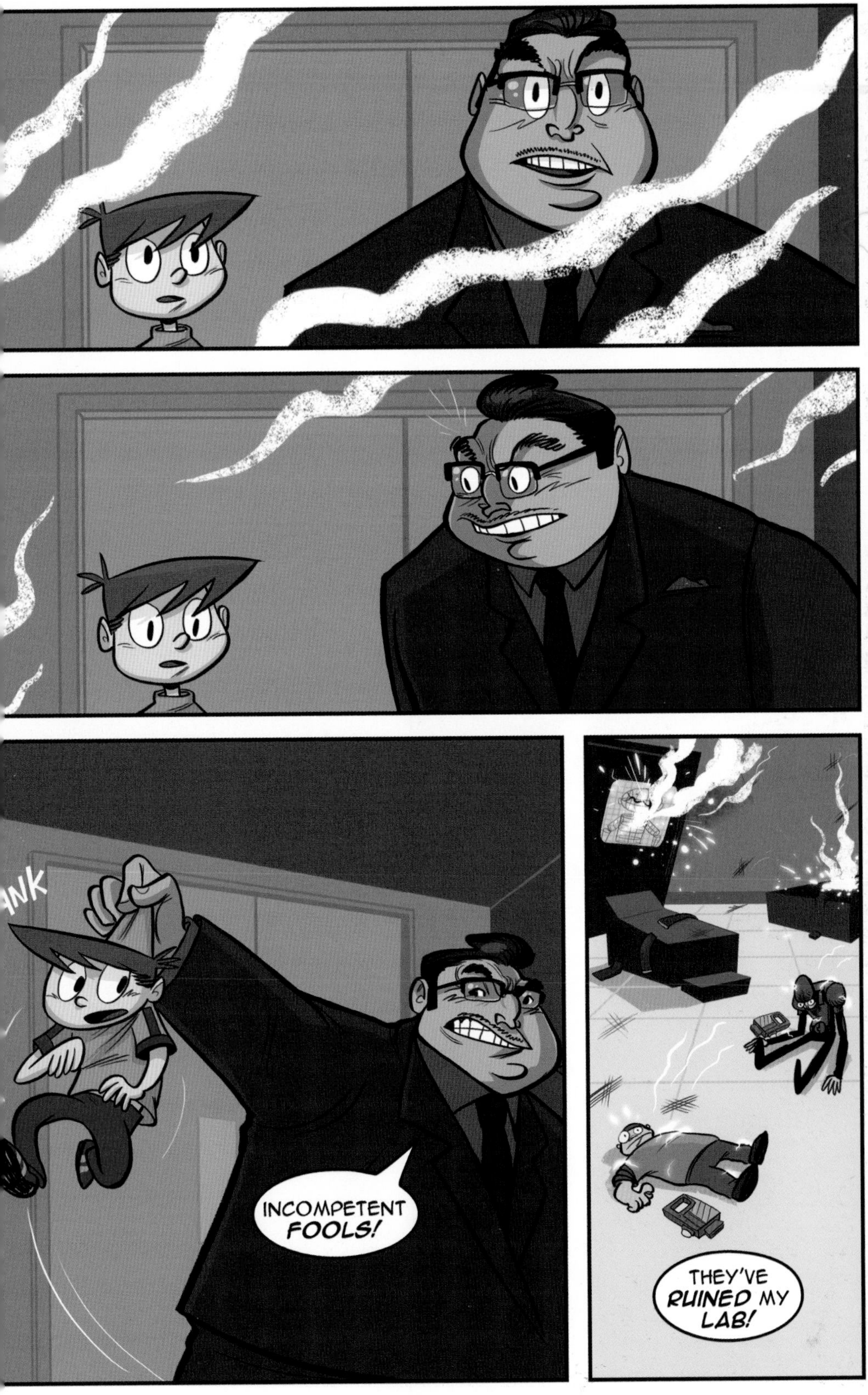
INCOMPETENT FOOLS!
THEY'VE RUINED MY LAB!

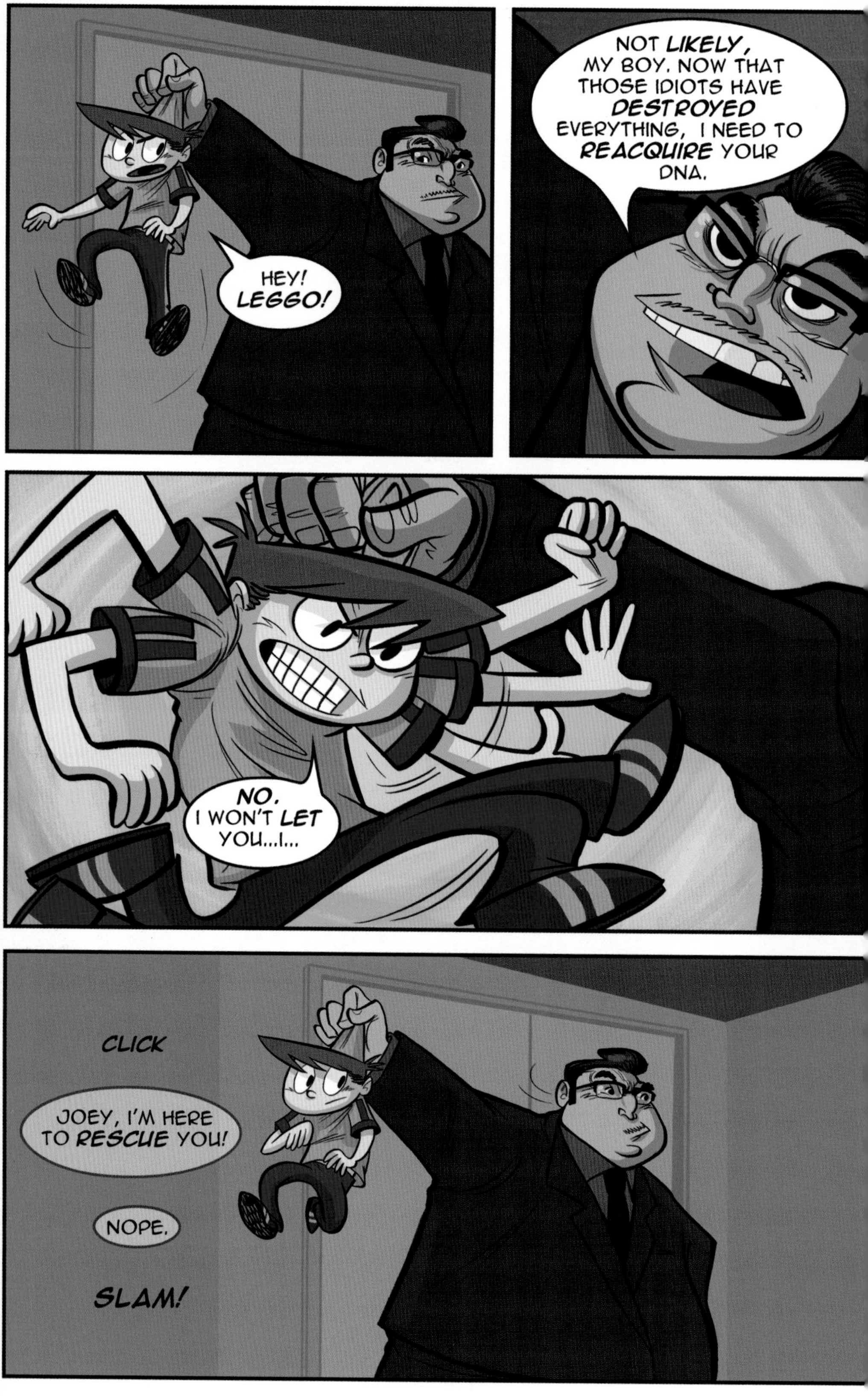
HEY! LEGGO!
NOT LIKELY, MY BOY. NOW THAT THOSE IDIOTS HAVE DESTROYED EVERYTHING, I NEED TO REACQUIRE YOUR DNA.
NO. I WON'T LET YOU...I...
CLICK
JOEY, I'M HERE TO RESCUE YOU!
NOPE.
SLAM!

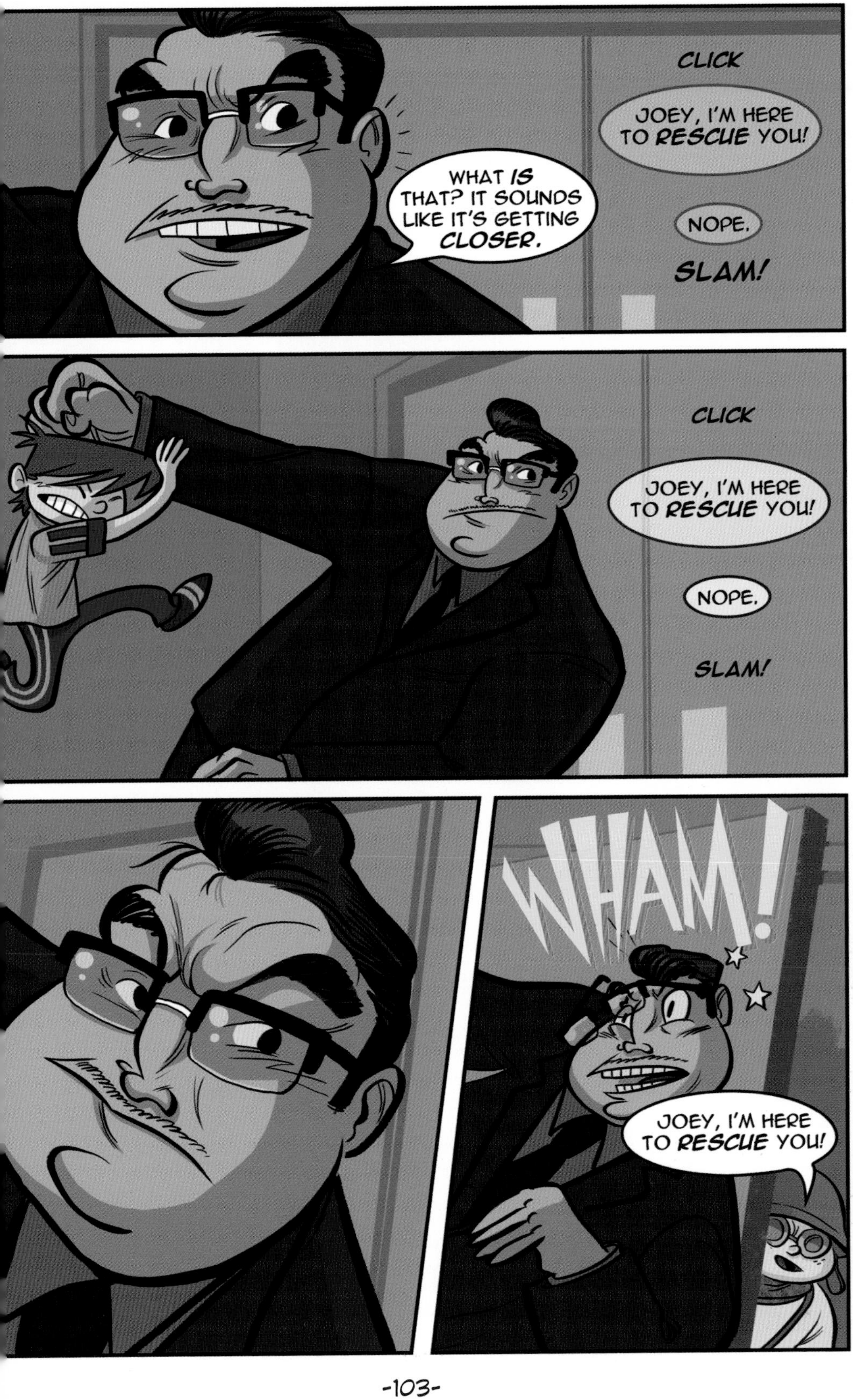
WHAT IS THAT? IT SOUNDS LIKE IT'S GETTING CLOSER.
CLICK
JOEY, I'M HERE TO RESCUE YOU!
NOPE.
SLAM!
CLICK
JOEY, I'M HERE TO RESCUE YOU!
NOPE.
SLAM!
WHAM!
JOEY, I'M HERE TO RESCUE YOU!

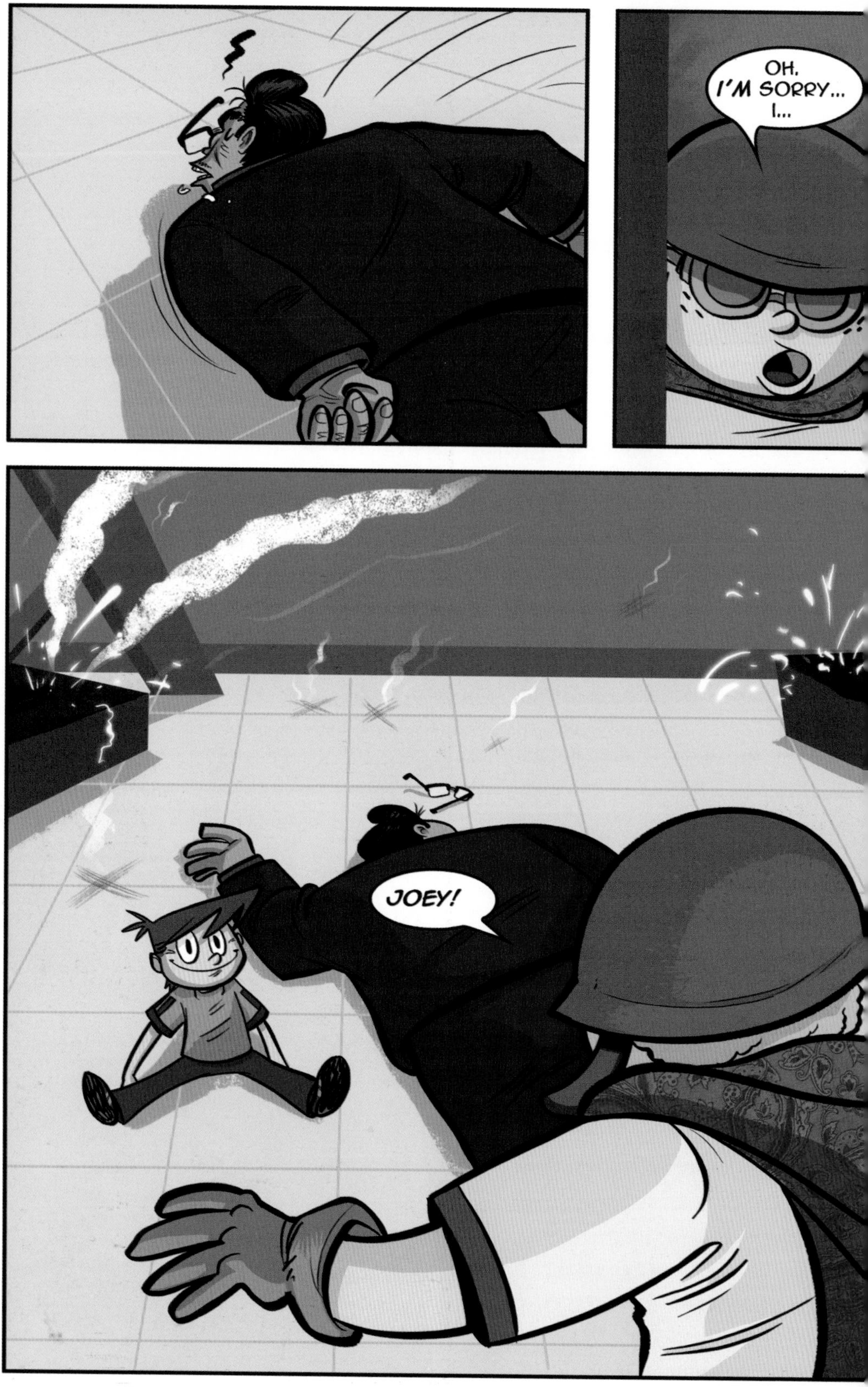
OH. I'M SORRY... I...
JOEY!

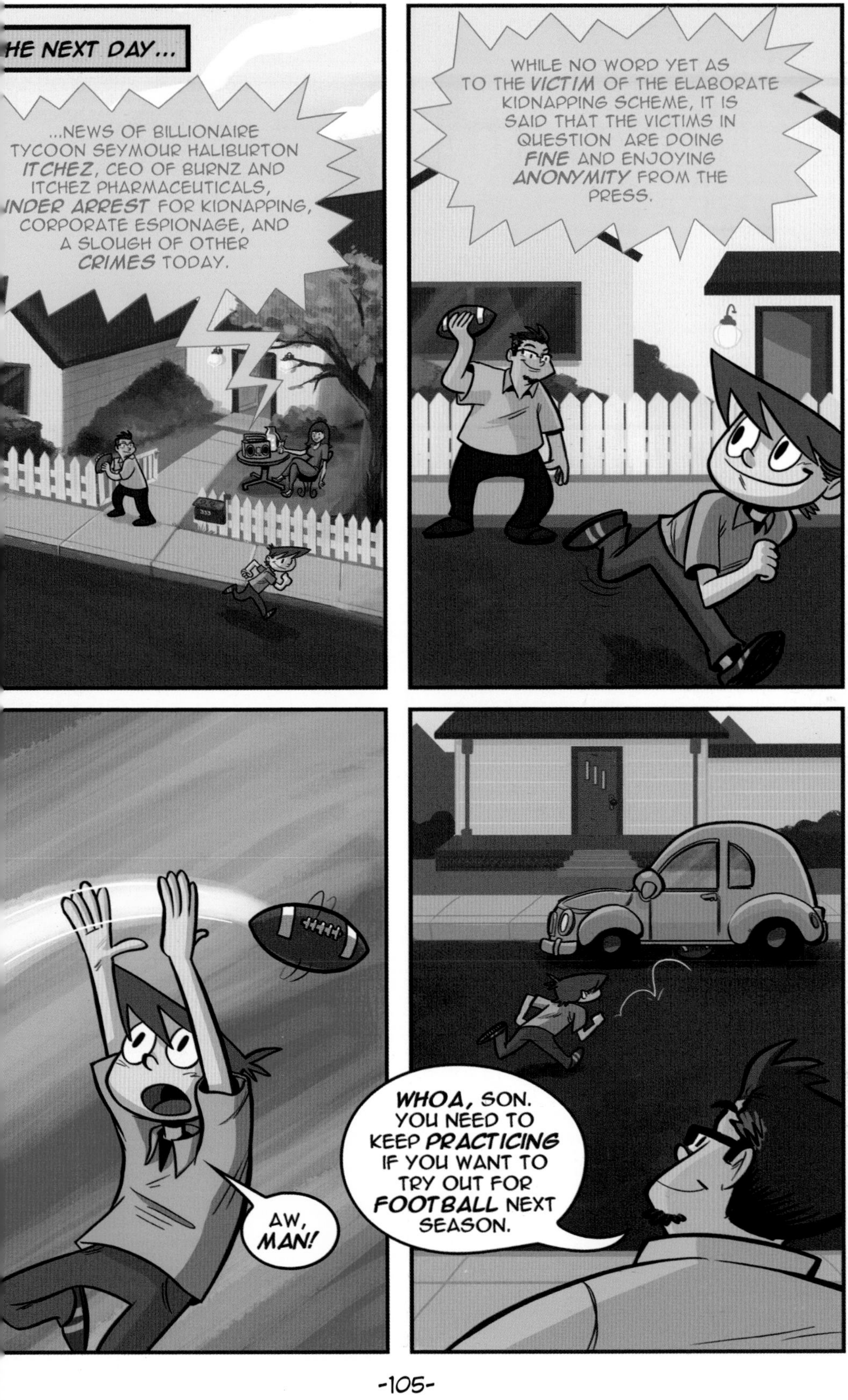
HE NEXT DAY...
...NEWS OF BILLIONAIRE TYCOON SEYMOUR HALIBURTON ITCHEZ, CEO OF BURNZ AND ITCHEZ PHARMACEUTICALS, INDER ARREST FOR KIDNAPPING, CORPORATE ESPIONAGE, AND A SLOUGH OF OTHER CRIMES TODAY.
WHILE NO WORD YET AS TO THE VICTIM OF THE ELABORATE KIDNAPPING SCHEME, IT IS SAID THAT THE VICTIMS IN QUESTION ARE DOING FINE AND ENJOYING ANONYMITY FROM THE PRESS.
AW, MAN!
WHOA, SON. YOU NEED TO KEEP PRACTICING IF YOU WANT TO TRY OUT FOR FOOTBALL NEXT SEASON.

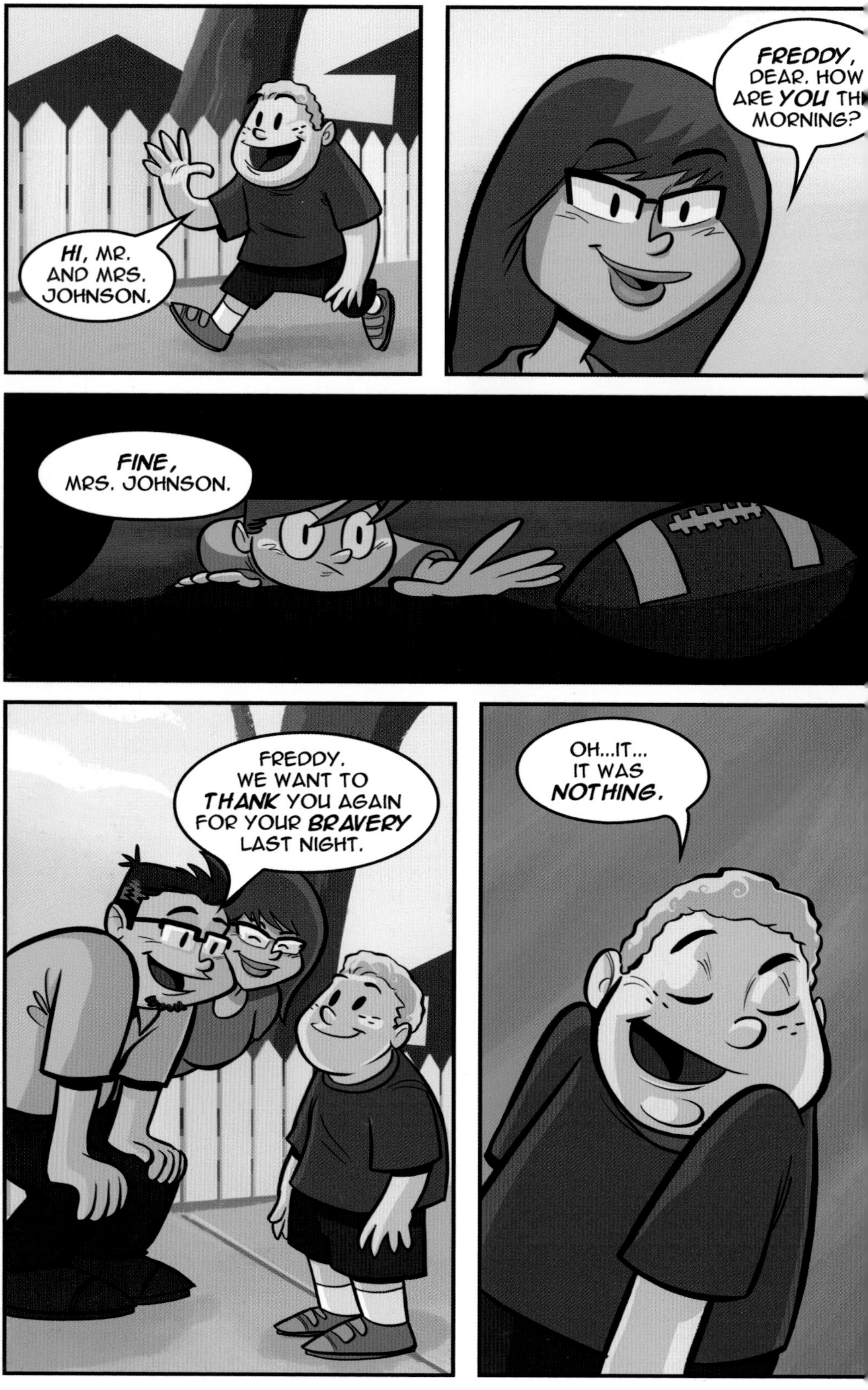
HI, MR. AND MRS. JOHNSON.
FREDDY, DEAR. HOW ARE YOU TH
MORNING?
FINE, MRS. JOHNSON.
FREDDY. WE WANT TO THANK YOU AGAIN FOR YOUR BRAVERY LAST NIGHT.
OH...IT... IT WAS NOTHING.

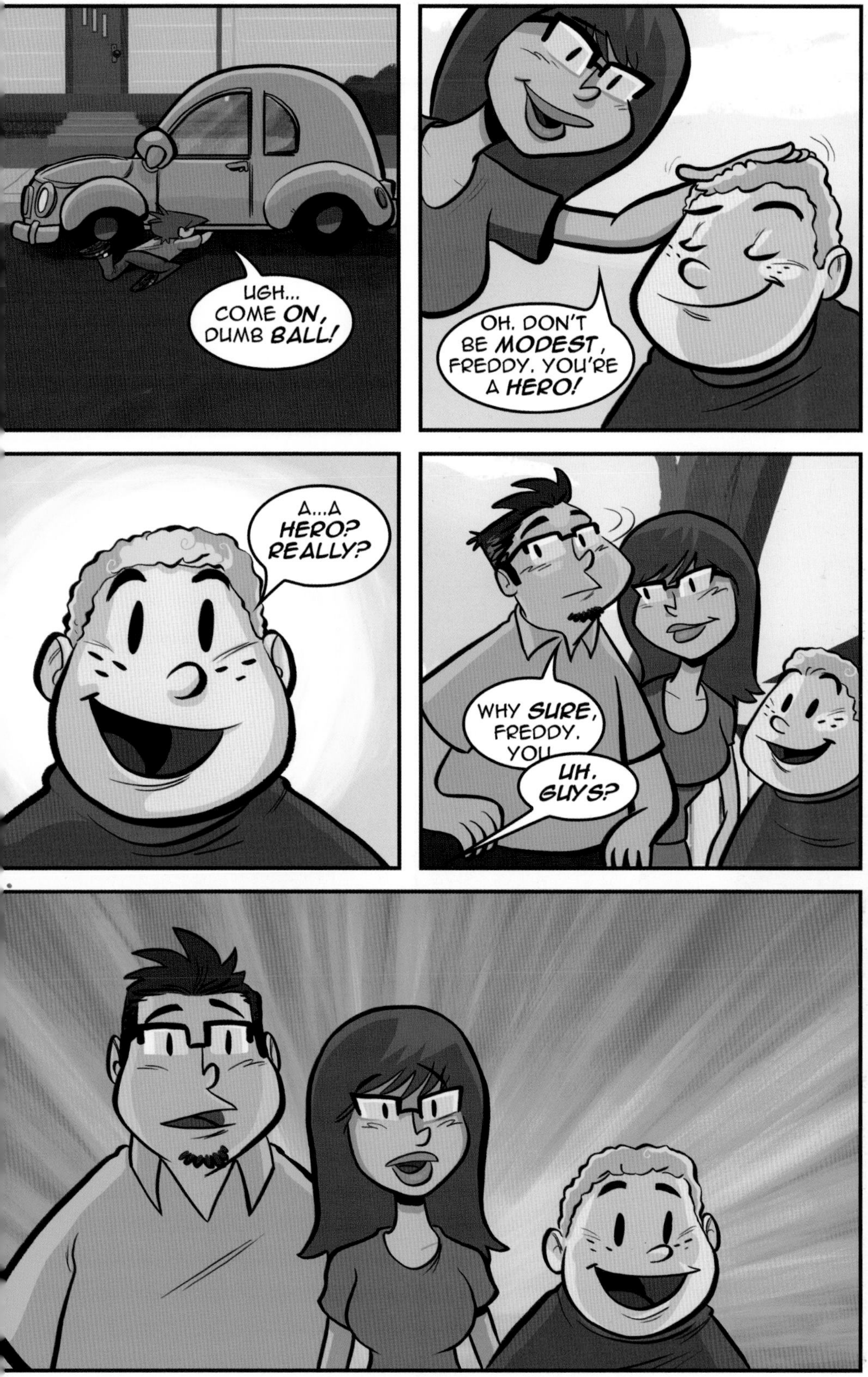
UGH... COME ON, DUMB BALL!
OH. DON'T BE MODEST, FREDDY. YOU'RE A HERO!
A...A HERO? REALLY?
WHY SURE, FREDDY. YOU
UH. GUYS?

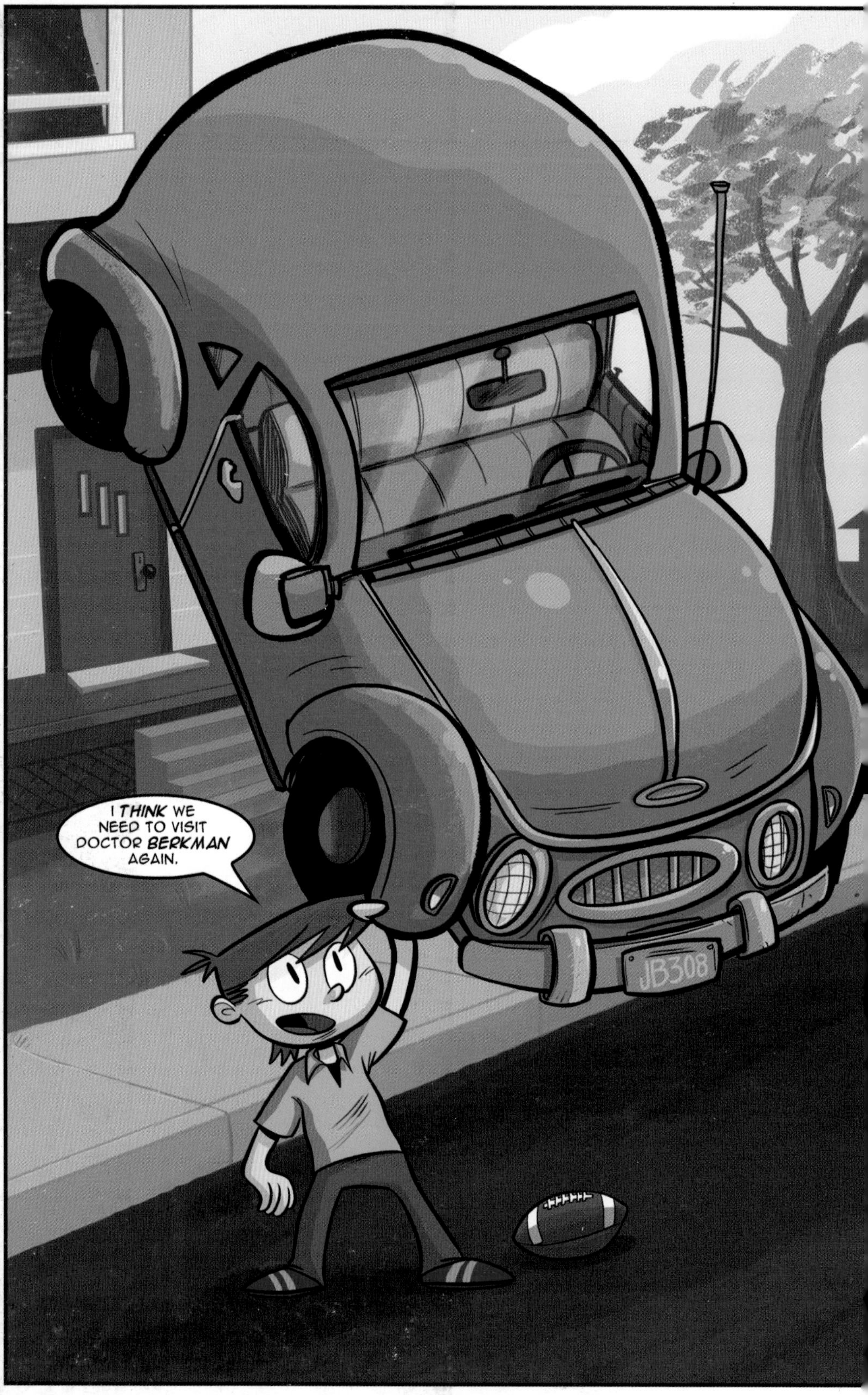
I THINK WE NEED TO VISIT DOCTOR BERKMAN AGAIN.
JB308